We're almost halfway across the river. The water's deeper, the current stronger. Nelson's up to his waist, I'm up to my chest. We hold our knapsacks over our heads. This would come up to the children's necks. How did they make it? Maybe they didn't.

Something catches my eye. It's barely breaking the surface, heading our way from upstream. It's hard to make out what it is, with the sun in our eyes and the light bouncing off the water. But it's dark brown. I think I can see holes in it. Nostrils? A snout!

"Nelson! To the west! It's coming toward us! Hurry!"

He sees it too. We churn through the water. Struggle to get to the other side. The crocodile's getting closer. I lurch forward. There's a break in the sandbar. Nothing under my feet. I can't touch bottom. I'm underwater, except for my arms and knapsack. My legs flail. I burst through the surface. "Help!"

Chanda's Wars

ALLAN STRATTON

With an afterword by Roméo Dallaire (Head of U.N.
forces during the Rwandan genocide)

HARPER TEEN
An Imprint of HarperCollinsPublishers

HarperTeen is an imprint of HarperCollins Publishers.

Chanda's Wars
Copyright © 2008 by Allan Stratton

Library of Congress Cataloging-in-Publication Data
Stratton, Allan.
   Chanda's wars / by Allan Stratton. — 1st ed.
      p.   cm.
   Summary: Chanda, a teenaged African girl, must save her younger siblings
after they are kidnapped and forced to serve as child soldiers in General
Mandiki's rebel army.
   ISBN 978-0-06-087265-6
   [1. Civil war—Africa—Fiction. 2. Kidnapping—Fiction. 3. Orphans—Fiction.
4. Blacks—Africa—Fiction. 5. Africa—Fiction.] I. Title.
PZ7.S9109Ch 2008   2007010829
[Fic]—dc22   CIP
                                                                              AC

Typography by Joel Tippie
10 11 12 13   CG/CW   10 9 8 7 6 5 4 3
❖
First paperback edition, 2009

Dedicated to young people caught by war

"Sensible commanders always grab whatever weapons are easiest at hand, and no weapon is easier to get or control than children."

Former Burundi Commander

Chanda's Wars

Part One

1

IN MY DREAM, Mama is alive and well.

We're on Granny Thela's cattle post outside Tiro. The bush land stretches farther than I can see. Cows graze freely in the grasses, cluster for shade beneath the broad-boughed acacia trees, and wander around thickets of scrub brush. Mama's sitting on a slab of rock in the shade of a termite mound. I'm by her feet. We're at the abandoned campsite where I found her dying six months ago.

It's a rainy-season dream, but the sky is clear. The sun is hot. Mama's cotton dress clings to her body. "What a glorious day to be alive," she laughs. I love her laugh; deep and rich, it lifts the day like sunshine. She fans herself with a palm leaf and soaks her feet in a bucket of water drawn from the nearby stream. Orchids grow out of her hair.

In the clearing, my little brother and sister twirl each

other in circles. Soly is five, but looks about seven. He's tall for his age, a tangle of legs, my baby giraffe. Iris is six, and tough like a nut. The combs in her hair are the size of her head. The two collapse in a dizzy squeal.

"You've kept them safe," Mama says. "I can rest easy." She smiles, and offers me a biscuit from the pocket of her apron. I'm about to say thank you, when she sniffs the air. "We have to go."

"But we just got here."

"There's going to be a storm."

She's right. Out of nowhere, clouds are rolling in.

I face the clearing. "Soly, Iris—we have to go." But the clearing has turned into savanna. Soly and Iris have disappeared in the tall grasses.

"They're playing hide-and-seek," I say. "I'll track them down."

Mama doesn't reply. I glance at her rock. She's vanished too.

"Mama?"

"Don't worry about me," says a white stork perched on the termite mound. "Get Soly and Iris to safety."

The sky is dark. There's a rumble in the distance.

I plunge into the grass. It's growing faster than I can

think. In a blink, it's over my head. Where am I? I check the treetops. I used to know them all, but everything's mixed up. New trees are everywhere. I'm lost.

"Soly? Iris?"

A flash of lightning. The storm's closing in. There's a machete in my hand. I hack frantically at the grass. I hack and I hack and—I'm out of the bush, at the side of the road leading to Tiro. Soly and Iris are nearby, watching ants swarm a dung beetle.

"What took you so long?" Soly asks, with big innocent eyes.

"Don't ever run off again," I snap.

"We didn't run off," Iris taunts. "You lost us."

"Enough of your lip. We have to go."

Too late. Lightning strikes a nearby mango tree. Thunder booms. The sky falls. We're thrown to the ground. Raindrops the size of melons explode around us. We take cover in a hollow baobab tree, as children flood from the bush on either side. They stream down paths out of cattle posts. Pour onto the road, ahead and behind.

The storm lets up. But the children don't go home. They run toward Tiro.

A boy races by. "They're coming!"

Who's coming? Who? We try to run too, but we can't. The road is mud. We slip, fall, get up, slip, fall, get up. Everyone's gone. The sun goes down. We start to sink.

"Tiro," I scream. "We have to get to Tiro." But we can't move. We're up to our knees in mud.

Out of the night, a bush breaks to the right. A branch snaps to the left.

Soly and Iris cling to my waist. "It's them! They're here!"

WHO ARE YOU? WHAT DO YOU WANT?

"Chanda! Wake up!" Esther shakes me.

I sit bolt upright on my mat. "Esther! What—?"

"Iris and Soly. They ran and got me. They said you cried out."

I see them cowering in the doorway. "It's all right," I say. "I'm fine."

"Are you possessed?" Soly asks in a little voice. "Iris says you're possessed." Iris pokes him. "Ow."

I glare at Iris. "Stop scaring your brother, Iris. I was just having a dream, and you know it. Now go back to bed."

Esther shoos them to their room. Thank god for Esther. We've been best friends since forever. When her parents died, Esther's family was scattered all over. She worked the streets for the money to get them back. One night, she got raped, her face slashed. I took her in. Now she lives with her own little brother and sister, Sammy and Magda, in two rooms off the side of our house. Mrs. Tafa, our next-door neighbor, says she's a bad influence. I don't care. She's Esther. If it weren't for her, I'd never have made it through Mama's funeral, or these past few months.

Esther returns, sits by my mat, and holds my hand. Under the light of the oil lamp, the scars from the attack cast shadows across her cheeks and chin. "It wasn't just a dream, was it?" she says. "It's the one about Tiro."

I look away.

Esther rubs my palm and takes a deep breath. "You used to get it every couple of weeks. Now it's almost every night. Chanda—"

"Don't say it."

"Why not? Pretending everything's fine won't it make it go away." She grips my hand tight. "Something's wrong. You need help. Somebody older. You know I don't like Mrs. Tafa. All the same, she was your mama's best friend. You should talk to her."

"No!" I yank my hand free. "Mrs. Tafa knows what happened to Mama. She'll try to bring in the spirit doctor."

"So?"

"Mrs. Gulubane's a fake."

"Then talk to Mr. Selalame."

"I can't. He's Mr. Selalame! I'd feel strange."

Esther throws her arms in the air. "What's more important, your pride or Soly and Iris? Nightmares have a reason, Chanda. If you don't see Mr. Selalame, I'm going to Mrs. Tafa."

"Is that a threat?"

"Don't be mad. Please," Esther begs. "I'm your friend. And you're in trouble."

2

Before Esther goes back to bed, we peek in on Soly and Iris. They're pretending to sleep. We draw the thin curtain across their doorway.

"Get some more rest yourself," Esther whispers as she steps into the night air. "There's another few hours till dawn."

"Sure," I say. I hold up the oil lamp till she's reached her place, then I bolt the door, get my satchel from beside my mat, and bring it to the table in the main room. There's no way I'm going back to sleep. I've had enough nightmares.

I pull out my binders and go over today's duties at the elementary school; the bit of money I earn as a replacement teacher keeps us going. At the beginning of the year, I babysat the kindergarten class for Mrs. Ndori, who was out with pneumonia. That's what they called it anyway. Next I looked after the grade fives. Everyone knew their regular teacher had been putting on weight, but nobody guessed she was pregnant till her water broke in the middle of a spelling bee. People still laugh: "How do you spell 'catastrophe'?"

Now I'm with the grade ones. Iris is in the class. She's not too thrilled about it. Neither am I.

My job came about thanks to my old English teacher, Mr. Selalame. He's helped me since my first day of high school, when I stayed late to help him unload boxes of used books from a missionary minivan. As we lined them up on his shelves, I was overcome by this need to touch their covers, feel their pages filled with words I'd never seen—a lot of them, words I didn't even know. Mr. Selalame beamed. He lent me as many as I could read, and told me how, if I worked hard, I could be a lawyer or a doctor. By last year, a scholarship seemed so real I could taste it. Then Mama passed away, and I had to drop out to raise Soly and Iris. Mr. Selalame talked to the principal at the elementary and, well, the rest is history.

The shade of the oil lamp is smeared with soot. It's hard to read. I yawn, put my binders back in my satchel, and close my eyes. I see the road to Tiro. Children without faces spill from the bush.

I jump up from the table. I won't go to sleep. No.

A gray light filters through the window slats. A rooster crows from one of the neighbors' yards. Soon it'll be sunup. Good.

Time to look after the chickens. I take the lamp and a jug and make my way to the cistern by the coop. The water level's lower than I'd like, what with my washing, cleaning, and the vegetable garden. Tomorrow's Saturday; I'll load the wheelbarrow with pails and spend the morning pumping at the standpipe.

Across the cactus hedge to my right, my neighbor, Mr. Tafa, starts his truck and heads off for work with United Construction. He likes to leave early, before Mrs. Tafa has a chance to start in on him. We wave to each other as he drives away.

I fill the jug in the cistern and set the lamp on a paving stone by the coop door. Inside, I pour water into the chickens' pan and edge my way through the gloom to the feed bag hanging from a spike on the far wall. I toss a few handfuls of seed on the ground. While the hens peck breakfast, I feel the corners of their nests. Esther's supposed to collect the eggs at night, but she always misses a couple.

Things rustle in the shadows. Flap at me out of the dark.

I imagine my dream—the things in the night—and stumble out of the coop. Hens. It's only the hens. I don't care. I grab the lamp and race to the house.

Inside, there's a commotion in the kids' room.

"What's going on?"

"Nothing," Soly singsongs.

"Yes, nothing!" Iris insists. "We're sleeping. So stay out."

I push aside their curtain. Iris is on her hands and knees trying to scoop up a million beads from an upturned bowl. And—oh my lord—she's undone her cornrows.

"Iris?!?"

"I was trying to bead my hair."

"You can't even braid it!"

"I can so. It was perfect, till you left with the light."

"I told her not to," Soly peeps. He's hiding under their sheet.

Iris punches him. "Baby."

I grab her by the elbow, drag her to the table, and get out the tong combs. "I don't have time for this, I really don't," I say, running my hands through her hair. It's four inches long and unbelievably dense. My hands snag everywhere.

"Ow," Iris squeals as I tease out the tats. "Ow, you're hurting."

"Sit still, or it'll hurt even more." There's a mass of knotted kinks. I dig in a comb. "I promised I'd bead your hair this weekend."

"You promised last week too," Iris pouts. "You're a liar!"

"And you're a brat." I yank hard.

"Ow! Ow ow ow!"

I smile: That'll teach her. After forty-odd minutes, I've worked out the worst of it. I quickly separate the hair into large sections and weave six thick braids.

"I want cornrows!" Iris squeals.

"Later." I get up and head to the counter to make porridge.

Iris crosses her arms. "I won't go to school with my hair like this."

"Yes you will, or I'll shave you bald."

Esther arrives at the door with her brother and sister, Sammy and Magda.

"Breakfast's late," I say, tossing my head toward Iris. I reach for the jar of maize meal. The lid's off. One look inside, and I seal it up tight. "Esther, can I speak to you in private?" I say calmly.

Three steps outside, I lose control. "The flour's crawling with insects. If Iris finds out, she'll blab. Then Soly won't eat his porridge ever again, and Mrs. Tafa will go on and on about how Mama always kept a clean house and what would she be saying if she were alive to see the mess I've made of it."

"Don't worry," Esther soothes. "I'll sift the flour while the rest of you are at school. Or I'll make bread: We can say the bugs are raisins."

I laugh despite myself.

"For now, stay here and pull yourself together," Esther continues. "I'll take care of breakfast." She winks encouragement and goes inside. I chant the alphabet to calm down—ABCDEFG, ABCDEFG—fill the watering pail at the cistern, and head to the vegetable patch.

A screen door squeaks open and bangs shut across the cactus hedge. It's Mrs. Tafa, off on her grand morning tour of the neighborhood. Her girdle won't fit anymore, so she's strolling out in her billowing yellow kaftan and matching parasol. She looks like a one-woman sunrise. It was bad enough when Mrs. Tafa had the only house on the street with electricity, running water, and a land line. She'd lord about, telling the neighbors how to stake their tomatoes, asking if their babies had ear mites, and covering her nose with her hankie to let them know they needed a bath.

These days, it's worse. Mr. Tafa brought her a cell phone from work. It's practically attached to her head. So now instead of simply yakking at the neighbors, Mrs. Tafa hollers their sins to the world. Folks run when they see her coming. That doesn't stop her: "There goes Mrs. Bande," she'll bellow into the cell. "I'd hide my tail too, if my yard looked like a rummage sale at the dump." Last week, she got on the local radio call-in show. "I'm at the Nylos' place on Fourth Street," she announced. "What a smell! Jacob Nylo should stop chasing young girls and dig out his outhouse."

Right now, Mrs. Tafa's on the cell to her husband, telling him what to pick up at the drugstore on his way home. I pray she doesn't see me. No such luck. "Why, there's Chanda," she hoots at the cell. "The poor thing's watering her excuse for a garden. Those bean rows are more crooked than Mrs. Gulubane's teeth. Yoo hoo! Chanda!" I look over. She's waving at me. I wave back. "Well, I've things to do, places to go," she brays at her husband. "Bye bye."

Mrs. Tafa sashays into the yard, struggling to find the cell's Off button. The trouble is, the buttons are too small for her to see without the little magnifying glass she hides in her sewing bag. She's always getting wrong numbers. I'll see her on the street, squinting and poking at the pad, then yelling at the stranger that answers: "Who the hell are you? I never phoned you! Get off my cell, or I'm calling the police!" After a dozen wrong numbers, she'll pitch it at a tree. No wonder it's covered in glue, sticky tape, and elastic bands. I'm amazed it's even working.

I keep my eyes on my watering in hopes that Mrs. Tafa will leave. Instead, she twirls her parasol and stares at me. I move slowly through the rows. She keeps staring. I pretend to check for aphids. More staring. Finally, when I can't stand it anymore, she says: "Any trouble last night?"

"No. Why?"

"Saw your light. Your light's been on quite a few nights lately."

"Soly's afraid of the dark," I shrug.

Silence. I examine the pale yellow leaves on the squash vine.

"You'd tell your Auntie Rose if there was a problem, wouldn't you?"

Auntie Rose. I hate it when she calls herself that. The name began when I was little. Mama and Papa had moved down from Tiro and settled us into the worker houses at the diamond mine. Mrs. Tafa's first husband, Meeshak, was a friend on Papa's shift; they died together with my older brothers in the great cave-in. Mrs. Tafa started acting like we were family. "Calling her Auntie Rose is such a little thing," Mama said, "and it'd mean so much to her." So fine, I call her "Auntie Rose" for Mama's sake.

"Chanda, dear," Mrs. Tafa says. "I asked you a question."

"Yes, Auntie Rose. If there was a problem, I'd tell you."

She dabs her forehead with her hankie. "I'm thinking of your mama, is all. She'd want me to know."

I nod. We say our goodbyes. Out in the street, Mrs. Tafa makes a big show of poking her button pad. "Howdy-do, Mr. Mayor," she blares into the cell. "What a pleasure to find you awake. I trust you're not hungover?" With that, she sails off on her tour.

The kids run out the door ready for school, Esther following with my satchel and a small bag of biscuits. I give Soly a hug. Iris glares past me, her hair wrapped in a kerchief. She grabs Magda by the hand and the two skip off, Soly and Sammy close behind kicking a stone between them.

When I started work at the elementary, I tried to walk with them, but they told me it made them embarrassed in front of their friends. To be honest, going alone is best for me too. I get to ride my bike. Bonang's a city of eighty thousand; it's all spread out, and we're in the far west outskirts. If I have errands to run after class, having wheels is a blessing.

"I'm going to the Welcome Center this morning," Esther says as we watch the children turn the corner. "But I'll be back to feed them lunch and supper. You'll be late, right? Talking to someone at the secondary?"

"Please, Esther. Don't make me tell Mr. Selalame my dream. I don't want him thinking I'm crazy, or that he made a mistake getting me my job. Please, please, I can't let him down."

"Then talk to your 'Auntie Rose.'"

I give her a hard look, grab my satchel, and jam it in my bike carrier. "Keep the stupid biscuits. I'm not hungry."

The ride to school is the only peace I get all day. Little Ezekiel Sibanda has smuggled in a carton of shake-shake from his papa's still. First thing I know, he and a friend are drunk at the back of the class. They fight, I haul them to the front, and they puke on my desk. I spend the rest of the morning wiping up vomit. I spend lunch hour explaining to the principal how I let it happen. Then I'm in the hall with Lena Gambe sobbing on my shoulder about some name-calling. Finally, to top my day, Iris decides to show me who's boss. She sits backward on her bench, won't turn around, and dares me to do something about it.

When the final bell rings and the students spill from the room, I collapse in my chair. I couldn't see Mr. Selalame now even if I wanted to. I'm too tired. Too, too tired. I'll wait till after the weekend.

My eyelids flicker shut. I'm on the road to Tiro. The ditches are rivers of blood. Soly and Iris are swept away.

My eyes snap open. I can't breathe. Mr. Selalame. I don't have a choice.

3

I BIKE TO the secondary, run down the hall to Mr. Selalame's classroom. He's working late, as usual. Right now, he's leaning out the window, clapping his blackboard erasers, singing a march. What do I do? Waltz in? Knock first?

I end up outside his door, staring. Some teachers have coffee stains on their jackets or stink of B.O. and alcohol. Not Mr. Selalame. He's the cleanest, handsomest, smartest man in Bonang. And he uses new words for fun. His newest is *ergo*.

Esther thinks I have a crush. One day when I couldn't stop saying his name, she said: "Remember, Chanda, he's got a wife and kids." I gave her the eye. "Of course I remember, Esther. When it comes to men, I'm not like *some* people." I hope she's forgotten. It was back when we could tease about boys, before her days on the street.

Besides, even if I do have a crush, it's not *that* kind of crush. Is it? I'm not sure. I've never had a crush like that—at least I don't think I have—so it's hard to tell. All I know is, I could watch him forever.

Mr. Selalame finishes clapping his dusters and centers them on the ledge under the blackboard. As always after a clapping, he has a tickle on his nose from the chalk dust. He rubs it with the back of his wrist. Then he turns around, wiping his hands with a handkerchief. We both jump when he sees me.

"Chanda!"

"Mr. Selalame!" I think he's embarrassed I caught him singing. I'm embarrassed he caught me spying.

"Come in," he laughs. "Sit, sit. Can I offer you a tea?"

"No, thank you." I hesitate, then slump into my old desk—middle aisle, two rows back—and stare through the hole in the upper right-hand corner where the ink bottle used to go.

Mr. Selalame props himself against the desk opposite me. "I see you've come about something important."

I nod. Mr. Selalame smells of fresh soap and peppermint. I try not to notice.

"I've been getting this nightmare," I say at last. As the words fall from my mouth, I want to jump out the window; I have a dream and I run to my old teacher? "Mr. Selalame, I'm sorry, I shouldn't have come, I have to go."

He raises his hand. "Not before you tell me your dream."

"It's stupid."

"Nothing you care about is stupid."

I look in his eyes. They coax the truth out of me, like Mama's. I check the door to make sure no one's listening. Then, even though I'm kicking myself, I take a deep breath and begin. When I'm finished, Mr. Selalame thinks a bit, clicking his tongue behind his teeth. "Your dream is always the same?"

I frown. "Sometimes the ditches by the road are full of crocodiles. Other times they're full of blood, and the children paddle by in dugouts. But it's always about Tiro. Tiro and Mama and my little brother and sister. Is it a warning? Is something terrible going to happen?"

Mr. Selalame smiles. "Relax," he says. "Dreams don't predict the future. They're about the present. You know that, don't you?"

"Yes." I lower my head. The truth is, I don't know it. I

say I do, because it's what Mr. Selalame wants to hear. But deep down, I'm not sure what I think. I don't believe in magic. All the same, I know there's more to life than what we see with our eyes.

"Your nightmare is a chase dream," Mr. Selalame says calmly. "Ergo, it's about feeling helpless. Trapped. Chase dreams come when we're stressed."

I sit up straight, shoulders back. "But I'm not."

"You are." He folds his arms. "You need to slow down, Chanda. Since your mama passed, you haven't taken a breath."

"There hasn't been time."

"Make time."

"How? There's always a problem with Soly and Iris—a scrape, a fever, a stubbed toe. Or Soly will cry, or Iris will throw things—and I know it's from missing Mama, and I want to make it better, but I can't. And when I'm not messing up with them, I'm working, or doing chores, or visiting Mama at the cemetery. And I haven't even started the friendship center in her memory. I promised to open one when she died, and—" I bang my head on the desk, twice. "I'm sorry. It's just, Mr. Selalame, I'm scared. Sometimes I fill up with this panic. I can't stop it. Why? What's wrong

23

with me? Mama always managed. She did what she had to. Why can't I be like her?"

Mr. Selalame checks his shoes, so we can pretend he doesn't see my eyes fill. "Chanda," he says slowly, "what about taking a break from your supply teaching?"

"No. My family needs the money."

"Not as much as you need your health."

"I can't afford to think about that."

"You have to. For the sake of your brother and sister. You can always patch clothes. Stretch a pot of soup. But if you make yourself crazy-sick, you won't be able to do anything. Then what?"

I breathe out till my lungs are empty. "You must think I'm a baby."

"No," he exclaims. "But you're not an adult either."

"I'm old enough. Mama was married at my age. She had babies."

"Is that what you want?"

I shake my head, rock on my hands. "All I want is to make Mama proud. I want her to know I'm taking care of things. That Soly and Iris are safe."

"She knows. She's proud."

"How can you say that? Everything's falling apart."

Mr. Selalame pauses. "You're too tired to see this, but I promise you: You're doing fine. One day Soly and Iris will be grown up. You'll go back to school. You'll graduate with that scholarship. You'll build your Mama's friendship center. Trust me. These things take time, that's all. Don't let your pride destroy your future."

He lets me think about that for a while, then he leans back slowly. "If I recall rightly, you have people in Tiro."

My throat dries up. "It depends what you mean by people."

"Relatives. Your mama-granny and grampa, some aunties and uncles, cousins—and isn't there an older sister? It's where your mama went when she got sick."

I nod.

Mr. Selalame strokes the side of his head like he's nursing an idea. "In your dream, you have to get to Tiro," he says slowly. "Maybe your mind is telling you, you need to return to your roots. Families are something to cling to when things get overwhelming. Maybe you need a visit to Tiro. It'd give you support. It'd give you a rest as well."

"No," I blurt out. "I'll never go back to Tiro."

Mr. Selalame leans in, eyes alert.

My ears burn. "Things happened in Tiro," I whisper.

25

"Things happened to Mama." I flap my hands. "Please, don't make me say it."

Mr. Selalame puts his finger to his lips. "If you want an ear, I'm here. Otherwise, I haven't heard a thing."

"Thank you. Thanks."

I don't know where to look. A silence swallows the room.

Mr. Selalame clears his throat. "So," he says carefully, "where else could we turn for some help? . . . How about your neighbor lady?"

"Mrs. Tafa?" My eyes twitch.

Mr. Selalame looks like he's stepped in a cow pie. "I guess it's not my day for ideas."

I find myself laughing. "I guess not!"

He smiles.

My eye catches the time on the wall clock. "It's late. Soly and Iris, they'll be waiting for supper. *Ergo*, I better go." I get up, stand awkwardly by the desk. "Mr. Selalame . . . thank you. Thank you for everything."

"But I didn't do anything."

"Yes. You did. You made a difference just being here."

He gives me a wink for encouragement. "Drop by anytime."

"I will." I stop at the doorway, heart bursting. "Mr. Selalame—you're the best teacher in the school. And you have the cleanest blackboard erasers in the whole world."

I flush and race down the corridor. *You have the cleanest blackboard erasers in the whole world?*

How embarrassing.

4

I RIDE TOWARD home, lighter than air: a chase dream. Now that I know what my nightmare is, it doesn't seem as scary anymore. In fact, I'm so happy to name it, I almost don't notice Mrs. Mpho standing at the side of the road. She waves me over with a dish rag, mad as a hornet: "I'll have you know my family's underpants are clean as the priest's!"

"What are you talking about?"

Her mouth drops open like she's out to catch flies. "Don't play the innocent. This very morning I was hanging my laundry, when Rose Tafa waltzed by. 'Why, Chanda,' she said into that phone of hers, 'Mrs. Mpho's forgot to scrub her undies again.'"

"Whoever Mrs. Tafa was talking to, it wasn't me," I say. "I was at school. Only the principal has a phone. If you want to complain, complain to Mrs. Tafa. I dare you."

I leave Mrs. Mpho cursing in my direction, and speed to Mrs. Tafa's, too upset to think. Mrs. Tafa is squeezed into her lawn chair, fanning herself with a fly swatter. Soly and Iris are at her feet, drinking her famous lemonade.

Iris points smugly at her hair. It's in tight, shiny cornrows, beads woven throughout. "Look what Auntie Rose did. She knows how to do it right. And I didn't have to say ouch once, did I, Auntie?"

"No, you were an angel," Mrs. Tafa beams. She peers up her nose at me. "If you don't mind my saying so, that girl's hair looked like a weaver's nest."

I try not to scream. "Auntie Rose." I clip each word. "How dare you pretend that I gossip with you on your cell phone!"

"Who says I do?"

"Mrs. Mpho."

Mrs. Tafa sniffs. "That woman's got coconuts in her head." She rearranges her rear end on her chair's vinyl seat straps. The aluminum legs wobble. I pray they'll buckle and send the old goat onto her backside with her dress over her head.

I turn to the kids. "Soly, Iris. Come with me. It's time for supper."

"Auntie's already fed us," Soly says.

My eyes bulge. "What?"

"You were late," Mrs. Tafa chides. "The poor things were starving."

"But Esther was making supper," I say.

"Esther. Cooking." Mrs. Tafa shudders. "Who knows where those hands have been? Besides, the children get far better food here."

Iris nods vigorously. "Auntie Rose gave us chicken and figs and sweet potatoes and things that came out of a can."

I grab my bike and storm to our yard, leaving the kids behind with Mrs. Tafa. Esther's chasing Sammy and Magda around the outhouse. She stops when she sees me. "Don't blame me," she says, before I can get out a word. "I went over to Mrs. Tafa's and called them to eat: eggs and maize bread. Mrs. Tafa told me that she was looking after things and for me to mind my own business."

"Esther," I say fiercely, "we're going for a walk."

We get Sammy and Magda to promise they'll stay in the yard till we're back. Then we march past Mrs. Tafa's, Esther struggling to keep up.

"Where are you going?" Soly calls out to me.

"Nowhere," I yell. "Eat some more figs, why don't you?"

"Are you mad?"

I stare straight ahead and keep stomping. We end up at the empty sandlot a few blocks away, sitting on the rusty swing set that the city put up, back when the place was supposed to be a park. I grab my side chains, push off the ground, and swing up hard with all my might.

"It's not fair," I say bitterly. "I'm losing the kids. Mrs. Tafa's got time and money. She can do things for them that I can't. Mr. Selalame says my nightmare's because of stress. Well maybe she's the stress. Maybe she's what I'm afraid is out to get them. I hate her. I hate her I hate her I hate her!"

"Chanda, slow down," Esther says. "You're going to swing right over the top bar and crack your head open."

"I don't care."

"The kids love you, Chanda . . . Mrs. Tafa, she doesn't matter . . . Listen to me!"

"No, you listen." I skid my feet in the dirt and come to a stop. "Mrs. Tafa's not just stealing Soly and Iris. She's ruining my name." I tell her about Mrs. Mpho and the cell phone story.

Esther frowns. Then suddenly, she laughs.

"What's so funny?"

31

"Think about it, Chanda. This morning, Mrs. Tafa pretended she was talking to you, but she wasn't talking to anyone. I'll bet it's like that all the time. She whoops into her cell like she knows the world, but really she's just blabbing to herself. It's like when Mrs. Gulubane mutters into her giant snail shell, pretending to talk to the dead."

My head swims. "You think so?"

"Of course," Esther hoots. "She's rich compared to most people around here, but that's not saying much. How would she know anybody important? Why would the mayor take her calls? As for our neighbors—how many have a phone? Who'd talk to her if they did? The only people she can call are her husband and the man at the radio call-in. Mrs. Tafa's a mean, old bully. Your mama was her only friend, and that's because your mama was a saint."

Esther's right. Even Mr. Tafa avoids her. He leaves for work early and gets home late; on his days off, he does odd jobs, like building Esther's rooms at the side of my house, or patching the tenant shacks at the far side of his property.

"Everyone's scared of her tongue," Esther says, eyes dancing, "but nobody pays her much mind. As for Mrs. Mpho—it's true about her underpants."

I laugh. Next thing I know, Esther and I are twirling our

swings till the chains are twisted tight. We lift our feet off the ground and spin, squealing like when we were little. We wobble dizzily to the road and make our way home in the near dusk.

Iris and Soly are already under the cover in their night-clothes. They're so quiet, I have to check to know they're there. When I stick my head into their room, Iris says: "Would you tuck us in? . . . Please?"

I pull the bedsheet under their necks and smooth it just so.

"Do you still love us?" Soly whispers.

"Of course. How could you ask that?"

He acts shy. "You were so mad. We were scared."

"Not me," Iris says. But I know she's lying.

I kiss their foreheads. "I love you now and forever," I say. "More than anything." Then I sit cross-legged at the side of their mat and tell them their favorite bedtime story—the one about the impala and the baboon—acting the parts with Soly's sock puppet and my hankie.

I kiss them good night again. My stomach dissolves. Mama. I remember how she tucked me in, how she kissed my forehead, told me stories, said how she'd love me forever. Mama. I miss Mama so much I can't stand it.

As I leave Soly and Iris, I touch their door frame for balance, get to the far corner of the main room, and roll into a ball on the floor, stuffing my hankie in my mouth so they won't hear me cry.

When I'm like this, I usually go to Esther. She holds me and rocks me and lets me babble, and it helps. But she didn't know Mama. Not really. She's the sort of friend that stays away from parents. All she remembers is that Mama smiled at her, offered her biscuits, and never kicked her off the property. So it's not the same. Not like she knew Mama, and knows what Mama means.

I'm going to start sobbing, I know it. I won't be able to stop. I need to get away. The sandlot. I'll go back to the sandlot.

I walk gingerly across the yard. To the left, music and happy talk drift up the street from the Lesoles. Mr. Lesole's a safari guide; he's mostly away in the bush. When he's home, he celebrates, spending his tip money on CDs for his boom box and food for his guests. Normally I like it—I even go over—but tonight, all I can think is: How can there be parties with Mama dead? How can the world go on without her?

I turn right toward the sandlot and hear a familiar

voice: "If I was you, I wouldn't be wandering far, this time of night."

Mrs. Tafa's in her lawn chair, alone in the dark under her tree, waiting for Mr. Tafa to come home. All of a sudden, she doesn't seem so mean. Just lonely. I'm filled with shame. Why am I mad about what she does for Soly and Iris? Why should they lose out because of my fear and pride?

I go into Mrs. Tafa's yard and sit quietly on the ground beside her lawn chair. We don't talk about our fight. Don't talk about anything. Just sit there. After a long time I swallow hard and say: "Thank you for doing Iris's cornrows."

"It was nothing," she says. "Something to pass the time, is all." A pause. "It's nice to have someone braid your hair, isn't it?" Another pause. "I could do yours someday if you'd like. Not as good as your mama, mind. But I could try."

I sob. Mrs. Tafa puts her hand on my shoulder. "It's hard, isn't it?"

I gulp air.

"Your mama was the finest woman who walked this earth," Mrs. Tafa says gently. "Oh, how she loved you kids. She was proud of you, especially. Before she went to Tiro, she said to me, 'Rose, no matter what happens, I can die happy. I know my Chanda will take care of things.'" Mrs. Tafa slaps her thighs. "But why talk about sad things, when there's so much good to remember?" She leans in to my ear. "I'm thinking of when you were little, how your mama'd blow on your tummy to stop you being grumpy."

I sniffle-smile at the thought of it. "I've tried that on Iris," I say. "She hates it."

"Iris is a special one, isn't she?" Mrs. Tafa chuckles, and recalls the time Mama was shelling peas and Iris got one stuck up her nose: "Your mama made her a necklace of husks so she'd stop crying." Soon, Mrs. Tafa and I are laughing and storytelling in the dark. Stories about Mama. Happy stories. Simple stories. Stories from our time in the worker houses at the mine, to a few years back when Mama won a prize at the street fair for her sweet-potato pie.

"You should have seen the way your mama and papa flirted at the mine hall," Mrs. Tafa winks. "The glint in your mama's eye when your papa'd do a jig. Folks knew they took care of business, all right."

I get all embarrassed, but I want to hear more. As long as we talk, Mama's alive. Please, I don't want to go to bed ever. When Mr. Tafa finally comes home, though, I know it's time.

"It's been ages since we've talked like this," Mrs. Tafa says. "Let's do it again." She watches from her stoop as I head to my door. At the last minute, I have a sudden need to run back. I fall on my knees and clutch her round the waist. "Auntie Rose, will the pain ever go away?"

Mrs. Tafa kneels down, arms around me. "Remember how it was with your papa?"

I nod.

She kisses the top of my head. "The missing never goes away," she says. "But after a time, the hurting's not so sharp. And in the end, if you're lucky, there's a glow."

An enormous hole opens in the pit of my stomach. "Why did Mama have to die? Why like that? I wish she'd never gone back to Tiro."

Oh, how Mama hated Tiro. At fifteen, Granny and Grampa engaged her to Tuelo Malunga, a boy from the neighboring cattle post; but Mama was scared of him, and ran off with Papa instead. Relatives said she was cursed for dishonoring the ancestors. They blamed her for everything. So for her to return there . . . Before she left, she said she wouldn't be gone long. But weeks passed and she didn't even call us. Then one night Mrs. Tafa blurted her secret: Mama wasn't coming back, not ever. She had AIDS. She'd been scared of what would happen to us kids if the neighbors found out, so scared she'd gone to die in a place where she was hated. I got on the next flatbed truck to Tiro. The relatives had left her at the abandoned ruin on their cattle post. They claimed they brought her food. All I know is, when I found her, she was alone in the bush, thin as a reed, huddled under a stained sheet buzzing with flies. She didn't recognize me. With the help of the Tiro health clinic, I got her home. Three days later, she passed.

I leave Mrs. Tafa's, crawl onto my mat, and toss and turn till the middle of the night. Mama. You didn't have to go to Tiro. We'd have taken the shame, the pain—anything, everything—to keep you with us. Why couldn't I stop you? Why?

I drift into my dream. Mama's alive. We're at the ruin where I found her, watching Soly and Iris dance. Mama turns into a stork. "Keep them safe," she says. "There's going to be a storm."

5

MOMENTS LATER, I'M shaken awake into a real-life night-mare. Esther says I screamed in my sleep again. Only this time when the children went to get her, their cries roused the Tafas, who thought we had robbers. Mr. Tafa ran over with his shotgun, followed by Mrs. Tafa in her nightie, wielding a fry pan. She's wormed my dream out of me. So now, while Esther comforts Soly and Iris in their bedroom, I'm stuck at the table in the main room getting preached at.

"Your ancestors have sent you a dream," Mrs. Tafa exclaims, drumming her stubby fingers on the wood boards. "If you don't get to Tiro, something terrible's going to happen. The warning is plain as the nose on your face."

Mr. Tafa yawns loudly. He leans against the front door, his shotgun propped beside him, waiting to escort Mrs. Tafa back home. I wish she'd take the hint. Instead, she

39

wrestles her left foot onto her lap, takes off her slipper, and squints at the callus on her bunion. "Let's go over that dream again: You have to get to Tiro. You don't make it. What happens? Disaster! How simple can a dream get?"

I think of Mr. Selalame. "Dreams don't tell the future."

"That's what they teach you at school," she snorts, "but we know different, don't we?" She picks at the pad of dry skin. "According to Esther, this waking-up-screaming has turned itself into a habit. Well, I'm here to tell you, it won't stop. Not till you get yourself to Tiro."

"I'm never going to Tiro again," I say. "Not after what they did to Mama."

"They never meant for things to end like that."

"I don't care."

Mrs. Tafa looks up from her work. Her eyes are gentle. "Chanda, it's nobody's fault your mama passed. Not your granny's. Not your Auntie Lizbet's. Not your other aunties, nor uncles, nor your older sister Lily. Your mama had that thing. Nothing could change that."

"They abandoned her in the bush."

"They didn't know any better. They're from Tiro, for heaven's sake, not Bonang." She grunts. "You wouldn't happen to have a peeling knife, would you?"

I fetch it from the rack by the sink, along with a small

dish for her scrapings. What with her eyesight, in two minutes her toe will be raw, and I'll be looking for a rag to staunch the bleeding.

"Thank you kindly." She takes the knife and whittles away like she's peeling a sweet potato. Her concentration is frightening. "It was bad enough, you didn't call the family about your mama's funeral. I offered you my phone."

"And I used it."

"Not till the night of the laying over when it was too late for them to get here. You didn't even call ahead to your granny and grampa. Your mama's own parents."

"They wouldn't have come anyway."

"You don't know that."

"And what if they *had*?" I snap. "What would they have said? That Mama died the way she lived? Cursed? Mama deserved a little peace at the end. Respect. Love."

Iris is peering in from the bedroom.

"What are you doing up? I thought Esther had you back in bed."

"I'm sorry, Chanda," Esther calls out. "I'm helping Soly."

"His diaper fell off," Iris announces.

"It's not a diaper," comes Soly's voice. "It's a feed sack with leg holes."

Poor Soly. I used to wrap him in a towel, secured by a

41

little plastic grocery bag. We switched the little grocery bag to a green plastic feed sack, cut to size and fitted with a drawstring, so he'd feel more grown-up. But Iris is no fool.

"I don't care what you call it," she yells, "it's still a diaper. And you peed all over."

"You didn't have to tell!" Soly cries.

"Why not?" Iris mocks. "You're a pee factory. And you're five! Five! I only wore a diaper till I was two. Wait'll your friends find out."

Soly wails.

"I mean it. I'm telling the world!"

"Don't you dare," I say. "Soly's problem is just between us. Now go back to bed."

"How can I? Our mat's all wet."

Esther appears behind her: "I've put down a new one."

Iris flounces back into the bedroom.

"Good night, Iris," I say. Iris doesn't answer. Esther winks. Now it's Soly's turn for attention. He waddles past Esther and up beside me, the towel around his waist, the feed sack tripping up his ankles.

"Yes?" I sigh.

"I just peed a little," he says.

"We'll talk about it tomorrow."

"Yes, but Chanda . . ." His eyes are big. "Are you going to Tiro? Are you leaving us?"

"No."

"Then what's going to happen?"

"Nothing. Everything'll be fine."

"That's what Mama said."

"Soly, go to bed."

"Come on," Esther says. "I'll tell you and Iris a story." She maneuvers him back into the bedroom.

I give Mrs. Tafa a tight smile. "Thanks for your prophecy."

She ignores my sarcasm. "By any chance do you have a rag? My bunion's raw. There's something the matter with that knife of yours."

I throw her a strip of cloth. She wraps her toe in silence and wriggles her foot back into her slipper. Then she looks me straight in the eye, her voice quiet, but firm: "No good ever came of a feud. No matter what your family did, or didn't do, they're still your family, and they're the only family you have. For years, I tried to tell your mama that, but she wouldn't listen. Well you listen now. Stop being selfish. Soly and Iris deserve a granny and grampa. Go to Tiro. Make peace for the children, if not for yourself."

"I appreciate the advice, Auntie Rose," I say. "Now,

please, it's three in the morning. In no time the sun'll be up, there'll be chores, and a day of teaching. I have to sleep."

"I'm telling you, there'll be no sleeping till you make things right with your people." She taps her nose. "Get to Tiro. Make peace. Otherwise, dear god, something terrible will happen to the children. If you don't believe me, ask Mrs. Gulubane."

I'm still uneasy about the dream part. But Mrs. Gulubane? I roll my eyes.

"Go ahead, laugh, you and your education!" Mrs. Tafa hisses. "Eight years ago, Mrs. Mpho couldn't have children. Mrs. Gulubane rubbed her belly with a potion and she's been making babies ever since. Then there's Mr. Lesole. She gave him a little bag of magic powder. For six years, it's saved his safari camp from General Mandiki and the rebels of Ngala. He'd be dead if it weren't for her. Chopped into bits with machetes! Everyone near the park too!"

"Auntie Rose, I don't mean to make fun of the spirit doctor. But the war is in Ngala. General Mandiki and his rebels have never crossed our border. Not once."

"What did I tell you? Mrs. Gulubane's magic is so powerful it even works on devils!"

Mr. Tafa's asleep, propped against the door frame. At

the mention of the word "devils," he tumbles over. His shotgun clatters on the cement. The sound of it startles him awake. "What? What?" He blinks, grabs the rifle, and jumps to his feet.

"It's nothing," I say. "We were just talking about the rebels in Ngala."

"Oh, them," Mr. Tafa yawns.

"They must have popped into your dream when you heard us talking."

Mr. Tafa stretches. "As long as General Mandiki stays on his side of the border, his rebels are no business of mine."

Mrs. Tafa smacks him on the shoulder. "It's time I got you home to bed, Leo."

Before she can smack him again, Mr. Tafa mumbles, "G'night." He stumbles out the front door ahead of her.

Mrs. Tafa turns in the doorway. "Make no mistake, Chanda," she mutters darkly. "Your dream is a warning from the ancestors. Take heed while you can."

6

IN NO TIME it's Saturday morning.

I load up the wheelbarrow with pails and go to pump water at the standpipe. Normally Esther would help, but she's taking Sammy and Magda to see their Uncle Kagiso. He's in from the country for the day, staying with their Auntie and Uncle Poloko. The Polokos can't stand Esther—they say the scars from her rape are the wages of sin—but they can't keep her away from her Uncle Kagiso when she's with the little ones.

At the standpipe, I get in line behind Mrs. Lesole. She's wearing a flowered cotton-print dress, a polka-dot bandanna, and orange flip-flops; there's three buckets at her feet, one for each hand and one for her head. "I hope the noise from our street dance didn't keep you awake last night," Mrs. Lesole says.

"I couldn't sleep anyway."

"My man's back to the safari camp tomorrow," she sighs good-naturedly. "There'll be more feasting tonight. Come. Bring Soly and Iris. He loves to play with them."

"I know," I smile. Since Mama passed, Mr. Lesole's been incredibly kind. Mrs. Tafa steams with jealousy when the kids talk about his games and adventures. "That man has quite the mouth on him, doesn't he?" she sniffs. "If he's so important, what's he doing in Bonang?" Look who's talking.

As it happens, Mr. Lesole's outfit, the Kenje River Safari Camp, is the most important tourist camp in Mfuala National Park. And Mfuala National Park is the most important tourist destination in the country—ten thousand square miles of dense bush, forest, and floodplain that starts forty miles north of Tiro and ends at the Mfuala mountain range that separates us from Ngala. "There's an even bigger park on the Ngala side of the mountains," Mr. Lesole likes to brag, "but nobody goes there because ours is better." The truth is, the Ngala park is where General Mandiki and his rebels hide out; anyone who goes there gets killed.

Mr. Lesole's camp is a private reserve on an oxbow in

the Mfuala foothills, near the border. There are no roads in. Tourists arrive on small planes and stay in fancy tents, with hardwood floors, maid service, and flush toilets, that cost more per night than most of us earn in a year. Each morning, Mr. Lesole leads them on bush walks, rifle at the ready in case they run into trouble with the animals. At dusk, he and a driver take them out in 4x4s.

"The night drives, that's when we see the kills," he'll whisper to the kids in a spooky voice. "I'm strapped in a seat on the hood of the jeep, my rifle under one arm. With my free hand, I scan the bush with a spotlight. I've seen lions take down impala, a leopard attack a bush buck, and a pack of hyenas tear into a Cape buffalo that got stuck in the mud during rainy season."

I love to listen to Mr. Lesole. Closing my eyes, I see mama baboons loping through clearings, with babies clinging to their bellies. Hippo pods sunning on the banks of a lazy oxbow. Vervet monkeys skipping up fever trees. Zebra grazing in wooded brush. Roan antelope dashing through thickets.

I wish I could see it in real life. Apart from bush rats, lizards, and a few warthogs, the game outside the parks was hunted out before I was little. Sometimes a bachelor elephant will roam beyond the park boundaries, but they disappear fast. Farmers burn old tires to keep them away, or poachers shoot them for their ivory tusks.

Mr. Lesole hates poachers. He reports every one he discovers. "Our animals are a natural resource," he'll say, "same as oil, copper, and diamonds. The tourist money they bring in helps keep our country alive."

Mrs. Tafa couldn't care less. When Soly and Iris mentioned Mr. Lesole's fights with the poachers, she went berserk: "Those damn beasts," she barked. "I'm glad they're gone. When I was a girl in the country, elephants ruined our farms. They killed the trees, ate the bushes, and trampled the crops. If rich tourists want to spend their money to go to some park and take pictures, fine. But spare me tears about the hunt. Who wants lions attacking their cattle, or hyenas picking off their children? Heavens, what's bush meat for, if not feeding the hungry? They don't put leopards in jail for hunting. Why should animals have more rights than we do?"

How can I argue with that? I wasn't alive in the old days. I can't imagine what I'd do if wildlife took my food and threatened my family. But when I see the animals on the back of Mr. Lesole's park map and hear his stories, I thrill

49

with pride. Elephants, lions, giraffes and hippos—they're part of what makes this place special. Blessed.

When I get back from the standpipe, I tell the kids that Mrs. Lesole gave them a personal invitation to today's party. Their eyes sparkle, then Soly gets concerned. "Can we go early? Once the grownups show up, Mr. Lesole won't be able to play."

We head to the Lesoles' midafternoon. Halfway, we smell the goat stew simmering over the firepit. Soly and Iris break into a run. "Mr. Lesole! Mrs. Lesole!"

Mrs. Lesole sits by the pot, wiping her forehead. Mr. Lesole is flopped in the hammock slung from his tree. He's poured into a ratty khaki outfit, fanning himself with the old Tilley hat he retrieved from his camp's lost-and-found box. His cheeks and chin are dotted with stray hairs; he doesn't have much to shave, so when he's on break he doesn't shave at all. If I was Mrs. Lesole, it'd drive me crazy.

At the sound of the kids, Mrs. Lesole waves greetings with her stir stick. Mr. Lesole leaps out of his hammock and pretends to hide behind the tree. The kids drag him out, crying, "Let's play Don't Die! Can we? Can we? Please?" Don't Die is a series of games Mr. Lesole invented to teach them how to survive in the bush. Naturally, he's up for it.

They start with Soly's favorite: Elephant Charge. Mr. Lesole lumbers around like an elephant, his arm-trunk twisting imaginary leaves to his mouth. When he goes near Iris, she freezes like she's supposed to, then backs off slowly as if she's moving downwind. Not Soly. He loses concentration and fidgets. Mr. Lesole rears back and touches his fingertips to his temples, making big imaginary ears with the spaces between his elbows and his head. He shakes his head so hard you can almost hear the big gray ears slapping. He rocks, swings a foot to and fro, stomps the earth, kicks it behind him. Then he raises his arm-trunk, trumpets, lowers his head, and charges. It's too late for Soly to freeze, but he holds his ground, yelling and clapping. Mr. Lesole stops in front of his nose. A terrible pause. He moves off. Soly beats his chest and yodels.

"Well done, you two," says Mr. Lesole.

"Elephants can't talk," Iris reminds him tartly.

Once, I asked if charges could always be stopped. "They're usually for show," Mr. Lesole said. "Whatever you do, don't run. If you run, you're jam."

"Yes, but what if the charge is real?"

He grimaced. "If the ellie's angry—ears flat back, trunk

tucked under its chin—you're in trouble. They can run twenty-four miles an hour. You can't. They can barrel through thornbush that'd skin you alive. If you climb a tree, they'll knock it down. Your only hope is to get downwind. But chances are, you'll be dead first."

I'm glad he didn't tell that to the kids; Soly'd be wetting his mat forever.

Mr. Lesole recuperates by stretching his lower back, while Soly and Iris prepare for the next adventure: Hyena Hideaway. Shouts of "We're ready" fill the air. It's time for Mr. Lesole to be a hyena and catch them sleeping outside their protective enclosure of thorny acacia boughs—here, made of chairs and benches. After Hyena Hideaway, there's Hippo Highway, Crocodile River, and dozens of other life-and-death thrills. Mr. Lesole would make a great teacher. A great papa, too, if he wasn't away so much.

When the games are over, Mr. Lesole flops back into his hammock. Iris and Soly pile on top, bounce on his belly, and pull his chin hairs till he tells them about his recent adventures. "Last month, there was this tough-guy tourist wanted a morning swim. We warned him the river was full of crocodiles. He didn't listen. Snuck off when we weren't looking. All we found were his sandals, a pair of sunglasses, and a beer can."

The kids squeal, and I send them off to help Mrs. Lesole prepare for the feast. Before joining them, I decide to have some fun. "So," I say, easy as a frog on a lily pad, "I hear-tell Mrs. Gulubane gave you a little bag of magic."

Mr. Lesole falls out of his hammock. "You heard what?"

"A bag of magic." I bug my eyes. "To protect you from the rebels of Ngala."

He gets up, brushing the dirt off his pants. "Says who?"

I look up at the sky and hum.

"It was Rose Tafa, wasn't it? That woman's mouth is bigger than her backside!"

"Can I see the bag?"

"I lost it on a night drive."

"I don't believe you."

"Fine by me."

I smile. "What's in it?"

His eyes dart around the yard. "Nothing to laugh about, that's for sure."

The way he says it, I get a chill. "I'm not laughing. Show me."

"This goes no further?"

"I promise."

Mr. Lesole fidgets inside the collar of his shirt and pulls out the magic pouch, hanging by a cord around his neck. I peek inside. "There's hedgehog and porcupine quills," he says furtively, "the dried wing of a nightjar, a talon from some bird of prey, and a handful of roots and bark chips I couldn't make out by the torch light. She ground them up in a skull with a pestle of bone. On my life, I won't repeat the spell she chanted, or tell you what she did in her trance. If you say any of this, I'll deny it."

"My lips are sealed."

"I've never gone near magic before," he continues, "but this Ngala business is different. Things have been fine, our side of the mountains. We act like they always will be, to keep the tourists coming. But we're whistling past the graveyard. Who knows what Mandiki will do next? Even *he* doesn't. They say he worships the skull of a dead spirit doctor. Carries it around in an ebony box wrapped in a monkey hide. You were a kid when he was in power. You've no idea what he's like."

Mr. Lesole is wrong. I was barely ten when the civil war started in Ngala, but Mama and Mrs. Tafa used to whisper about it all the time when they thought I was playing with my dolls. Of course their whispers made me listen even harder. I remember Mrs. Tafa reassuring Mama that even if Mandiki crossed the mountains, he'd have the whole of

Mfuala Park to travel through, and another forty miles of cattle posts, before he'd get to our relatives in Tiro. She was right. Mandiki's guerrillas stayed in the park on their side of the border, launching attacks on their own people. Every so often there's a headline in the market papers: "Ngala village torched; villagers burned alive," or "Ngala farmer's tongue cut out: a warning not to talk." Worst of all, Mandiki kidnaps children. He uses them as slaves, decoys, human shields. They become child soldiers. If they try to escape, they're killed—kicked to death, or chopped to bits with machetes. One day, after I'd seen a newspaper picture of a farmer nailed to a tree, I asked Mr. Selalame if he thought the Ngala war would ever end. His shoulders slumped. "Nobody wants peace. If Mandiki loses, he'll be executed. But if Ngala wins, the foreign funds it gets to fight terrorism disappear. Its leaders need that cash to pay for their limos and mansions."

Neighbors start to arrive for the feast. Mr. Lesole slips the magic pouch back inside his shirt and greets them, while I collect the kids to go home. When we find Mr. Lesole to say goodbye, he's at the side of the road talking with the Sibandas, who've hauled up pails of shake-shake in wheelbarrows. Mr. Lesole's parties take away the night trade from their *shabeen*, but as long as they can sell their booze by his house, they're happy. Mr. Sibanda ladles some brew into a recycled juice carton and hands it to Mr. Lesole.

"You're welcome to stay for the party, Chanda," Mr. Lesole says.

"Thanks. But I have to get the kids to bed."

"It's too early," Iris pouts.

"You listen to your big sister," Mr. Lesole smiles. He gets down on his knees and gives the children a cuddle.

"I hate it when you leave for the bush," Soly says. "Can't we go with you? I want to see the animals."

Mr. Lesole knuckles his forehead. "One day, when you're big, I'll get you a job as a busboy. How's that?"

"Really?"

"Sure thing. That's how I got started. In the meantime, here's a little something for your very own." He pulls a worn copy of the park map from his hip pocket. "Next time you miss me, just look at this map, close your eyes, and imagine me tracking a leopard. I'll give you a wave in your dreams."

"What do I get?" Iris demands.

"Iris!" I say. "Mind your manners."

Mr. Lesole just laughs. "You get this." He plops his Tilley hat on her head. It droops over her nose, but she's delighted.

"What do we say?" I prod.

"Thank you."

"Oh, and here's something for the big kid." He grins, and offers me a tiny pair of binoculars. "They call them 'opera glasses.' Some American lady brought them on safari. They fell out of her bag, and the jeep ran over them. One of the lenses is cracked, but it still works, sort of. Take it on a walk. Or spy on Mrs. Tafa."

Mrs. Lesole gives me a bowl of stew, maize porridge, and bread to take home. What a relief not to have to cook supper. I give thanks, promise to return the bowl first thing in the morning along with some fresh eggs, and we say our goodbyes.

As we head up the road, I see Mrs. Tafa at our gate, her cell phone pressed to her ear. She waves us to hurry. Who's she pretending to talk to this time? I wonder. The President? The Pope?

But when we reach her, Mrs. Tafa does something strange. She hands me the cell. "It's for you."

7

"Chanda?" The voice coming out of the phone is familiar, but I don't recognize it. "Chanda?" it says again.

The connection is bad. It sounds like the call is coming from far away. I press the phone to my ear and plug my other ear with my finger. There's talking in the background. The loud *cling* and *clang* of an old metal cash register. Oh my god. I'm talking to Lily, my older sister who stayed in Tiro when the rest of us came south. She must be using the phone at the general dealer's.

But why is she calling? How did she know the number to reach me?

I glance at Mrs. Tafa. She's staring at me like I'm her evening's entertainment. Suddenly, everything makes sense. Mrs. Tafa's called Tiro and left a message about my dream. She's arranged for Lily to call collect. I glare at Mrs.

Tafa, turn my back, and move off a piece.

The line crackles. "Chanda, are you there?"

"I'm here," I say tightly. "If this is about my dream, I'm hanging up."

"Granny's standing beside me." Lily says. "She's wanted to talk to you for a long time." The noise in the background is suddenly muffled. It's like Lily's cupped her mouth to the phone, so Granny won't hear. "When your neighbor called about your dream, Granny said it was an omen. If I put her on the line, will you be nice?"

"It depends."

"She's been crying since Mama died. Please. Be nice."

"Fine."

The receiver is passed to Granny. I hear Lily's voice in the background: "Granny, you have to talk into this part here."

"Hello? . . . Hello? . . . Chanda?" It's Granny. She sounds lost.

Mrs. Tafa's breathing over my shoulder. I give her a look. She backs off.

"Hello, Granny. It's me, Chanda."

"Chanda . . ." Granny's voice is so old. It was old before, but never like this.

There's a lot of static. "Granny, I'm sorry, I can't hear you."

"I'm sorry too," Granny says. More static. "Things got said that should never have been said. Things got done that . . . Chanda, I want to see you."

My head swims.

"Chanda, are you there?"

"I'm here." My eyes well. My knees are jelly.

"Please come visit," Granny says. "Please. Your grampa and me, we're too old to travel down."

I can't think. I can't see.

"We want to bless our grandchildren before we die. We want to heal the family curse."

"Granny . . ." The words choke out. "Granny . . . I can't talk . . . I'm sorry . . . I . . ."

I drop the phone in the dirt and run toward the house. Esther's in the yard with Sammy and Magda, back from visiting their uncle. I wave them off, run into my room, and cover my head with my pillow.

Outside, I hear Esther soothe Soly and Iris.

"What's wrong?" they ask.

"Nothing," Esther says. "Your sister's just thinking. You know what it's like when you need to think?"

They sound uncertain. When Esther has them ready for bed, they call for me to tuck them in. I do. Then Esther and I step into the yard. Esther sits cross-legged on the ground, her back slouched against the cistern. I rest my head on her lap, look up at the moon, and tell her about Granny's phone call.

Esther strokes my hair. "I think you should go," she whispers. "And not just for a few days. A month at least."

"Never. I made a vow."

"People can change their minds." She smooths out a tat.

"Anyway, I can't go. If I went, what would happen to you?"

"Chanda, I can manage. Really." She cups my face in her hands. "My health's been good. And if I get sick, or something happens, I've got friends at the Welcome Center. I can count on Mrs. Tafa, too." Her eyes twinkle. "She can't stand me, but she'll do anything to get you to Tiro."

We smile.

Esther hesitates. "Chanda, I used to have fights with Mama and Papa about boys. I gave them a hard time. But when the end came, they knew I loved them."

"What does this have to do with me and Granny?"

Esther pauses. "When your granny and grampa pass,

they're never coming back. If you don't go to Tiro, how will you feel when the priest puts them in the ground? How will you feel, knowing you kept Soly and Iris from receiving their blessing?"

I think hard all Sunday. Then Monday, I go to the secondary, early-early.

I find Mr. Selalame in the staff room. He makes us tea and sits on an armchair with the stuffing coming out, while I sit kitty-corner on what used to be a sofa. I pour out my heart, letting him know about everything: Mama, Tiro, Granny's call, and what Esther said.

Mr. Selalame blows gently on his tea. "So how *would* you feel, if your grandparents passed before giving their blessing?"

"Terrible," I say. "Terrible and guilty, knowing my pride kept Soly and Iris from getting something special. But how do I forgive what they did to Mama?"

Mr. Selalame takes a long, slow sip from his mug, then carefully sets it down beside the pile of essays on the coffee table in front of us. "You loved your mama very much."

I nod.

"Do you ever think maybe she loved *her* mama, your

granny, the same way?"

"I guess. I don't know," I say, so quiet there's hardly a sound. "Probably."

"Probably, yes?"

"Yes." The room is so still I can hear the clock on the far wall.

"Your granny and your mama had a falling out," Mr. Selalame says at last. "It hurt your mama to her dying day." I lower my eyes. He waits till I look up. His eyes are deep pools filled with everything I've said. "Chanda," he continues, "what would your mama have done if your granny'd called and said she was sorry? What would she have done if your granny had offered a blessing?"

I can't breathe. "She'd have been on the next bus to Tiro."

8

WE PACK THE evening before we leave. If we didn't, I'd be awake all night worried that we'd forget something. Mainly we fill our pillowcases with clothes, but I find a place for the spyglasses from Mr. Lesole. They'll be something for Soly and Iris to play with. I also slip in the bookmark Mr. Selalame gave me last year when Mama was sick. It's got a picture of the sun rising over the plains to remind me there's hope in new beginnings. Lastly, I hide some green plastic feed sacks to put over Soly's diaper-towel.

The kids are bringing mementos too, tucked in their "treasure chests," a pair of old metal lunch boxes, painted black. Iris fills hers with ebony combs from Mrs. Tafa, paste jewelry from Esther, a few crayons, and her swath of torn mosquito netting. (Some days, she pretends it's a bridal veil, other days that it makes her invisible.) Soly packs his with stones he's collected on the way from school, the sock puppet he likes to sleep with, and Mr. Lesole's map of Mfuala Park. To make sure the map is safe, he rolls it inside the lunch box thermos.

I was worried the kids would be scared of the trip. They've never been outside Bonang, except as babies, and the only relative from Tiro they've met is Auntie Lizbet, who came down a year ago for our baby sister's funeral; they remember her "funny shoe," meaning her club foot, and that's about it. I didn't have to be concerned. They're head over heels with excitement. Mr. Lesole's park map has a mini-map of the country in the top left corner. On the mini-map, Tiro is only a quarter inch from Mfualatown. Soly and Iris think they'll be seeing giraffe and zebra from Granny Thela's front door.

Their only fright comes when Mrs. Tafa drops by at bedtime. "Leo's taking me to the hairdresser's at the crack of dawn," she says. "But he'll have me back to see you off by lunchtime."

"Lunchtime!" Iris wails. "We may be gone by then!"

Mrs. Tafa laughs. "Not if I know Obi Palme!"

Obi Palme is the bus man who drives the open-air flatbed truck between Bonang and Mfualatown, the trading center by the entrance to Mfuala National Park. Officially, he's supposed to leave Mfualatown at dawn, pass through Tiro by breakfast, and get here by noon, returning through

Tiro by supper, and to the park by dusk. In real life, Mr. Palme shows up midmorning to swap stories and smoke cigarettes with the merchants setting up their stalls at the park gates. He hardly ever gets away till noon. And since he stops everywhere to let folks hop on and off the flatbed, we're lucky if he drives through Bonang by midafternoon and gets to Tiro by midnight. There's even times he's rolled back to Mfualatown the following morning because of trouble with the engine—or because he's run out of gas, on account of the fuel lines leak and the gauge doesn't work. At least there's never a problem with the fan belt; Mr. Palme keeps a bag of old pantyhose in his glove compartment for emergency repairs. He gets them from friends in the hotels who fish them out of tourists' wastebaskets. "At least, that's the story he tells his wife," Mrs. Tafa winks.

In a blink it's morning. Departure day. As I rub my eyes, I feel a glow. Maybe my dream—Tiro, the loss of loved ones— came from the shock of finding Mama at the ruin. Going back to Tiro, seeing my relatives, I'll have the chance to face down that horror: to bury the past in the present.

Right after breakfast, Mr. Selalame bicycles by on his way to class. "All the best." He gives me three cards: one from my students with their names in crayon on a piece of construction paper; the second from the teachers at my school; and the third from him and his wife. Next thing I know, he's halfway down the street, waving goodbye. The trip suddenly feels real. My stomach flips.

Neighbors drop over all morning. The kids are skittish as chickens before a storm. They chase each other around the outhouse, get me to give them rides in the wheelbarrow, and brag to Esther about the adventures they're going to have. Then they hug her as if they're never going to see her again, and fret about whether Mrs. Tafa will be back from downtown before we leave.

As it turns out, the Tafas don't return till early afternoon, but it doesn't matter; the bus is still an idea, somewhere in the distance. As Mr. Tafa helps Mrs. Tafa out of his truck, Soly and Iris race to see who can get to them first. Mrs. Tafa drops to her knees so she won't be knocked down. They crawl over her like ants on a mango pit.

"Careful of Auntie Rose's new hairdo!" I holler, as her kerchief comes undone.

"You think I'd really go to the hairdresser's on a day like today?" Mrs. Tafa hoots. "Where's your sense, girl? I went shopping! Leo, get those wicker baskets over to Chanda's."

67

She pats her forehead with the kerchief. "We can't have you showing up in Tiro empty-handed, can we? What would your mama say?"

Mrs. Tafa's bought us each a new set of clothes. "By the end of the ride you'll be plenty dusty," she says. "Wet your dirty tops in the bathroom sink at the last rest stop, wipe yourselves clean, and change into these. First impressions are important." Mrs. Tafa's also bought gifts for my relatives. New socks for my uncles and Grampa, pot holders for my aunties and Granny, plus two tins of gingered pears, a jar of marmalade, and a box of chocolates.

"This last little gift has seen better days, but it's still in good working order," Mrs. Tafa says. She hands me a small cardboard box. Inside is her old cell phone patched with sticky tape. "It's topped up for an hour."

I'm overwhelmed. "I can't accept this."

"Nonsense. The Mister's got me a new one," she says. "Besides, I won't have you children getting homesick. If ever you feel like a one-legged dog at the races, home is only a call away. To tell the truth, getting your news'll be good for me."

I hesitate, but then I look at Esther. I miss her already. Making sure she's all right will help me rest easy.

"Thank you."

"You're welcome," Mrs. Tafa beams. "Esther here's been kind enough to program my number. She's also programmed the number of the general dealer in Tiro, so you can check for truck delays the day you return. Promise you won't waste my time card calling him for groceries."

"I promise."

"And no excuses about being in a dead zone, you hear? There's towers all through the north to keep those fancy safari camps hooked to civilization. And another thing—"

"Enough, Auntie," I laugh. "I'll call."

"See that you do." She picks a twig from Soly's hair, then licks her thumb and wipes a smudge from Iris's forehead. "Mind you behave."

The truck to Tiro rounds the corner. We run to the side of the street and flag it down. "Take care of these three, Obi," Mrs. Tafa says to our driver. Mr. Palme grunts and helps us scramble up onto the flatbed.

Mrs. Tafa's face trembles. Her eyes embrace us. "Be good."

"Don't worry, we will." For a second, it's like saying goodbye to Mama.

The truck lurches forward. We blow kisses. Bonang disappears in a cloud of dust.

Part Two

Part Two

9

WHENEVER MRS. TAFA drives Mr. Tafa's truck, she goes so fast you expect to be killed, thrown through the windshield or crushed in a pileup. The ride to Tiro with Mr. Palme is different. All I expect to die from is boredom.

For the first hour, the flatbed is packed with other travelers, but they've mostly left by the time we pass the Kawkee turnoff. Some have hopped off with their fishing poles to try their luck in the river and wetlands above the dam. Others have headed into the village to visit relatives, or to see Dr. Chilume, the herbal doctor whose farms are a short way off.

The farther we get from Bonang, the more the highway's in need of repair. Soon the paving disappears and we're driving on dirt. Gravel's been laid down on either side of the villages dotting our route to protect against erosion, but most of it's been washed away anyway, along with chunks of the road.

An hour north of Kawkee, the highway narrows to a single lane. The truck slows to a crawl as we wait for mule carts and bicycles to move to the side. We stop entirely while our driver, Mr. Palme, argues with an oncoming tractor about who should back up. The tractor ends up perched on the edge of nothing. We pass, and it regains the road, as the dirt shoulder crumbles.

After about an hour, the highway widens back to two lanes. Rainy season is over, and already the smaller streams that run into the ditches have started to disappear. The sedges and reeds beside their banks are turning yellow in the hardening mud. We jolt through miles and miles of scrub brush. Trees close to the road have been chopped for kindling. In the distance, though, we can see scattered mopane, acacia, and baobab trees.

Soly and Iris love the baobabs. They don't get to see many in town. I let them peer through Mr. Lesole's binoculars at the squat, bulbous trunks, some over sixty feet around and a thousand years old, their topknot of branches looking like a tangle of roots. They giggle as I tell them stories about how the baobab got its shape: "Once, the baobab was the most beautiful tree in the forest. But it wouldn't stop bragging. So

God said, 'I'll teach you not to boast.' He ripped it up and stuck it back into the ground headfirst, with its ugly roots up in the air for all the other trees to laugh at." Or my favorite: "God gave every animal a seed to plant. He gave the baobab seed to a hyena, but the hyena was so stupid he planted it upside down, and it grew that way."

"The baobab tree got its revenge, though, didn't it?" Soly says. "When it gets big and old, it goes hollow, and people can hide inside from the hyena."

"From lions, too," Iris adds, not to be outdone. "From everything."

"That's right," I smile and stroke the top of their heads.

The sun starts to set as we reach the rest stop at Rombala, the halfway point in our journey. There are a couple of picnic tables next to the gas pumps. I packed some maize bread and dried chicken, but after bouncing around all day in the back of the pickup, none of us is hungry. We settle our stomachs with water from the roadside pump.

Rombala is a trading post with an army base nearby. It's got its own paper, *The Rombala Gazette*, that publishes once a week. A few crumpled sheets from last week's edition have blown against a leg of our table. Before I toss them in the garbage, I check to see if there's anything interesting to read.

There's a front-page story about the town's new chief.

She's the niece of the past chief, and the first woman ever chosen for the post.

There's also news about a hollowed-out pumpkin found smashed near the home of a local spirit doctor. Nearby, the neighbors discovered a necklace of beads carved from the stalk. The spirit doctor says a rival used the pumpkin to fly over his property to spy; the flying pumpkin fell to earth owing to a spell he cast. His rival has a broken leg. The rival says he broke it tumbling off a ladder, not from crashing in a pumpkin, but the timing is considered suspicious. Mrs. Gulubane should move to Rombala, I think. The deeper we go into north country, the more folks believe in magic.

Turning the page, I see the headline "National pact with Ngala." There's a photograph of General Mandiki. He's standing on a pile of headless bodies, brandishing an AK-47, a necklace of human jawbones over his medals. Child soldiers with machetes pose at his side. Mandiki looks like a crocodile. Cold, dead eyes. Leathery skin. Finger stubs with thick, fungal nails. An extended jaw with a wall of crooked teeth. The rumor is, when he was president of Ngala, he ripped those teeth from the mouths of his enemies and had them implanted in his own.

According to the article under the picture, the Ngala army has marched into its national park. A sweep uncovered Mandiki's main camp, but he and the rebels had already scattered. The article says they're probably moving in small raiding parties of about twenty. Ngala has no idea where any of them may be heading. Our government's pledged that any of Mandiki's men who slip across our border will be shot on sight.

The rest of the paper is announcements: a buy-and-sell column, a calendar of upcoming events, and a posting of births, marriages, and deaths. The dead are almost all in their twenties and thirties. According to the gazette, they all passed of pneumonia, cancer, and TB. There's no mention of AIDS.

It's too dark to read anymore. I throw the paper in the trash and get Soly and Iris back on the truck, as Mr. Palme loads new passengers. There's a couple of peddlers, a barefoot man with a toothbrush sticking out of the pocket of a filthy nylon jacket, a middle-aged couple with two sacks of sweet potatoes, and a granny with three small grandchildren, two chickens, and a goat.

The men sit at the end of the flatbed and smoke. The granny sits with her grandkids and livestock, staring ahead, eyes vacant. When the baby cries, she gives it her thumb to suck. The couple sit near the cab with Iris and Soly and me.

Iris and Soly are worn out. They hug the potato sacks and fall asleep. I try to sleep too, resting my head on my pillow of clothes. But lying flat makes the truck's rattling worse. I sit up, propping myself against the back of the cab. Somehow I drift off. When I come to, the couple with the sacks are gone, and Soly and Iris are wide awake. I keep my eyes closed, curious about what they talk about when they think I'm not listening.

"Granny Thela has long yellow teeth," Iris declares. "They're so long she uses them to scratch her chin. Grampa Thela is worse. He has porridge brains. When he tips his head over, the porridge spills out of his ears, and that's what they eat for breakfast."

"Ewww."

"Then there's Auntie Lizbet and her funny shoe. Her left foot is really a hoof."

"I remember the hoof," Soly says solemnly.

"And remember her tail, swishing under her dress? And the sharp little horns under her bonnet? Auntie Lizbet's a witch. If you're not careful, she'll come in the middle of the night and eat you."

"She will not."

"Will too. And then she'll throw up."

I open my eyes. "What are you two talking about?"

"Nothing," Iris says. "Just things."

"Is Auntie Lizbet a witch?" Soly asks.

"No," I say with a sharp look at Iris. "But little girls who tell lies grow lizard scales, and nobody wants to go near them."

"Ha ha ha," Iris yawns, and crosses her eyes at me.

We rumble along the road in silence. Soly snuggles into my side. "How much longer?"

"Not much."

We pull into Shawshe, the last rest stop before Tiro. I get us cleaned up and changed in the garage washroom, while Mr. Palme fills a soft tire. He honks his horn for us to leave. Another hour, we'll be in Tiro.

There's a nip in the night air. I'm covered in goosebumps. I hold Soly and Iris close and rub their arms to keep them warm.

"Remember," I tell them, "we're going to be guests. So be polite. Make Mama proud. Give Granny and Grampa big hugs. And whatever you do, don't stare at Auntie Lizbet's club foot."

10

THERE'S A DIM glow in the sky to the right. The firepits of Tiro. We turn off the highway. A few hundred yards of potholes, a bend in the road, and we come to a place where the brush and grasses have been cleared back. Just ahead, I see the bare lightbulb shining over the front door of the general dealer's.

Mr. Kamwendo's store is exactly like it was when I came for Mama six months ago. The stuccoed walls need patching, the whitewash is faded to near gray, and there's weeds growing in the broken roof tiles. The only difference is, the neon Chibuku sign in the window is dead.

We pull up at the gas tank to the left. I look across the lot at the cluster of people huddled on Coca-Cola crates around Mr. Kamwendo's firepit. Four of them get up to greet us. "That's our Granny Thela, with the black shawl,"

I tell the kids. "And that's our older sister, Lily, carrying our baby cousin Abednego in a sling. The man in the toque running ahead of them is Mr. Kamwendo, the general dealer."

"And who's he?" asks Iris, pointing at the stranger slouching along at Mr. Kamwendo's heels.

"No idea," I say. From what I can tell, he's about my age. His face is set in a frown, but he's still pretty handsome. Tall, lean, with a strong jaw and forehead. I wish it was daylight, so I could see more.

Mr. Kamwendo's out of breath by the time he reaches us. His whiskers are whiter than I remember. "Chanda," he exclaims, "it's good to see you again!" As he helps me off the truck, he whispers in my ear: "You coming means a lot to your granny. She's been talking 'bout nothing else." Then in a big voice: "And you must be Iris and Soly. I'm Sam Kamwendo."

He lifts them down. Soly presses behind me, but Iris plays tough. She puffs out her chest like she's queen of the town. All the same, she takes my hand.

"That your stuff?" Mr. Kamwendo says, pointing at our bundles.

"Mm-hmm," I nod.

Mr. Kamwendo turns to our stranger. "Look lively, Nelson."

Nelson plants a hand on the truck's floor and springs onto the flatbed. He tosses our things to Mr. Kamwendo without a glance in our direction.

Granny's stopped a few yards away. Lily has a protective arm around her.

"Granny." I step forward. She barely comes up to my shoulders. I bend down. She opens her arms and swallows me up in her shawl. It smells of smoke and earth.

"Chanda." She tries to say more but she can't. I can feel her ribs under her sweater. I'm afraid to hold her tight for fear she'll break. She hugs me for what feels like forever.

I pull away gently. "Soly, Iris, I'd like you to meet your granny." I motion for them to give her a hug too, but they just stare, openmouthed.

"It's late. They're tired," Granny says. "In this shawl I must look like an old crow." She smiles at them. "We can have a hug tomorrow. How would that be?"

"Better," says Iris, in a voice that says: If we have to get hugged at all.

I look around for other relatives, but there aren't any. Why not? Don't they want us? I mean, I'm not expecting the world. My cousins are grown up, the male ones tending cattle with the herd boys, the females tending families of their own. But what about my aunties and uncles, my grampa, or Lily's husband, Mopati?

Lily reads my mind. "Everyone wanted to be here. But Auntie Lizbet's tending Grampa's joints, and Uncle Chisulo and Uncle Enoch are fixing the mule cart—the axle broke when we left to get you. Auntie Agnes and Auntie Ontibile, they're minding the soup. Still, they're all waiting to greet you at the compound—except my Mopati, he's training our son at the shanty." She nods toward Nelson. "Nelson's a son of Granny's neighbors. His people offered their cart, and him to drive it."

I turn to Nelson. He's standing off to the side, our pillowcases and wicker baskets at his feet. "Thank you," I say. He gives me a sideways look and shrugs.

"Nelson's a real charmer, aren't you, Nelson?" Lily laughs.

"If you say so." He grabs our belongings in both hands and heads to the mule cart tethered at the far side of the general dealer's. We follow. "Get in," he says. Lily and I help Granny up and make a comfortable spot for her with the stuffed pillowcases. Nelson balances the load, then he unhitches his mules. He walks to the inside of the road, guiding them with his right hand, holding the reins to the side of the yoke.

"G'night," Mr. Kamwendo calls out.

We holler "g'night" back, except for Nelson, who keeps his eyes focused ahead. "Aren't you going to ride with us?" I ask him. "We could make room."

"I'm fine walking."

"Nelson's worried about the weight," Lily whispers. "The mules are tired. They worked all day. They'll be working again tomorrow."

So no wonder he's rude, I think. I decide not to add to his burden. First impressions are important, as Mrs. Tafa says. "I'll walk too," I say, and jump off.

The mules react. Nelson tightens his grip on the reins and braces himself against the yoke. "Whoa." He whirls on me. "What are you trying to do? Spook the mules? Shift the load? Tip the cart?"

"I thought I was helping."

"If I want your help, I'll ask for it."

"Nelson!" Granny barks.

"Beg pardon, Mrs. Thela." He looks to my left.

I get back in the cart, cheeks burning.

Iris whispers to Soly: "He sure told her."

Lily's home is a short detour from the general dealer's. We let her and the baby off. "I'll be by tomorrow morning," she says.

"No hurry," Granny replies. "Chanda and the children will want to sleep in."

"Good luck to that," Lily laughs. "The roosters of Tiro can wake the dead. And Nelson's place has a yardful. They strut and crow like trackers on payday. They learned that from you, didn't they, Nelson?"

Nelson snorts. "We should get going." He leads the mules around, and we begin the long trek down the village line, parallel to the highway.

When I was little, Tiro was just a gas stop on the way to Mfuala Park. Blink and you'd miss it. There was the general dealer's and a flat stretch of ground where folks came to trade twice a month. Then the government built a health clinic opposite the dealer's, along with a grid of water pipes under a square mile of big, empty lots. Soon there was a blacksmith's, a weaver's, a tinker's, a barber's, a feed store, and a school. All sorts of folks moved in from the country for the convenience. They built compounds next to friends from nearby cattle posts, so they'd keep the same neighbors in town. Others stayed on the land.

My family held out till Granny and Grampa got feeble. By then, the only lots available were on the far outskirts by the cemetery. Now every day, while my aunties run errands around the village, my uncles commute with the other men to their posts in the country, where their cattle are tended overnight by sons and hired herd boys.

There's a rustle of grass to my side. A field? I look back. Pockets of glow flicker up from the front yards behind us. The village line comes to an end. Nelson whispers something to the mules, and we swing right. The rickety cart tilts as the left front wheel lumbers over a rock. Where are we? Nelson must see by starlight. How? I'm glad I'm in the cart.

A few minutes later, beacons of light ahead. As we get close, I make out three lamps in front of three mud homes on three sides of a yard, a blazing firepit in the center. It's Granny and Grampa's compound. Their place is the one in the middle; they share it with Auntie Lizbet. Uncle Chisulo and Auntie Agnes live to the left; Uncle Enoch and Auntie Ontibile to the right.

My uncles' broken cart is over by Uncle Chisulo's. One end is on cinder blocks. My uncles are wedging a wooden wheel onto the new axle, while Aunties Agnes and Ontibile fuss at the soup pot hanging over the fire. A fifth person gives everyone instructions with her cane: Auntie Lizbet. With her wizened breasts and lumpy thighs, she looks like a rotten pear.

"Your grampa must be asleep," Granny says. "Your Auntie Lizbet's taking a break, bless her heart." Bless her heart? When I came to find Mama, sainted Auntie Lizbet swung that cane to crack my head open. Mama had been left alone, dying, at the abandoned ruin on the cattle post. Auntie Lizbet said she deserved it. She said it was god's will, and the will of the ancestors.

By the time we pull up, everyone's come to bid welcome. Uncle Chisulo lifts Granny out of the cart like she was a feather pillow, while Uncle Enoch wrestles our bags over the side of the cart by pushing off with his belly. Their wives, Auntie Ontibile and Auntie Agnes, are right behind, wiping their hands on their aprons. They're identical twins. I tell them apart by the dent in Auntie Ontibile's forehead, from where she got kicked by a goat when she was little.

Last to join us is Auntie Lizbet. I shoot her a look that says: Remember what you did to Mama? What you said to me? Her head drops. She turns away.

I'm all in knots. Aren't I here to heal old wounds? Isn't

that what Mama would do? Why can't I forget? Why don't I forgive? What's wrong with me?

"Thanks for the ride," Granny says to Nelson. He nods. I smile awkwardly. A chorus of g'nights, and he leads his mules home.

"You three will be staying in my room," Auntie Lizbet says. "I'll be in with your granny and grampa."

"We thought that'd be best," Granny adds. "You'll have some privacy, and your auntie will be handy if Grampa's legs cramp up in the middle of the night."

"Good, yes, thank you," I say. All I want to do is put the kids to bed, flop on my mat, and sleep till Judgment Day. But everyone's planned a welcome party, so after we drop our bags inside, we come back out to sit around the firepit.

I open Mrs. Tafa's wicker baskets and give them all their presents. Mrs. Tafa chose well. My uncles are pleased with their socks. My aunties admire the stitch work on their pot holders. And Granny cradles the preserves.

"I'll bring out the biscuits," Auntie Lizbet says. "Just the thing to put that marmalade to the test." She hobbles to get them. Iris follows, staring in bug-eyed wonder at her foot.

"Iris! No!" I cry.

Auntie Lizbet whirls around, catching Iris in the act. "What are you gawking at?"

"Your hoof," says Iris.

The world stops breathing.

"My . . . what?" Auntie glares.

"Your hoof!" Iris exclaims again. "It's so . . . so . . . clumpy."

Auntie Lizbet grips her cane. "Who taught you your manners, girl?"

"Nobody," Iris says brightly.

"Nobody?" Auntie Lizbet pounds her cane. "Nobody???" She suddenly bursts out laughing. "Can you beat the nerve of the little thing!" She peers at Iris over her spectacles. "So, nobody taught you manners?"

"No, Auntie," Iris says, innocent as you please. "Not a blessèd soul."

Auntie puts on a stern look. "Well, we'll have to see about that, won't we?"

"Oh yes," Iris says.

Auntie beams. "What a little sweetness."

Iris bats her eyes at me. I could smack her.

11

As SOON AS the party's over, I put the kids in bed, roll onto my mat, and fall asleep.

Mama is sitting beside the termite mound. "There's going to be a storm."

My head is thick, but I know one thing for sure: "This isn't real, Mama. It's just my old dream."

"All the same, there's going to be a storm."

I close my eyes and kick myself. "Wake up, wake up."

When I open my eyes, the mound is gone. But I'm not on the mat in Auntie Lizbet's room either. I'm back on the flatbed to Tiro. It's night. Did I dream I arrived, or am I dreaming now? Soly and Iris are beside me, hugging potato sacks. Next to us, a granny with three kids lets the baby suck her thumb.

There's a rumble. Mama was right. There's going to be a

storm. A crack of lightning. Thunder. No, it's not that! It's rocket fire!

The granny turns to me. Under the light of a green flare, I see the face of a crocodile. Dead eyes. A wall of teeth. This isn't a granny. It's General Mandiki.

Mandiki pulls his thumb from the baby's mouth. His thumb is a machete.

A missile explodes against the flatbed. We fly through the air. Crash into a ditch. The potato sacks split open. They're full of human heads.

Mandiki stands above us. He swings his machete.

"Run!"

I sit bolt-upright. I'm on my mat in Auntie Lizbet's room. A nightmare. I've had a nightmare, that's all. Thank god I didn't scream. Granny and Auntie Lizbet would've taken me to a spirit doctor. But why am I dreaming about Mandiki? Of course. I slap my forehead. I saw the general's picture with the bodies in *The Rombala Gazette*. Mr. Selalame is right. Dreams are about the present. My mind was on our trip.

I reach out in the dark and brush Iris and Soly's shoulders. We're safe. I smile at my silliness. My nerves, my nerves. I'm such a coward.

It's a good thing we're here. I need the rest. I do. I really do.

I lie down again. Float into the night.

Roosters crow. Somewhere there's roosters. Oh yes, there's roosters across the way at Nelson's. Maybe Granny and the aunties have some too. I cover my head with my pillow. Drift off again.

I blink. What time is it now? The shutters are closed and the curtain across the bedroom door is drawn, but I can feel the sun's up. Soly and Iris are out of bed. I hear the rattle of dishes. They must be having breakfast.

I hear Auntie Lizbet. "What we say is 'please.'"

"'Please,'" Iris mimics.

"Good girl," Auntie Lizbet says. "And then we say, 'thank you.'"

"Thank you," Iris repeats. "Thank you, Auntie Lizbet, for teaching me 'please and thank you.'"

"You're welcome." There's a twinkle in Auntie Lizbet's voice.

I can't believe it. Mama taught Iris "please and thank you." I taught her "please and thank you." She's such a little brat, pretending we didn't. Oh well, if it puts Auntie

Lizbet in a good mood . . .

I roll over.

"Chanda?" Soly's in the doorway. "Chanda, are you still sleeping?"

"I was." I rub my eyes.

"Can I play with Pako?"

"Who's Pako?"

"Nelson's brother. He's nine. Granny says it's all right. Is it?"

"If Granny says so."

He gets his lunch box from beside his pillow. "I'm going to show Pako the map." A few minutes later I hear the two of them outside my window. "When I grow up, I'm going to work at the Kenje River Safari Camp with Mr. Lesole. It's the red dot near the mountains. Mr. Lesole's a big boss there and he's my friend."

"Aren't you afraid of lions?"

"Well . . ." Soly replies carefully, "I wouldn't walk up and pet one. But Mr. Lesole says they mostly hunt at night. I'd be in bed then. And you get warnings. If a lion's around, the impalas get jumpy. And anyway, unless they're old or sick or starving, they stay away from people. Mr. Lesole says our meat's not as tasty as antelope or porcupine."

"How does he know?" Pako laughs. "Is he a lion?"

"Don't be stupid," Soly sighs. "Want to play Hyena Hideaway?"

"What's that?"

"A game. First we need some stools and benches . . ."

By the time I get up, everyone's outside, except for Grampa, who's snoring. I rub my eyes and go into the main room. There's a table, chairs, and a rocker, and in the left corner, a sink and open shelves draped with a curtain. Granny and Grampa's room is at the back; Auntie Lizbet's (our room) is to the side. The layout's a lot like our place, actually, except the bedrooms at home are next to each other.

Granny's place is different in other ways, though. Our home is in the city. It's cinder block, with a cement floor and a corrugated tin roof. Here, the floor is dirt, the roof is thatched, and the walls are mud bricks, made from a mixture of earth, dried cow dung, and the soil of termite mounds. I've decorated our house with drawings that Iris and Soly made at school. Here, everything's bare. The other thing different about here is the smell of old people.

I stick my head out the door for some fresh air. The yard is alive with work.

Auntie Ontibile and Auntie Agnes sit together scrubbing laundry on their washboards. Auntie Lizbet hangs it to dry on lines strung between our houses. Iris is at her side, handing her clothespins, and pushing the tub of cleaned wets in front of them with her foot. Auntie Lizbet doesn't have her cane; she uses Iris's shoulder for balance.

"Welcome to the land of the living!" Granny laughs when she sees me. She's sitting on the bench by the firepit with Lily, Lily's baby, and a middle-aged woman I've never seen before. There's a pot of seswa and a kettle of water simmering on the coals. Lily's nursing her baby. Granny and the woman are having tea and biscuits. The woman soaks her biscuits before eating. She's missing her front teeth.

I look up at the sun. It must be past eleven.

Granny waves me over. "Let me introduce our neighbor from across the way," she says. "Our families go back years. She came by to meet you. I was telling her what a great help Nelson was, getting us home last night."

So this is must be Nelson's mama, I think. I try and straighten my hair. I'm such a mess. At least my skirt is clean.

Nelson's mama rises. She has the look Mama had before she went away. Thin as a rake, her eyes are large and yellow, her cheeks gaunt, the skin stretched tight to her skull. Her bright green dress hangs limp from her shoulders. It's like she's swimming in cloth.

I forget about everything. "Don't bother getting up."

Her eyes flicker. She knows I know her sickness. "I'm fine," she says. "Just a little arthritis." She winces as she takes my hand, but her grip is strong. Mama's grip stayed strong till the end, too. "So you're Chanda Kabelo."

"Yes," I say.

"I'm Grace Malunga. Tuelo Malunga's wife."

I gasp. Tuelo Malunga! The man who almost married Mama! The man she was afraid of! Of course. The Malunga cattle post is next to Granny and Grampa's. Like everyone else, they built next to each other in town, to stay neighbors.

"Mrs. Malunga," my lips flap. "Mrs. Malunga, Mrs. Malunga, I've heard so much about you."

"Is that a good thing?"

"Yes." I can hardly say no.

"I always let Chanda's family know about your boys," Granny winks.

The boys. Oh yes, Granny made sure to tell Mama each time Tuelo Malunga had another boy. Eight boys. No girls to need dowry. It was as if Granny liked to rub the

Malungas' good luck in Mama's face. As if she were saying, "Mrs. Malunga has sons to take care of her in her old age. Eight sons. Eight. It could have been you. You, if you hadn't run off. You, if you hadn't broken our hearts and shamed us."

The Malungas. I've heard all about the Malungas. Tuelo Malunga. Mrs. Malunga. And Nelson's their son. I sink onto a stool.

Mrs. Malunga steps back to give me a good once-over. "I'm impressed," she announces, her words as firm as her handshake. "Your sister Iris is quite the worker. Your Soly's played well with my Pako all morning. And as for you, my girl, you're as lovely as your Granny's reports."

I'm confused. Granny told her I was lovely? After what I said and did when I came for Mama?

"You made an impression on Nelson, too," Mrs. Malunga adds drily. "'She's a real handful,' he tells me this morning, saddling up for the post. 'Well,' I said, 'pepper adds spice to the seswa.'"

"Chanda's got pepper all right," Lily hoots, giving her baby a burp. "She's a basket of piri-piri."

The three of them laugh.

I hate that. Since when am I meat spice? The trouble is,

if I don't laugh along, they'll say my head's as big as a melon. I change the subject. "Where's Soly?"

"I think the boys went over to our place," Mrs. Malunga says.

Granny stirs the pot. "It's getting near mealtime. Grace is joining us. How be you make yourself useful and call them back?"

I'm happy to get away. I cross the road to the cluster of shacks on the Malunga property. Lily was right. There's roosters everywhere. The yard is covered in crap. I wave at a couple of Mrs. Malunga's daughters-in-law. They're by the granary, mending work pants, surrounded by half-naked toddlers. They seem to know who I am and why I've come.

One of them points to a lane through a field that leads to what looks like a wood lot. "They're at the cemetery paying respects," she says, her hand in front of her mouth. Is she missing teeth like Mrs. Malunga? I pretend not to notice.

The drying grasses along the route are well trampled. I'm at the graveyard in no time. It's surrounded by a post fence strung with barbed wire to keep out goats and cattle. The trees are old. The villagers must be afraid to chop here.

Like the cemeteries circling Bonang, the Tiro yard is outside the town limits. I spot a few moritis: rusted metal enclosures over the burial mounds, with frayed canvas and nylon tops; a name and birth and death dates soldered to the front, the letters breaking away. Tiny homes for the dead. But moritis are expensive. Most of the graves are marked with paving bricks and homemade wooden crosses. At least Tiro is small enough that family can be buried together. In Bonang, AIDS kills so many so fast that families like mine get scattered everywhere.

Stepping into the cemetery, I think about Mama. I say a prayer. The air is still. I listen to the insects: the rustle of beetles, the whisper of moths.

Then, to my right, the cries of children, and a rhythmic thumping on earth. I look over. Soly and Pako are a hundred yards off, faced away on their hands and knees. I sneak up behind them. They're in front of a freshly filled grave. Each is holding a rock in both hands and pounding it on the dirt. "Ai! Ai! Ai!"

"Soly?" At the sound of my voice, the boys drop the rocks and leap back. Soly squeals with relief when he sees it's me. Not Pako. A scruffy boy in need of a bath, his eyes are hunted.

Soly recovers. "Pako, that's Chanda."

"Sorry to scare you." I smile. "It's lunchtime. What were you boys doing?"

Pako gives Soly a warning glance. "My papa died three weeks ago," he replies flatly. "I was showing his grave."

My head reels. Tuelo Malunga—dead? Why didn't anyone tell me? I want to ask about the rock pounding, but the way Pako looks at me, I don't. "I'm sorry about your papa," I say instead. "We lost our mama a few months back. It hurts, doesn't it?"

"I guess." He looks across the field toward his house.

"Pako's papa died of a bewitchment," Soly says, low and serious. "He has brothers here too." He points at four nearby stone markers. Another shock. Granny never sent word about the dead Malunga boys either. Only the births.

"Matthew would've been my twin," Pako says, pointing at the smallest marker. "If he was alive, he'd be nine like me. He strangled on the cord when we were coming out. My brother Yoo, next to him, he died when I was little. I don't remember him much. Just how he kept crying, like my younger brother Shadrak, over there. Their bones were weak. They'd fall and break them. This marker, at Papa's feet, it's the baby from last year. It was born sick. I'm older than all the dead ones, when they passed, so maybe I'm going to be lucky."

I swallow. "I'm sure you are." For the first time I realize his jaw is crooked. Was he born that way, or have his bones been broken too?

"Anyway, my brothers, they have markers," Pako says, "but Papa's getting a moriti. Wrought iron, Mama promises, with a gate and a lock. A strong lock."

"Good," I say. "Good."

A pause.

"So . . . it's time for lunch?"

"Uh . . . yes."

Pako shows us a shortcut out of the cemetery, a dried streambed nearby where you can slip under the barbed wire. There's a footpath from here that leads directly across the field to his family's yard. The whole way back, Pako checks nervously over his shoulder. When the graves are out of sight, he lets out a holler, twirls around, and beats himself three times on the head.

What a strange boy. If Soly's going to play with him, I better keep an eye out.

12

IT'S NIGHTTIME. AUNTIE Lizbet is worn out. This afternoon, while Soly taught Pako how to play Elephant Charge, Iris asked Auntie to take her on a walking tour to the general dealer's and back. To Granny's amazement, Auntie Lizbet agreed. Granny and I watched them walk hand in hand down the road. "You should bottle that girl, she's a tonic," Granny laughed. "She's one of the few people to make your auntie smile, much less take to town without a cart."

Well, I thought, let's bottle Auntie Lizbet while we're at it. She's one of the few people to make Iris act like a human being. Iris likes Esther for her jewelry, the Lesoles for their stories, and Mrs. Tafa for her treats. That's about it. She ignores Soly, except to scare him. With me, she's plain mean.

Mrs. Tafa's told me not to worry, it'll pass: "The poor thing's grieving your mama. She's lost and angry, and you're the one minding her. Who else is she going to get mad at?"

"She could get mad at you," I said.

Mrs. Tafa shook her head: "I'm a mama. Her mama's what she's missing. It's what she's looking for."

"But I'm her mama now."

"You're her sister; it's different."

"I know, I know." Still, when I see the way that Iris sticks to Mrs. Tafa and Auntie Lizbet, I feel so jealous.

Anyway, Auntie and Iris's walk to the general dealer's turned out to be too much of a good thing. Mr. Kamwendo had to get Auntie a lift back home with a trucker who'd stopped for gas. Now her feet are puffed up like sausage fruit. She's sitting at the table in the main room, her good foot soaking in a pot of warm water, her club foot raised on a chair. Iris is on her knees, gently rubbing the club foot, touching the distended arch and webbed toes as if they were the most wondrous things in the world.

Granny's on her rocker knitting. Soly's in bed, and I'm cleaning the food bowls. Everything's quiet, except for the soft moan coming from Grampa in the back room. We haven't been brought to him yet. "Your grampa's not himself today," Granny said this afternoon. "Maybe tomorrow. I know he wants to see you."

"What's wrong with him?" I asked.

"Oh nothing. Don't you fret about that moaning. It's a sound he makes in his sleep. If he was in pain, we'd know about it, believe me."

So here we are, thinking our thoughts, big and small, when out of nowhere, Iris says: "Auntie, why didn't you ever get married?"

Auntie Lizbet nearly chokes on her tongue. "Who says I wanted to?"

"Well, didn't you?"

"Wouldn't you like to know."

"Yes, please and thank you."

Auntie raises her eyebrows. "Well, if you must know, I never got married because I never got married."

Iris scrunches her nose. "That's a reason?"

"I don't know. But it's the one you're getting."

"You must have had lots of fellows."

"Maybe I did, maybe I didn't."

"Weren't there any you wanted?"

"It's too far back to remember. Now hush with the questions."

Auntie's eyes are misty. According to Mama, she wanted a husband more than anything in the world, but no man would have her. How could she fetch water, haul wood, and run after children with that club foot of hers? They made jokes about her. It put a hurt on Auntie's heart, a hurt that hardened to stone. Mama told me to remember that, whenever Auntie was cruel, and to try and forgive. All I know is, looking at Auntie, I never want to be in love. Love's just another thing to break your heart.

Suddenly, shouts from across the road. Iris jumps up. I run to the window.

"Nothing to worry about," Granny says, eyes on her knitting. "Just the Malunga boys, home from the post."

"What are they doing?"

"Not much of anything I expect."

"And none of our business, besides," Auntie adds.

"Nelson's walking off down the road," I say, peeking through the shutters.

"Always does when things get lively."

A bottle smashes. A woman curses, screams. It's not Mrs. Malunga. A daughter-in-law? "We should do something."

"Sit yourself down," Granny snaps.

More shouting and screaming.

"It's love pecks," Auntie says. "Nothing but love pecks.

The Malungas scratch and claw, nine months later there's a baby."

In a few minutes, the shouting settles down.

"You see?" Auntie says. "All done. Nothing to worry about." She sticks her club foot in the pail of water and lifts the wet one onto the chair seat. "How be you do Auntie's other foot?" she coos to Iris.

Iris looks from Auntie to me and back again. She tosses her head and resumes her work as if nothing's happened. But the noise has bothered Soly. "Chanda?" he calls out. "Chanda, can you come here, please?"

I go into the bedroom. Soly is curled up, hugging his pillow. I sit cross-legged beside him. "Don't worry. The fighting's over."

"It's not that," he says.

"Then what is it?"

"Chanda," he says slowly, "can spirits come out of the ground?"

"Why do you ask?"

"I don't know. But can they? Can they come out of the ground and hurt people?"

"Who's been telling you stories?"

"Nobody."

"Is 'nobody' Iris?"

He shakes his head.

"I see. Then is 'nobody' Pako?"

He looks away.

I turn his head toward me and ask the question I've wanted to ask all day. "Soly . . . this morning in the cemetery . . . what were you and Pako doing at Mr. Malunga's grave?"

Soly bites his lip. "We were praying."

"Pounding a grave with rocks isn't praying."

"So don't believe me then." He squeezes his pillow.

"Soly, if you don't tell me the truth, I can't help you."

"But it's a secret."

I lie down beside him. "Soly," I whisper, "you can tell me. No one will ever know."

"Promise?"

"I promise."

Soly hesitates, then he hugs me around the neck and presses his mouth to my ear. "All right. But this is very very very secret . . . At night . . ."

"At night. Yes?"

"At night, Mr. Malunga comes out of the ground. He flies from his grave and into Pako's room. He beats Pako like he did when he was alive. Pako wakes up with bruises. His papa wants him in the graveyard with his brothers."

"That's why the two of you were pounding the burial mound?"

Soly nods. "We were trying to keep his papa in the earth. But what if it didn't work? His papa will know I pounded his grave. He'll come for me too."

"No, he won't," I say. "Spirits don't rise from the grave. Not even Mr. Malunga."

"But Pako's bruises—"

"Pako hits himself in his sleep. Or his brothers hit him."

"How do you know that?"

"I don't, but I'm pretty sure. I'll have a quiet talk with his mama."

"No! You promised you wouldn't tell. He'll get in trouble."

I hold him close. "Soly, things are happening at the Malungas'. Bad things. We need to help, don't we?"

"I don't know," he says. "Just don't tell. If you tell, I'll never talk to you again. Not ever."

13

THE ROOSTERS CROW. My head is splitting.

I get up, have breakfast with Granny, Iris, and Soly.
Auntie Lizbet is in the back room, feeding Grampa. When
she comes out, she says: "Your grampa's more himself this
morning. He'd like to see you."

We cluster at the door.

"Gently, gently," Granny says. "Your grampa doesn't get
many visitors. This is a lot of excitement. Don't be upset if
he's a little confused."

Grampa's room smells of old food. It's dark. At first I
don't see much, but as we kneel beside him, my eyes get
accustomed to the dim. Grampa's propped up on pillows
on his mat. He's wearing a bib with bits of dried things on
it. Auntie Lizbet tells him who we are, and asks us to lean
in, one at a time. Grampa feels our faces. He pauses on

mine, his fingers fluttering like butterflies. "Lilian? Is this Lilian?"

"No, Papa," Auntie says. "Lilian is passed. This is her daughter, Chanda."

"Chanda?"

"Yes. Your granddaughter. Chanda."

"Chanda. Ah yes."

"And this is your granddaughter, Iris. And your grandson, Soly."

Grampa fidgets. "Iris? . . . Soly?"

"Yes."

"And Lilian? Where's Lilian?"

"Lilian is passed, Papa."

"Ah yes. Lilian has to marry Tuelo."

He has a spasm in his legs, and we're ushered out.

"Grampa's ears are huge," Soly says quietly.

"And there's hair in them," Iris adds.

"That's because he's old," I tell them.

"Why doesn't he know about Mama?" Soly asks.

"He does," I pretend. "He just needs to be reminded, that's all."

Auntie Lizbet takes Iris and Soly into the yard.

"Watch me skip, Auntie," Iris says. "I can skip to over two hundred."

Granny stands with her back to me, watching the children, her hands pressed to the windowsill. "They never knew him when he was himself," she says quietly. "Do you remember your grampa from when he was strong?"

"Yes," I say. But not like she hopes. I remember Mama bringing me to visit when I was little and Granny and Grampa were on the cattle post. They'd take us to Auntie Amanthe's burial stone at the abandoned ruin. "Amanthe would be alive today, if you'd married Tuelo Malunga," Grampa would say to Mama. Then he'd stare, and Granny would feed us tea and biscuits. I tried not to eat, even if I was hungry, because if I dropped a crumb, they'd get angry. I was afraid of them. They were so big. And now . . . Now they're so small.

"Your grampa used to be young, once," Granny says. She breathes in deep. And again. And again.

I go up behind her. I hold her. She trembles.

When Granny collects herself, she goes into the back room for a lie-down. I try and get the kids' things in order. We haven't shared a sleeping space since I moved into Mama's old room. Somehow, Iris's torn mosquito net has gotten mixed up with my clothes. The cell phone I'd wrapped so carefully in my underthings is lying in the corner. Was Iris playing dress-up in my panties? I'll strangle her.

I turn on the cell to make sure it's still working. It is. There's three messages. Mrs. Tafa! I feel guilty. I should have called to let everyone know we arrived safely. How could I be so thoughtless? I slip the phone in my pocket and wander out back to the woodpile for a little privacy.

Two rings and Mrs. Tafa picks up. I decide to be nice and call her "Auntie" like she likes: "Hello. Auntie Rose, it's Chanda."

"Hallelujah! The blessèd cell works."

"I just called to say we're fine. Sorry I didn't phone earlier."

"Never mind. What a relief! And the children? The children are fine too?"

"Yes. Why do you ask?"

"No reason," she clucks. "And you're sure? You're sure the children are fine?"

"I'm sure! How's everyone there?"

"Oh, couldn't be better. Except for Mr. Lesole."

"Mr. Lesole? Isn't he up at his camp?"

"Was." There's a tick in her voice. "They flew him back yesterday."

"Why? What's the matter?"

"Just flu, I expect. He's kept indoors. I'll give him your best. Not a word to Soly and Iris."

"No, not a word."

"And . . . and," she hesitates, "you're *sure* you're all fine?"

"Yes!" I'm starting to get annoyed.

"All my love to you and the little ones, then."

"Thanks, and—Auntie Rose, before you hang up, could I speak to Esther, please?"

"I'm afraid she's off with Sammy and Magda."

I hear Esther shouting in the background: "I'm here! I'm here!"

"Why, look who's coming up the road," Mrs. Tafa lies. As she passes the phone to Esther, I hear her whisper: "Don't say a word to upset Chanda. They're only rumors. We don't know anything for sure."

"Chanda!" Esther says. Her voice is so clear, I close my eyes and I'm home again.

"Esther, it's so good to hear you. What's happened to Mr. Lesole?"

"Well, like Mrs. Tafa says, everything's fine down here."

"Except for Mr. Lesole. Tell me the truth. What's happened? What are you hiding?"

Esther laughs like I've told the funniest joke in the

world. I'm about to explode, when she says in a low voice: "Chanda, sorry, Mrs. Tafa's watching me like a hawk from her lawn chair. I'm as far away as I can get. Last night, Mr. Lesole came home in an army jeep. He had a bloody coat over his head. Soldiers are guarding his house. Mrs. Lesole is wailing. Government cars have come and gone all morning."

"Why? Why?"

"One of the guards says, when the tourists were sleeping, poachers attacked the safari camp. They left the tourists alone. But they stole the camp's guns and cleaned out the safe. Mr. Lesole tried to stop them. They did something to him."

"What?"

"Nobody knows. The soldier wouldn't say. There's all these rumors. Mrs. Tafa thinks the poachers wanted revenge. Mr. Lesole's sent poachers to jail."

"But Mr. Lesole also said poachers don't go near the camps. They're too afraid to get caught."

"I know," Esther says. "Here's something else that's strange. When Mrs. Gulubane dropped by, Mrs. Lesole ran out of the house. She screamed how Mrs. Gulubane was a quack and threw a small bag at her head."

I gasp. Mr. Lesole's magic pouch. The one to ward off the rebels.

"Chanda, what?"

"Nothing."

"Don't lie. You know something. What?"

"Nothing. Really. Mrs. Lesole's upset. She could be screaming about anything. And Mrs. Tafa, she could be right about poachers getting revenge."

Esther laughs. A little too loudly.

"Is Mrs. Tafa coming over?" I ask.

"Yes." Esther laughs even louder. "I have to go." I can feel her turning around, turning her back on Mrs. Tafa. She talks fast, deadly quiet. "Chanda. Chanda, about the rumors. About what the poachers did to Mr. Lesole—"

"Yes?"

"There's these sounds—these terrible sounds coming out of his place."

"Sounds?"

"Animal howls. Animal cries. It's like it's Mr. Lesole, but it's not. Like he's trying to talk, but he can't."

"What do you mean, he can't?"

"Chanda . . . The rumor is they cut out his tongue."

14

I HANG UP in a daze. Slip the cell phone into the pocket of my skirt. What's happened? I have to find out. How? The general dealer's. Mr. Kamwendo always has the radio on. Maybe there's news. Or maybe someone driving down from the park has stopped for gas. If something important's gone on, there'll be word.

I pray that Mr. Lesole's all right. That, at worst, it's poachers who attacked, and he just got beat up. If that's what happened, they'll catch them, put them in jail, and Mr. Lesole will get better. But what if it's Mandiki? What if his rebels have broken into small groups, like *The Rombala Gazette* said? A raiding party could *look* like poachers. Maybe they'd *want* it to look like poachers to keep people off-guard, till they were set for a big attack.

Stop it. It's crazy to panic. Think where the news came

from. Mrs. Tafa. She's full of gossip and rumors. She probably got Esther all worked up. But what about the sounds? Well, maybe the Lesoles bought a goat or something. Maybe it's in a back pen for slaughter. Even so, why the soldiers?

I wish I didn't have this stupid cell phone. If I didn't, I wouldn't have had that conversation. I wouldn't be feeling so . . . so . . . I put on a smile and return to the front yard. Pako's come over; he's playing with Soly. Iris is still skipping for Auntie Lizbet. Auntie's clapping along, singing a skipping chant I'd half-forgotten from when I was little.

"I'm going to the general dealer's to say hello to Mr. Kamwendo," I call across the yard. "Can I get you anything?"

"No," Auntie says. "Just be back in time for lunch."

Iris is distracted. She trips. "I was at two hundred and thirty," she shouts at me. "I was setting a record. You wrecked it!"

"Sorry."

Auntie gives me a stern look and turns with a smile to Iris. "We'll start a new record. How's that?"

"All right," Iris fumes, "but it won't be the same."

* * *

Mr. Kamwendo is sitting under the tin awning in front of his store, at the center of a semicircle of men who've dropped by for a jaw. Music from his radio blares through the screen door. He's chewing tobacco, an old spittoon at the side of his chair. He gets up slowly and waves as I approach. "What can I do for you?"

"Not much. I just came by to see if there were any letters for out our way."

He chuckles. "No more than usual."

"Actually," I toe the dirt, "I was wondering if you've heard any news from Mfuala Park."

"Not that I recollect." He turns to the others. "You boys heard anything from the park?" They shrug no.

"Nothing about poachers?" I ask.

Mr. Kamwendo spits a drool of tobacco juice into his spittoon and taps the corner of his mouth with his juice rag. "There's a trial about to start in Shawshe, if that's what you mean. Eight fellas from Mfualatown shot a hippo, what, maybe six months ago. A ranger was in on it. Quite the operation. Split the meat amongst five families. Had a foreign buyer for the head. They're lookin' at two years each, six for the ranger."

"No," I say, "this trouble, it'd be from a couple of days ago."

He shakes his head. "Then sorry. Haven't heard a thing."

"Nothing about the Kenje River Safari Camp?"

"Why?" Mr. Kamwendo teases. "You planning a holiday with the tourists? You should've seen a travel agent back in Bonang." The men laugh.

I laugh too, then: "It's just, there's a rumor they had a problem with poachers."

"Not so's I know. But we never hear much bad from the camps. They don't want to scare away the tourists. Neither does the government." He shakes his head. "Gotta say, though, it don't sound right. Poachers, they tend to stick clear of the camps. Park's so damn big, why risk gettin' caught? Them boys in Shawshe are in for one helluva ride."

"That's what I thought."

"Anyway," he smiles, "if you want my advice, don't fret. There's always plenty of stories around. If poaching's up, they'll hire more rangers. Plant a few soldiers by the park towns. Whatever it is, it'll sort itself out."

I work hard around the yard all afternoon. Granny tells me to relax, but I have to keep busy to clear my head. I want to ring Mr. Lesole, to know what's happened for sure. But I'm afraid. Even if I could get his number, would the soldiers let him take my call? And if they did, what would I say?

We eat around the firepit and watch the sun go down. My uncles and aunties come out and join us. My mind's a mess, but I try to be good company. No one can know what I've heard. Especially not Iris and Soly. Like Mr. Kamwendo says, there's always stories around. Why make folks crazy with rumors?

Time passes. Uncle Enoch tells a joke about two porcupines in love. He laughs so hard, bits of maize cake fly from his mouth. We laugh at his joke, and at him laughing at his joke. Auntie Agnes and Auntie Ontibile sing a folk song about the coming of the rains. We sing along. Uncle Chisulo drums a beat on his cheeks, chest, and thighs.

All the while, Iris sits cross-legged on the ground beside Auntie Lizbet. During a lull, she rests her head against Auntie's knee. "Auntie," she asks into the silence, "do you ever miss not being a mama?"

"Oh, sometimes, I guess," Auntie says simply, staring at the coals in the firepit. "But if I was a mama, all my love would have to go to my children, wouldn't it?"

Iris thinks a bit. "I guess it would."

"Then I wouldn't have any left over, would I?"

"No, I guess you wouldn't."

"So maybe this is best," Auntie says, stroking Iris's hair. "This way I have lots of love, all stored up, to give to little girls who don't have mamas."

A pause.

"Little girls like me?"

"Little girls like you."

Iris smiles. She doodles a finger on Auntie's club foot. "When I grow up, Auntie, I want to be just like you."

"Hush now, hush. Don't wish for that."

"But I do."

We sit in comfortable silence and watch the smoke drift skyward. Before long, we hear Nelson and his older brothers riding back from their cattle post. Their noise carries from over a field away. By the sounds of things, his brothers are into the booze.

Granny goes to the road and flags down their mule cart. "A little reminder. Tomorrow's the big feast to honor my grandchildren's visit. I want you boys here in good time."

"We'll do our best," says the one with the hip flask.

Granny wags her finger. "I want more than that. Before the celebration, our families have important business to discuss. Understood? Nelson, if your brothers get lazy, you crack the whip."

His brothers laugh: "It's us who crack the whip."

I catch Nelson sliding me a look. When he sees me seeing him looking, he snaps his head back to the road and flicks the reins. "Don't you worry, Mrs. Thela," he says as the mules move forward, "we'll pen the cattle late afternoon."

"That's my Nelson." Granny waves, and returns to our circle.

"You're having a feast on our account?" I ask.

"Of course," Granny says. "Your being here is important. To all of us."

I lower my eyes. "Thank you."

"Not a word of that. We're the ones grateful." Granny hesitates. We listen to the crackle of the fire as she struggles for the right words. "Sometimes things happen in a family," she says slowly. "Terrible things. Things that tear a family apart. We go to the ancestors for wisdom. But sometimes our healing comes through the young. A new generation gives hope that the sins of the past can be forgiven. That the mamas and papas, the grannies and grampas, can find peace when they think to the future."

Everyone stares at me. This time I'm the one who should say something. But what? I take a deep breath. I look each of them in the eye. "My brother, my sister, and I—we're glad to be here," I say. "At first, we were afraid. For that, I'm sorry. You've made us welcome. You've made this home. Whatever problems there've been in our family, I swear I'll do my best to put them right."

"Dear girl. Dear, dear girl." Granny offers her hands. I kneel down and kiss them. She kisses my forehead in return. "Bless you, child of my child. I give you my blessing."

Murmurs of "bless you, bless you" from my aunties and uncles, as Granny blesses Iris and Soly too.

"Tomorrow will be such a celebration," Granny says. "Tomorrow, Chanda, you must take your ease. No raking the yard, no fetching water, no helping with the meal like you did this afternoon. Reflect. Dream of your life to come."

I feel shy. I look over to the Malungas. They've rolled into their yard. I watch as Nelson's brothers stagger to their homes and yell for their wives to put food on the table. Is there going to be a fight? Do I go over? Ruin everything here? Soly puts a worried finger to his lips. Then—laughter behind the Malunga doors. My shoulders relax. Everything's fine. At least for now.

My eye catches Nelson, holding back with the mules. He unhitches them slowly, wipes down their flanks, and leads them to the shed. The whole time, he's staring over, all casual, like he's focused on something far away. But what he's really staring at is me. This time, I'm the one who turns away.

15

I GO TO bed. Granny's blessing, the love of the aunties and uncles, fills me with such peace. Nothing can change the past. But can the past be forgiven? Can forgiveness change the future? I think of Soly and Iris. For their sake, I hope so. I'm all the family they've got. They deserve more. Like Mrs. Tafa says, they need a granny, a grampa, aunties and uncles, cousins.

I fall asleep, filled with the wonderful things that can follow from Granny's blessing. But sometime in the night, I'm not sure when, my old dream starts, like a storm cloud rolling across a sunny day: As always, things begin well. Mama is alive. We're at Granny and Grampa Thela's cattle post, near the abandoned camp where I found her. Mama smiles at me, orchids in her hair. I want us to stay like this, but I know what's coming. "Wake up," I tell myself. "Wake up, before it's too late!"

This time, I do. I sit up, heart beating fast. I'm safe in my room.

What time is it? I rub my eyes, get out of bed, and step outside in my housecoat. It's not quite night, but it's not dawn either. The air is a dark, dusty blue. I can make out the shapes of the houses, the granary, the wash place, and the outhouse. My aunties'll be up soon, getting my uncles ready for the cattle post.

I shiver. The cattle post. The abandoned ruin. Mama.

A second ago, I was fine. Now everything's raw. I see me when I went to Mama. How I held her. Brought her home. How she died. Mama. Mama is gone. Forever. But the pain's still here. Now. Six months later. I want it to stop. Please, let it stop.

A need overwhelms me. To go where I found her. I don't know why. I just have to be where she was.

I move fast. If Granny or Auntie Lizbet find out, they'll stop me. I tiptoe into the house, find a cup, a bar of soap, and a towel. Then I hurry back outside, fetch a pail of water from the cistern, and go to the reed wash place beside the outhouse. The abandoned camp—it's an evil place to my relatives. But to me, it's holy. Sacred. I have to be clean.

"You're thinking crazy," says a voice inside me. "You

don't believe in superstition. Spirits. Ritual." I know. But right now, no matter what my head says, my heart tells me this is important.

I pour water over myself with a cup from the pail, wipe myself with soap, then sponge, rinse, and dry. In no time, I'm back in my room. I change under my sheet in the dark. Soly rouses. "What are you doing?"

"Shh. Nothing. Tell Granny I'll be home by lunch."

"All right." He's back asleep. Will he remember to tell Granny? Probably not. What if she worries? She won't. She'll think I'm having a walk, reflecting like she told me to. Which I am, sort of. And anyway, I won't be gone for long.

I head across the yard. Auntie Ontibile and Auntie Agnes have lit their morning lamps. I see them move about in the glow pouring through the slits of their front shutters. My uncles stretch in their nightshirts.

There's still no sun, but the dark is lifting. The sky is gray-blue. A rooster breaks the silence. I'm on the road now, heading toward the general dealer's and the highway. There's no one else as far as I can see. Before, when I went to find Mama, I drove out with a nurse and helper from the Tiro health clinic. This time I'm alone. Alone on a country road. Am I insane? This is something Esther would do.

I should turn back. I should ask my uncles to take me. No. They were the ones who brought her there. They'd be shamed. Besides, my uncles'll be coming to the post any minute. If I run into trouble, they'll be right behind me.

But what if a car drives by? A man could grab me, take off, rape me. No, not if he doesn't see me. If I hear a car, I'll hide in the ditch till it's passed. Besides, I have my cell phone in my front pocket. If a car stops, I'll do like Mrs. Tafa. I'll yell their license plate number into my cell at the top of my lungs. Then we'll see who runs.

I relax when I get to the turn at Mr. Kamwendo's. A few other folks are off to an early start. Once I hit the highway, there's a cart or a bicycle every few hundred yards. I fall in line, walk north for about twenty minutes. At last I reach the giant baobab on my left. There's a dirt trail heading into the bush. This is the cutoff used by my uncles, the Malungas, and the other families on nearby posts.

I slip across the highway, run a few yards up the trail, crouch, and look back. The carts and bicycles that were behind me pass by. No one's following me. Good.

I get up and follow the path. The rainy seasons have made new twists and turns in the trail since I was last here, and some of the trees have been cut down. All the same, the land comes back to me. It's like going downtown in Bonang and finding buildings collapsed, or a mall going up, or stores with new owners. No matter how different things are, I'm never lost. The map of it's in my bones.

I get to the three boulders that mark the southeast corner of Granny and Grampa's post. The abandoned camp is a hard walk into the scrub brush to my right. The new camp is a mile farther down the trail. It was built far away for a reason. The curse of the ancestors.

The story is like this:

When Mama refused to marry Tuelo Malunga and ran off with Papa, Granny and Grampa offered Tuelo a marriage with her younger sister, Auntie Amanthe. That stopped trouble between the families. But it didn't stop problems at the post. The well water went bad. Babies got sick. Granny and Grampa called in the spirit doctor. He sacrificed a cow, chanted incantations, and sprinkled magic powder in front of doorways, under eaves, and across the pathways leading to the compound. But things got worse. Within the year, Auntie Amanthe was dead. Tuelo Malunga brought her body back to Granny and Grampa. His family didn't want it buried on their post;

they said that it had been touched by a curse. The spirit doctor said they were right. Mama's disobedience had shamed the ancestors; they'd cursed the compound because of her. He said unless the camp was moved, all the cattle would die and every new baby would follow Auntie Amanthe into the ground.

Six months ago when I came to find Mama, Granny said our relatives had taken her to the abandoned camp to hide her sickness from the village. But I think there was another reason. For over twenty years, they'd blamed Mama for their bad luck. I think they returned her to the abandoned camp so the curse would die along with her, in the place where it started, where the evil first showed itself.

Near the three boulders, the cattle on the post graze freely, and for the first half mile I navigate quickly over a network of tracks; but my uncles and cousins have steered the cows away from the abandoned camp, and the end of my journey is hard. The grasses may be dying back, but they're still up to my waist, and I have to take care not to run into thornbushes or trip in nest holes burrowed by lizards, birds, and bush mice.

Every so often I check the sun to gauge my direction. I'm also helped by the old cart path that runs off the main trail. When the path was in use, the cart wheels rutted the ground, and the rains broadened and deepened the furrows. Now that they're overgrown, they could be mistaken for old streambeds. But I know what they really are—ghost tracks leading to Mama.

The brush and the grasses end. I'm at the camp.

The ruin where I found Mama is straight ahead. All that remains is the crumbling outline of where the mud walls used to be, and the ring of mopane poles that kept them in place. Some of the poles have toppled. Others stand like flagpoles at the center of termite mounds.

I go to where I found her. I lie in the spot where she lay and close my eyes. "Mama," I murmur. "Mama, it's Chanda. I'm here. Tell me what to do."

I don't know what I'm expecting. Perhaps the feel of her presence? Or, when I open my eyes, to see the stork from my dreams? Whatever I was hoping, it doesn't happen. When I open my eyes, I don't see anything unusual. Just things. Ordinary things. And then—a revelation that dawns like the still quiet of sunrise. These things I'm looking at, they aren't ordinary at all. They're the things Mama saw while she waited to die.

To the right, more ruins: a remembrance of the shacks

of my aunties and uncles. I think of the life that was shared there, the laughter, the joy and pain. Beyond my feet, the enormous termite mound and the tumbledown pole fence that penned the cattle; I picture the cows wandering home at dusk, without a clock or a minder. Then far on my left, a patch of river rocks, marking the graves of my ancestors, buried here on the land before the village cemetery was built. Auntie Amanthe's rock is in clear view.

When I found Mama, her mind was gone. She was talking to Auntie Amanthe's spirit. Talking as if Auntie Amanthe was alive. She talked to her in the Tiro clinic van too. "Don't marry Tuelo," she said. "There'll be bad luck. I know things." *Was* Auntie Amanthe with us after all? *Can* spirits come out of the ground? No. What am I thinking?

I suddenly notice something else. I leap to my feet. Turn in all directions.

The camp is in a clearing. When I was young, it didn't seem strange, and when I came for Mama I was too upset to notice anything. But now I see with new eyes. This is no ordinary clearing. It's as if someone—or something—has drawn a circle around the outskirts of the camp. Beyond the circle, the earth is alive with vegetation. But inside, even after years of abandonment, there's not a single living thing. Not a tree, not a bush, not even a blade of grass. It's like I'm standing at the center of death.

Enough. There's always a reason for things. At least that's what Mr. Selalame says. Maybe the earth was poisoned. Maybe even poisoned by the spirit doctor to prove his power with the dead. But reason can't explain the tingling in my forehead. The hair rising on my neck.

I freeze. Someone's watching me.

"Uncle Chisulo?"

Silence.

"Uncle Enoch?"

Silence.

I stick out my chest and elbows. Plant my hands on my hips. "I'm Chanda Kabelo. My uncles have guns. If you're a stranger, get off our post, or they'll blast you to kingdom come!"

A laugh behind me. I whirl around. See nothing. "I'm warning you. My uncles will get you. One of them's insane."

Another laugh. This one from the side.

I swing to face it. A fruit bat swoops in front of my eyes. Startled, I scream and race backward into the tall grass. I reach for the cell phone in my pocket, but I trip on a mopane stump, do a somersault, and sprawl into a nest of army ants. They bite. I flip over.

The stranger plants a foot on either side of my waist. He stands over me, silhouetted by the sun.

16

"GET AWAY FROM me, you sonovabitch!" I grab fistfuls of ants and sand and throw them at the man's face. He steps away. I scramble toward the path. He grabs me from behind.

"Hey, there, city girl," he laughs. "Settle down or you'll get hurt."

I know that voice. "Nelson?"

Nelson lets go of me. I stumble back ten feet and stare at him, brushing ants and dirt off my skirt. He's wearing a red bandanna around his neck, loose trousers, and a baggy shirt. A few of the top buttons are missing, exposing a muscled chest. I'll bet he cut them off on purpose, for the girls.

"What are you doing here?" I demand.

He flashes a row of straight white teeth. "Your granny asked me to find you. Your sister said you'd disappeared."

"I didn't disappear. I told my brother I'd be back by lunch."

"Who cares?" His voice goes dead earnest. "Do you know the trouble you could be in right now? A girl alone in the bush?"

"I was careful."

"Careful? You're not careful. You're a city girl!"

If I argue, I'll get mad. If I get mad, I'll act like an idiot. "Since you followed me," I say calmly, "you'll know I'm right. I was never in danger."

"I didn't follow you. Your uncles left before you were missed. Why do you think your granny came to me?"

"If you didn't follow me, how did you know where to find me?"

"Easy." He picks a blade of grass. "I tracked you."

"That's impossible. There were too many others on the same route."

"So?" he grins. "There's a trick for that. Someday, I'll tell you, if you're nice." He chews the end of the grass. "I've tracked things my whole life. Stray cows, city girls—it's the same thing."

"You're saying I'm a cow?"

"No." He squinches his nose. "Cows are smarter."

"So I'm a cow, only *stupider*."

"Sure." He sweeps his arm across the barren campsite. "Look at this place. What cow would be stupid enough to come here?"

"Is that supposed to be funny?"

"Not as funny as you," he smirks. "You should see yourself. This big stuck-up city girl with ants crawling out of her nose."

"Stop calling me 'city girl.'"

"How about 'little girl'?"

"Don't call me 'little' or 'girl' either. You're only seventeen yourself."

"Whatever you say, cow child."

"Goodbye, Nelson. I'm going home."

He runs his fingers over his hair. "Not without me."

"Yes, without you. I know I'm breaking your heart, country boy, but you're obviously too good for me." I throw my shoulders back and start down the old cart path. Nelson follows, a steady ten feet behind me. I whirl around. "Go away."

"Sorry, cow child. I promised your granny I'd see you home."

I glare. Nelson smiles. If only I could spit like Iris.

* * *

We reach the highway. There's a whirring in the sky, a rumble on the ground. Three military helicopters fly over us, leading a convoy of army jeeps. They're headed toward Mfuala Park.

I want to keep Nelson at a distance, but my nerves won't let me. "We didn't see any soldiers on the way up," I say. "Is this normal?"

Nelson shrugs. "Up here, the army comes and goes like the seasons. If you ask me, it's good to have soldiers in the bush around Mfualatown. Especially now we've signed the friendship pact with Ngala."

"You know about the friendship pact?"

"Of course. Do you think I'm stupid?"

I hesitate.

He gives me a fierce look. "You city folks think we're all stupid in the country. Well guess what. We've got radio and weeklies. I read *The Rombala Gazette* at the dealer's when it's in." He sees my surprise. "Yes, I can read, cow child. I can write a bit too, even figure out the cost of cattle feed. I have grade six, you know."

"I didn't mean to insult you."

"I don't care what you meant."

A second convoy passes. I bite my lip. Nelson is

amused. "Those jeeps really scare you, don't they? You, a girl who walks alone to the post at dawn?"

"I'm not used to them, is all."

"Well, relax. If I was the government, I'd send lots of soldiers to the park too. And I'd hoist the flag at the private safari camps. A show of force is good. It warns Mandiki not to cross the border."

I try to hold my tongue. But my fear blurts out anyway: "What if he's already crossed?"

"What do you mean?"

"Exactly what I said. What if Mandiki's crossed the border? What if his rebels are in our park?"

Nelson sighs like I'm an idiot. "We'd know."

"How?"

"A government plane patrols the border every day. They'd be spotted."

"A lot you know. The Mfuala National Park is over ten thousand square miles. It'd be like spotting mice in savannah."

"Once they're in the bush, sure," he agrees. "But first, they'd have go through a mountain pass. They couldn't risk it by night. They'd have to use torches, and the light would give away their position.

That leaves the day. And by day they'd be exposed."

"No, they wouldn't. The Mfuala peaks are covered in cloud."

"Who cares? The air force has heat sensors."

"What good's a heat sensor over a place filled with wildlife? It can't tell if it's picking up rebels, lions, kudus, or bush buck. Look at Ngala Park. Mandiki hid undetected for six years."

Nelson twirls in exasperation. "All right. Fine. You want the best proof Mandiki hasn't crossed the border? Here it is: Nobody's missing their lips and tongues."

I start to shake. I gasp for air. I can't stop.

"Sorry if that upsets you," Nelson says, "but the rebels have mutilated folks from the very beginning. They do it to keep them from talking. They do hands, too, if the person can write. I thought a genius like you would know that."

"I do." I squeeze my arms. "I have a neighbor who works for the Kenje River Safari Camp. I heard the army flew him home. Soldiers are guarding his house. He's being questioned. There's a rumor his tongue's been ripped out by poachers. But what if it isn't poachers? What if it's Mandiki?"

Nelson looks at me in wonder. "Whoa! You don't even

know for sure your neighbor's been hurt. You don't know why he's being questioned either. A lot of poaching rings have someone on the inside. There's a case right now in Shawshe. How do you know your neighbor hasn't been setting up kills? Maybe that's why he's being held."

"No. Mr. Lesole hates poachers. He reports them."

"That's what he says, anyway," Nelson snorts. "Even if he reports them, so what? He could be doing it to cut down the competition. Or to throw off suspicion."

"How dare you attack Mr. Lesole!"

"I'm not. I'm just saying, don't jump to conclusions." He rolls his eyes. "I mean, listen to yourself. You hear a rumor from hundreds of miles away. A single rumor about poachers. And suddenly, your little brain sees rebels running all over the countryside. You really must enjoy scaring yourself."

I have to admit, when he puts it that way, I feel pretty foolish.

Nelson speaks slowly, mouthing the words like I'm a two-year-old. "Mandiki is in Ngala. He's been there for six years. It's where he's going to stay. If he's crazy enough to cross the border, those soldiers you saw will be there to stop him. Right?"

"I guess so."

"You guess so?"

"All right. You're right."

"I'm always right," he laughs. "Those army convoys mean security. Forty miles of security. Don't you forget it."

Part Three

17

WE'RE BACK IN Tiro by midmorning. Nelson's talked all the way home. Apparently, he's an expert on everything. The country. The city. The army. The rebels. The meaning of life. He's so full of himself I could throw up.

Granny claps her hands when she sees us. "Thanks for getting my girl home safe," she says to Nelson. "Remember to get your brothers home too. Early and sober. There's important business to discuss before the celebration."

"Sure thing, Mrs. Thela." Nelson tosses me a wink and runs backward down the road, throwing Granny and me elaborate waves.

"That boy's trying to impress you," Granny laughs.

I raise my eyebrow. "Trying."

"Good girl," Granny smiles. "Keep him guessing."

ALLAN STRATTON

A pause. I give Granny a sidelong glance. "I'm sorry I made you worry."

I expect a lecture on selfishness, but it doesn't come. It's as if Granny wants nothing to break the goodwill of last night's blessing and this evening's celebration. All she says is: "No harm done. But next time, for the sake of these white hairs, have an auntie or uncle go with you." She gives my arm a friendly pat. "Come, you'll want a nap after your walk."

"I should help to get things ready."

"Not a word of that. Tonight is in your honor. I want you as fresh, rested, and beautiful as you can be."

She leads me through the yard. Everyone nods greetings as we pass. Auntie Lizbet is adding bright beads to the ends of Iris's cornrows. They're on a bench next to the firepit, where Auntie Agnes is turning a goat on a spit. My sister Lily sits nearby, baby Abednego strapped to her waist. She wraps carrots, sweet potatoes, and pumpkin in damp leaves to slow-roast in the hot ash. Meanwhile, Auntie Ontibile is decorating the clotheslines with ends of bright cotton, old balls of foil, and tin cans that have been pressed flat and cut into the shapes of trees and stars.

I look around. "Where's Soly?"

146

"With Pako," Granny says. "I expect they're at the cemetery. What a good boy. Always paying respects to his papa."

If she only knew.

As promised, Nelson gets his older brothers home in good time. A change of shirt and they come over with Mrs. Malunga. Their wives remain behind with their children and Pako. Soly and Iris are with them too. Iris wanted to stay with Auntie Lizbet. "You can sit on my lap at supper," Auntie smiled, "but first, us grownups have things to talk about."

I'm not sure why the family wants to include me in the discussion. I know nothing about their goings-on. Still, it's a compliment to be counted with the elders, so I pretend to be happy about it, even though I expect to be bored.

The Malungas praise the preparations. Both families' tables have been set together and are piled with platters of goat meat, pots of vegetables, bowls of spiced tomato sauce, and fresh maize bread. For dessert, there's a basket of tangerines and a tin of Mrs. Tafa's gingered pears. Mrs. Malunga is especially impressed with Auntie Ontibile's cutouts, glinting in the late afternoon sun.

Nelson introduces me to his brothers Samson and Runako. They're not drunk yet, but they're not sober either. I can smell the manure on their skin and trousers. Samson's only in his mid-twenties, but his nose is already bubbled and pocked from alcohol. Runako is a few years younger; his left eye is slightly crossed. They lean in to me more than I'd like. I cross my arms over my chest.

After the welcome chitchat, Uncle Chisulo calls us to the circle of chairs and benches around the firepit. Granny leads me over by the elbow. She sits us across from Nelson and Mrs. Malunga. The others fill in the gaps. Samson and Runako sit together. A space opens up on either side of them. Everyone's too polite to say so, but no one wants to be near the stink. Runako slouches back on his chair; his trousers ride up his calves. There are open sores on his legs. I shudder. I'll bet his wife is sick too.

As the eldest male present—Grampa is indoors sleeping—Uncle Chisulo delivers a formal greeting and invokes the ancestors, praying that our meeting and celebration will be a blessing to all. We murmur agreement, then Uncle Chisulo asks Granny to share a few words.

Granny lifts herself up. "Everyone's had a chance to meet my granddaughter," she says. "A few of you more than others." She nods to Mrs. Malunga and Nelson. "As you know, Chanda's mama passed six months ago, leaving the poor girl with the care of her younger brother and sister, and the maintenance of a large property with a cinder-block house."

"I've seen it," Auntie Lizbet interrupts. "The property's as big as her next-door neighbors', and those neighbors have a row of rental rooms. Very nice, if you take my meaning."

Everyone is impressed. They nod congratulations. My pride gets the better of me. "Auntie's right," I enthuse. "It's very big. One day, I'm going to build a friendship center on the extra land. It'll be in memory of Mama."

People shift in their seats. It's like I've thrown a live skunk into the party.

Granny clears her throat. "As I started to say," she continues, "our Chanda is a hard worker. A good mama to her brother and sister." Hearty agreement from my aunties.

"Yes indeed," Lily adds. "My sister may be from the city, but she can cook, clean, carry water, mend clothes, and raise children, as well as me or our aunties. She'll make a fine wife."

"A fine wife, yes," Auntie Lizbet nods vigorously. "And

as we've hinted, her property, her large property, means she has money."

I flush with embarrassment. Auntie means well, but the Malungas will be thinking I'm spoiled. I hurry to correct the impression. "Auntie's mistaken," I say. "I have no money. If I sell our home, I'd have to buy another."

Mrs. Malunga understands. "Raising money is difficult for everyone," she confides. "When my Tuelo passed, he left our herd to our oldest, Samson and Runako. When their children are grown, they'll be able to manage the herd without Nelson and Pako. Those two will need to bring cattle of their own to the post. And the cost of cattle these days . . ." She raises her hands to the sky.

Samson and Runako could share their inheritance, I think. But they twiddle their thumbs and look in the air, as if things are beyond their control.

"I speak for our family," Uncle Chisulo says. "Papa is no longer able to farm. Enoch and I have cattle to sell. A sale would give us the money to connect our homes to Tiro's water pipe. We could have indoor sinks and washtubs. Maybe even an indoor toilet. A cattle sale would be good for us."

Mrs. Malunga nods. "But we have no money to buy."

I stare at my nails. When can we eat? I begin to realize the talking has stopped. I look up. For some reason, I'm the focus of attention. Why? I don't know anything about the cattle market or indoor plumbing. I sit up straight. "Well," I say brightly, "we all have the same problem, then. No money."

There's an awkward silence. Clearly I've been given a test and failed it. But what was the test? What was the question? I'm confused.

Granny smiles gently. She takes my hand and speaks to the circle. "My grandchildren are all alone in Bonang. No mama, no papa, no aunties, no uncles. Not a living soul. We are their only kin. My dearest Chanda has brought her brother and sister here to us to heal an old family wound. Last night, before god and the ancestors, I gave them my blessing."

"Granny?"

She squeezes my hand. "Child of my child, last night you spoke of this place as a home for you and the little ones. Your grampa and I, your aunties and uncles, your sister Lily, and our dearest friends the Malungas, would like to make it so."

"Pardon?"

"Nelson has agreed to accept you as his wife."

I look at Nelson. He shrugs and looks away.

"My boy says you have a tongue and a temper," Mrs. Malunga laughs, "but these can be cured."

I glance from face to face, utterly bewildered.

"Chanda," Granny says calmly, "the curse—the curse that we will not speak of out of respect for your late mama—this curse began with a marriage denied between our two families. You and Nelson, the next generation, have been brought together to mend this divide. It is a joy for all. No longer must you struggle alone in a far-off city. You can live here, loved and supported, by your family and your new family-to-be. Your property in Bonang is the dowry that will make this union possible. With it, your husband Nelson will be able to buy our cattle—cattle that he needs. And this payment will be used to make life better for all of us." She pats my knee with affection. "Especially for your aging granny and your Auntie Lizbet with her foot."

Everyone glows with satisfaction, except Nelson. They lean forward to hear my reaction, suspended from their seats in expectation of my gratitude.

Instead, what explodes out of my mouth is: "NO!"

They stay smiling. Frozen like statues. It's like they haven't heard.

Granny beams. "I know, it's too good to be true, isn't it? But it *is* true. The answer to our prayers."

"No!" I repeat. "No! Not *my* prayers. My home is in Bonang. I have a job. I have Soly and Iris to raise. And then I want to finish school. Granny, I have dreams."

My aunties and uncles frown. Then they begin to speak, louder and louder, one over the other: "Your home is with family." "You've no need of a job." "Why finish school?" "Why build a center?" "What better dream than a husband?"

"For goodness' sake, Chanda, " Mrs. Malunga declares, "there's no need to fear for Soly and Iris. Nelson will take them in. He's already promised."

"Even if he didn't, we would," Auntie Lizbet insists, pounding her cane on the ground.

"No! No!" I'm standing now. Stomping my feet. "Mama gave me that land. She gave it to me in trust. If I sell it for dowry, I'll have nothing. Soly and Iris and I—we'll be dependent forever."

"Not dependent," Granny says. "Supported by a loving husband."

"I don't need a husband. I have my neighbor lady and my best friend."

"Your neighbor lady has her own problems," Auntie Lizbet snaps. "As for that slut of a friend: Word has it she's a beggar-whore, face slashed and scarred as a country road."

"Esther's no whore!" I cry. "Even if she was—better a whore than a Malunga."

Runako and Samson leap to their feet. "What?"

"She's an ingrate," Auntie Lizbet rages. "Selfish as her mama!"

"Selfish?" I whirl on Auntie Lizbet. "You'd sell me to a family of brutes for indoor plumbing—and *I'm* selfish?"

" 'A family of brutes'?" Samson raises his fists.

"Beat me! Prove it!" The words fly from my mouth faster than I can stop them. "Mama was afraid of your papa."

"She was a crazy bitch."

"Was she? My friend is scarred, yes—but what about the scars in your own family? Mrs. Malunga—how did you lose your teeth? Was it your husband, Tuelo, or one of your big, strong sons?"

"Take that back!" Runako yells.

"No! I've seen you drink. I've heard the fights. I know about the broken bones. Pako's bruises. The way he pounds your papa's grave with a rock."

"He pounds Papa's grave?"

"Yes! So his spirit will stay in the ground! So it won't rise up and beat him like your papa did when he was alive!"

Samson's eyes blaze red. "Pako?!?" he yells to his yard. "What have you been doing? What have you been saying?"

"You shamed Papa," Runako roars. "You shamed our family, you little sonovabitch!" He charges across the road, Samson at his heels.

"Pako! Pako!" Mrs. Malunga cries.

We leap to our feet. All of us screaming, "Run, Pako! Run!"

18

THE BROTHERS SWOOP down like eagles on a mouse. Their wives try to stop them. It's no use. Runako knocks his backward with an elbow. Samson sends his flying with a fist.

Pako has only one way to run. The cemetery. He races to the shortcut. It's strewn with debris. He knows every root and pothole. As Runako pounces, Pako hops over a stump. Runako bangs his foot, stumbles into a rut, twists his ankle, and topples to the ground. Samson trips over him, banging his head on a rock. They're back on their feet in no time, angrier than ever.

"We're going to kill you, Pako! You hear me? We're going to kill you!"

Pako reaches the edge of the cemetery, Samson right behind. Samson flings his arm forward to grab his brother. But Pako dives. He rolls under the barbed-wire fence.

Samson's too big. He's running too fast. He drops too late. The teeth of the barbed wire rip into his face. Blood pours from his cheeks and forehead. He flails around on the dried streambed, howling like a stuck pig, as Pako disappears into the grasses outside the cemetery's main gate.

The rest of us catch up, except for Soly and Iris, who look on nervously at the edge of the Malungas' compound.

"Keep away from the blood!" I say. "It's got virus. You'll need plastic bags for your hands."

Samson's wife shoots me a dirty look. She ignores the cut under her own eye from where Samson hit her, gets him to his feet, and helps him away. Runako gets attention too. His wife takes his weight, and he hobbles off yelping about his ankle.

There are no words to describe the looks that pass between my family and Mrs. Malunga. "We'll deal with this," Uncle Chisulo says. Mrs. Malunga nods without expression.

"I'm sorry," I say. "I'm sorry. I didn't mean for any of this to happen."

Nobody says a word. They don't even look at me. They just turn their backs. I don't exist.

I stand alone in the twilight, at the edge of the cemetery,

as my family returns to their homes, slowly, silently, heads bowed. Soly and Iris stare. I open my arms. Instead of running to me, they back away, turn, and follow Auntie Lizbet. They know what's happened without being told. I've shamed the family. I've shamed them.

It's the middle of the night. I'm by the firepit. The coals are dead, the lamps blown out. Everybody went to bed hours ago, except for me and Nelson. Nelson, because he's off looking for Pako. Me, because, well, I'm afraid to go inside. Nobody's told me I can't. But I can't.

Dear god, let Pako be all right. If anything happens to him, it'll be my fault.

One thing's for certain: We're going back to Bonang tomorrow. After what's happened, there's no way we can stay.

The night's so still, I can hear the inside of my skin. I'm suddenly aware of a presence. I look up. I can't see him, but I know he's nearby. "Nelson?"

"Not bad for a city girl," he says quietly. His voice is coming from my right.

"How long have you been here?"

"A while."

"Have you found him?"

"I haven't gone looking yet."

"I thought . . ."

"You never think." He waits for me to argue. I don't. "When things are like this, I disappear," he says. "Don't worry. It's not the first time Pako's run away. I'll track him down at first light. I have an idea where he is."

"Will he be safe?"

Nelson exhales slowly. "Who's ever safe? . . . I can bring him food till my brothers calm down, if that's what you mean."

There's a long pause. "You knew about Granny's plans before I got here, didn't you?" I say. He doesn't answer. "That's the real reason you picked us up when we arrived, instead of my uncles. The families wanted you to get an eyeful."

He clears his throat. "It wasn't my idea."

"You could have told me. You could have warned me."

"I'm sorry." Another pause. His voice catches: "Just so you know, I'm not like them."

"I know that."

"No you don't."

"I do."

Silence.

"Nelson? . . . Nelson?"

But he's vanished.

Granny comes out at dawn to set the fire for morning tea. Neither of us says anything. We both know I'll be gone soon. I watch as she lays the kindling.

Inside, Iris and Soly have just woken up. "Why are you packing our pillowcases, Auntie?" Iris asks.

"Because your sister's taking you back to Bonang."

"But I want more time with you," Iris pleads. "Please, Auntie, please, it's not fair."

"There's lots about life that isn't fair," Auntie Lizbet says.

Iris and Soly begin to cry.

"There, there," Auntie comforts. "Let's kiss those tears away." She's crying too.

Granny lights a scrap of thatching with her oil lamp and touches it to the dried grasses at the base of the kindling. "We thought you'd be happy," she says at last. "We all did. We were so excited."

"I know."

"We thought you wanted us."

"I do. I . . ." My voice trails off.

We sit in silence, watching the kindling catch fire. "Nelson's a good boy," Granny says softly. "We'd never have put you in danger." She rubs her hands in the heat, then reaches over for the pot of water.

"You tried to make Mama marry Tuelo," I whisper.

Granny freezes. "What do you mean?"

"Tuelo Malunga, Granny. You know what I mean."

"In the bush, you don't see folks much; the posts are far apart," Granny says evenly. "We thought Tuelo had high spirits, that's all. We didn't know."

"Mama knew."

Granny swallows hard. "Ah well." She hangs the pot of water over the fire to boil and turns to go back inside.

"Should I go to the Malungas?" I call after her. "Should I say something?"

Granny looks me in the eye. "I think you've said enough. Don't you?"

19

Nobody eats much at breakfast. Granny fusses with Soly's shirt collar. Auntie Lizbet strokes Iris's hair. I sit apart. After the food is cleared, Aunties Ontibile and Agnes come over from their places to say goodbye to the kids, while my uncles lift our things into their cart.

Iris and Soly ride into town, pressed against Granny and Auntie Lizbet. I walk behind. I tell myself that walking is best, there's no room in the cart. But the truth is, nobody wants to sit beside me.

The general dealer's is still locked up when we arrive. Mr. Kamwendo sleeps on a cot in the back room. He's usually open by now, in case anyone needs anything for the posts. Not today.

Nelson's squatting by the front door. "Sam must have turned his hearing aid off," he says to Uncle Chisulo. "I've been banging for the past ten minutes."

"What's wrong?"

"Nothing I guess," Nelson says. "Still looking for Pako. I tracked him here, to around the gas pumps. I'm hoping he's with Sam."

As if he's heard his name, Mr. Kamwendo opens the screen door and steps outside. He stretches in the morning air.

"Late night?" Uncle Enoch says.

Mr. Kamwendo rubs his eyes. "Don't ask. That damn flatbed didn't roll in till close on midnight. Leak in the transmission. Must've been two by the time she left for the park."

"The children are going back to Bonang," Granny says.

"It's Chanda's fault!" Iris blurts.

A look passes between my relatives and Mr. Kamwendo. "Well," he says with an awkward cough, "I wouldn't expect the flatbed today. I did a patch, but she needs proper fixing."

Frowns from my relatives. Delight from Iris and Soly.

"Why don't you all go back to the compound?" I say. "I'll wait here for news."

The idea that I won't be around seems to make everyone happy. Even Soly and Iris. I try to give them a quick hug, but they shy away. Uncle Chisulo turns the cart around. "Me and Enoch will be back in a half hour," he says to Mr.

Kamwendo. "Can you have a pound of nails, a dozen spikes, and a ball of twine ready? We're mending the herd boys' quarters." Mr. Kamwendo nods and waves them off.

"Soly. Iris. I'll see you soon," I call out. Soly peeks at me, his face a wall of hurt; it says, You told my secret, how could you? Iris gives him an elbow and he looks down. My insides dissolve as I watch them disappear down the road.

Meanwhile, Nelson picks up a small stone. "Sam," he says, tossing it casually from one hand to the other, "did you see Pako last night?"

"Didn't see much except the underbelly of that damn truck," Mr. Kamwendo laughs. When Nelson doesn't laugh back, his voice goes serious. "The kid's off again?"

Nelson nods. "His trail ends here. By the signs of it, he arrived around midnight. I've circled three times. He never left the service area. At least not by foot. Any cars through here in the early hours? Trucks, carts, bicycles?"

Mr. Kamwendo shakes his head. "Just the flatbed bus. A lot of angry passengers, let me tell you." He smiles. "Isn't it always the way? Damn bus always waits for a full load to break down."

Nelson frowns. "Sam, if you don't you mind . . . Could you call Mfuala Park? See if Pako stowed himself on board?"

"You don't suppose he'd run as far as the park, do you?"

"He's walked halfway before. And this time"—Nelson glances in my direction—"this time was bad. Besides, like I said, his tracks come here and they don't leave. If that bus was the only way out, well . . ."

"I'll see what I can find out," Mr. Kamwendo says. He goes inside to phone. Nelson and I wait in the yard. It's as if we're total strangers. I watch the carts and bicycles heading out to the highway for the posts. Nelson drops the stone from his hand, catches it with the edge of his right foot, flicks it up in the air, and keeps it there, bouncing it back and forth from toe to knee to foot and back again.

Mr. Kamwendo returns in a few minutes, scratching the back of his neck.

"What's wrong?" Nelson asks.

"The flatbed never arrived at Mfualatown."

"What happened to it?"

Mr. Kamwendo shrugs. "Transmission likely conked out for good, I figure."

Nelson's nose wrinkles up. "Why didn't Mr. Palme call in for help?"

"On what? Obi's radio's been broke for weeks, and he never charges his cell. Serves the damn fool right. I've warned him: 'One of these days, you'll be caught in the middle of nowhere, needing a tow.' Sure enough, look what's happened!" He slaps his thigh and laughs. "If Obi's passengers were mad last night, I'd love to see 'em now!"

Nelson and I aren't in the mood for humor.

"Cheer up," Mr. Kamwendo says. "If Pako's on the flatbed, Obi'll take care of him. Right now, I expect home's looking pretty good to the little fella."

"Let's hope so," Nelson says.

I have a different worry. "If the truck needs a new transmission, how long could we be stuck here?"

"Dunno," Mr. Kamwendo squints. "A couple of weeks maybe."

"But we have to leave today."

Mr. Kamwendo pulls a plug of chewing tobacco from the pouch in his pants pocket. "Tell you what. I'll keep an eye out for rides going south." He pops the plug in his mouth. "Don't fret. I'll make sure it's decent, with a woman in it. And I'll make a big point of taking their license number. If you offer to pay what you'd have given the bus driver, you'll hitch a ride no problem."

I start to breathe again. "Thanks." Across the street, the health clinic's opening. I see the doctor, the nurse, and the assistant who helped me get Mama home when I brought her out of the bush. "I'll be across the street at the clinic. All right?"

"It's no never-mind to me," Mr. Kamwendo smiles.

I head over. The clinic staff all remember me. I thank them again for their kindness, and tell them how Mama passed in peace. They give me a hug. "Mr. Kamwendo's trying to get me and my brother and sister back to Bonang," I say. "Can I help out around here till a ride shows up?"

"You're manna from heaven," the nurse rejoices. In no time, she has me mopping the floors, wiping the windows, disinfecting the folding chairs, and taking out the trash. I'm so busy I barely realize the morning's passed without a word from Mr. Kamwendo. I wander over to see what's happening.

Mr. Kamwendo shakes his head. "Not a soul's pulled in. I've never seen it so dead." He offers me a bag of banana chips. "A going-away present," he says. "You must be hungry."

I am. And restless. I gobble the chips and wander out to the highway. Aside from a few carts and bicycles, it's completely empty. No cars. No trucks. Nothing. I wait ten minutes. Fifteen. Still nothing. It's creepy.

Suddenly, I hear a rumble. A huge cloud of dust whips up the road. In no time, six army trucks swing past me into Tiro. I race after them. They brake in front of the clinic. Dozens of soldiers leap into action. They heave piles of sandbags off the trucks to other soldiers on the ground. A wall of bags begins to build around the clinic.

I run to Mr. Kamwendo. "What's going on?"

He shakes his head, openmouthed in wonder. Tobacco juice drips off his chin. He doesn't notice.

A crowd forms around us, nervous and curious: the men from under Mr. Kamwendo's awning, the patients pushed out of the clinic, folks off the street—and anyone else who's heard the commotion.

I see Nelson. He sidles up beside me.

"Those soldiers," I say. "Some of them are our age."

"Why the surprise?" Nelson mutters. "What else can you do if there's no work? Not even room for you on your own post?"

Is he thinking about him and Pako? Am I supposed to feel guilty?

A lieutenant steps to the front, flanked by four sergeants, automatic rifles slung around their shoulders. The lieutenant is in his early twenties, too skinny for his uniform.

"Attention!" he bellows into a bullhorn. "There's been a situation to the north. An incident involving bandits. For your security, a squadron is being posted in each village from Rombala to Mfuala Park. Further, by order of the government, a dusk-to-dawn curfew has been imposed throughout the district. After sunset, anyone moving outside their town or cattle post will be considered a bandit, and shot on sight. To repeat, during curfew, a shoot-to-kill order will be in effect."

Furtive glances through the crowd. Men tug at their belt loops. Mamas touch their youngsters' shoulders.

"During the day," the lieutenant continues, "travel between villages and posts will be permitted by foot, cart, and bicycle. However, the highway is hereby closed to motor vehicles."

"But I have to get to Bonang!" I yell. "How do I get to Bonang?"

"And what about my gas station?" Mr. Kamwendo hollers.

Now everyone's shouting. They need to go to a birth in Shawshe. A wedding in Rombala. A funeral in Mfualatown. "What do you mean the highway's closed?!" I'm pushed forward with the crowd. We're shaking our fists. The sergeants swing their rifles. They fire into the air. We fall back.

A new army truck roars up to the clinic. The lieutenant signals. The soldiers unload it. This time they're not heaving sandbags. They're handing off corpses. Corpses wrapped head to toe in bloody sheets. A hush falls over the crowd.

"Last night, the Mfualatown bus crashed twenty miles north of here, after being attacked by rocket fire," the lieutenant says. "These bodies were found in the area, along with looted bags and suitcases. There are no known survivors. We'd appreciate any help you can give with identification."

The corpses are laid side to side. The last in the row is small. The height of a child. Nelson bites hard on his hand.

The soldiers uncover the faces one by one. The first is a man with receding hair. A moan rolls through the crowd. Everyone seems to know him. Wait. I know him too.

"That's Obi Palme, the bus driver," Mr. Kamwendo tells the lieutenant.

Mr. Palme. My insides go cold. I remember him filling up the tire in Shawshe. Now he's on the ground, eyes wide, mouth open, as if screaming to us from the dead.

The soldiers continue down the line. At each body we

hold our breath, afraid we'll see someone else we know. The third is a woman. At the sight of her, a man runs forward, beating his chest. "Jeneba! My sister, Jeneba!" Friends hold him back. He collapses.

The soldiers reach the last body. The child. One of them kneels down. Nelson can't bear it. He looks away. The cloth is lowered.

"Nelson," I gasp. "The child . . . It's not Pako."

Nelson rocks on his feet. For a second, his eyes fill with joy. Then instant confusion and fear. "If that's not Pako," he gulps, "where is he? What's happened to him?"

20

NELSON BOLTS FROM the crowd.

Others head off too. They scatter in all directions, spreading the news throughout town. Soon I'm alone, except for Mr. Kamwendo and a few others who've stayed behind to watch the soldiers sandbag the clinic.

Nelson's words ring in my ears. What's happened to Pako? I have a sick feeling. I sink to the ground. Stick my head between my knees and chant: "ABCDEFG, ABCDEFG."

"Chanda?" Mr. Kamwendo squats down beside me. "Chanda, are you all right?"

My throat's a rope full of knots. "I—I don't know. I—I—"

"Everything's fine." He squeezes my shoulder. "You heard the man. It's bandits. We've had 'em before. They'll run when they see the army."

"But what if he's wrong? What if it's not bandits?"

"Who else could it be?"

I choke out my fear: "Mandiki. The rebels."

"What?" Mr. Kamwendo checks to see if anyone's listening. They aren't. All the same, he waves his hand to hush me. "Look for trouble, trouble will find you," he says.

But I won't be hushed. I can't be. Not now that I've started. "Two days ago, I asked if you'd heard of any trouble at the Kenje River Safari Camp. The thing is, the man down my street works there. Folks at home say his tongue was cut out."

Mr. Kamwendo's eyes go tight. "It's you should have your tongue cut out, talking wild like that. You want to start a panic? There's no reason to think things are any different from what that soldier said."

"Really?" I give him a sharp look. "If it's only bandits, why post soldiers? Or barricade the clinic? Or close the highway? Or shoot-to-kill during curfew?"

"Better safe than sorry," he snaps. "You oughta be glad about the troops. They're here to protect us."

"How? They're barely as old as me."

"With an AK-47, it don't matter if they're six or sixty."

"It matters if they don't know what they're doing," I say.

"Our country's at peace. Our troops have never fought. What'll they do under fire? They can't even sandbag." It's true. The wall around the clinic is ragged; bags tumble off the top.

Mr. Kamwendo wipes his forehead with the back of his sleeve. "Enough of that. They're good boys."

"Sure they're good," I say. "Good and useless."

Mr. Kamwendo gets up. "It's best you move along," he says quietly.

"Mr. Kamwendo?"

"Shoo. Shoo. I'm too old for bad luck."

"What do you mean 'bad luck'?"

"You're like your mama. No respect. Just questions, tales, stuff to scare folks half to death. No wonder your people don't want you." He wipes his hands on the back of his pants. "I've done good by you. I've tried to help out, more fool me. Now move along. Please." He hurries inside. The screen door bangs shut.

If folks weren't looking at me before, they're looking now.

"What?" I shout. "What?"

They stare. Frightened. Suspicious. Angry.

I start to run.

My sister Lily's in her front yard with her baby, talking to a neighbor.

"Lily!"

She looks up, waves me off with a hand. "No," she calls out. "Whatever it is, no." The neighbor disappears. Lily heads to her house.

"Lily, wait!" I catch up to her at the door. "The army's in town. They've closed the highway."

"So I hear."

"Soly, Iris, and me—we'll need a place to stay."

"The children are welcome at Granny's, aren't they?"

"Yes, but they're with me. Mama put me in charge."

"Then take them wherever you want."

"I have nowhere to go."

"That's not my problem. You brought this on yourself." The baby cries. Lily pats its back. "Now excuse me. I'm busy." She goes inside. I try to follow. She blocks the doorway.

"Please, Lily," I say in a small voice. "Take us in. We're family."

"After the way you shamed us?"

"I'm sorry. I'm sorry."

"I don't want to hear it. This is between you and the

elders. I have a place in this family. I won't let you spoil it. Not for me, and not for my children. Sooner or later you'll be back in Bonang. We have to live here."

"What should I do?"

Lily gives me a long, hard look. "Swallow your pride," she says. "Crawl back to Granny. Tell her you'll do what she wants—you'll eat the Malungas' dirt if you have to."

"No. I can't."

"Are you family or not? If you are, act like it. If not, stop slipping us on and off like a pair of old flip-flops." She slams the door.

My body tingles. I float out of Lily's yard. There's a clothes pole near the side of the road. I lean against it. Everything goes black. Am I fainting? Out of the darkness, I see my dream stork flying toward me. I hear Mama's voice: "Mrs. Tafa."

I blink. The world swims into focus. I'm still on my feet. But I'm not scared anymore. Mrs. Tafa. Yes. I'll call Mrs. Tafa. She's talked to Granny before. To Mr. Kamwendo, too. She's an adult. They'll listen to her. She can fix things. Or pay for a room at the local rest house. Mrs. Tafa. If everything works out, I'll never laugh at her again.

I reach into my right skirt pocket for my cell phone. It's

empty. Strange. I try the left. It's empty too. What? I fumble frantically. Nothing. This is crazy. I remember putting the cell in my skirt after I talked to Esther. I haven't used it since. And I haven't changed skirts.

Did it fall out? Impossible. My pockets are deep. So where is it? When was the last time I saw it, touched it? There was my walk to the cattle post. I remember patting my pocket on the way. I felt it; I had it. Then I'm at the ruin. Nelson scared me. I ran. I reached for the cell but I tripped, somersaulted backward onto an anthill. It had to be then— then—with my skirt flying over my head. Oh my god! My cell fell out at the post, in the grasses with the ants.

My mouth's dry as sand. I can't go to the ruin. I'm too afraid. There's rebels in the bush. Where, I don't know, but somewhere. So how do I get it back? I have an inspiration. I don't need the cell. I can call from the clinic, or beg a special favor from Mr. Kamwendo.

The afternoon sun is hot. I long for the clinic's shade. By the time I get there, the army trucks are gone. The square is practically empty. A sergeant studies a map laid out on the hood of a jeep. Four soldiers stand at ease, guarding the clinic's corners. A fifth blocks the entrance, rifle at the ready.

I approach cautiously. "I have to see the doctor."

"The clinic is closed. House visits only."

"But I need to use the phone."

"The clinic is closed. House visits only."

"At least tell the doctor I'm here. The nurse. The assistant."

"They're out. The clinic is closed—"

I stamp my foot. "Listen to me. I have to use the phone. Now. How old are you, anyway?"

The sergeant looks up from his map. "This girl giving you trouble, soldier?"

"Sir. No, sir."

"You giving this soldier trouble?"

I shake my head. "I just need to use the clinic phone. It's an emergency."

The sergeant scowls. "Clear off, or you're under arrest."

My heart stops. "Yes, yes." I bow. "Right away."

But before I can take a step, there's a yelling and clattering from the general dealer's. We all whirl around. It's Mr. Kamwendo. He's attacking the left side of his eaves with a rake. Two night owls take flight. Mr. Kamwendo turns to us, his face a mask of terror. "Owls," he says. "Owls roosting in my eaves." He sees me. Points a bony finger. "It's you that brought this. Things were fine before you came. Now there's bandits. Owls. Death."

I look from Mr. Kamwendo to the soldiers and back again. They stare at me like I'm a witch. I run.

Mrs. Tafa. I need Mrs. Tafa.

There's no choice. I have to get to the cattle post.

21

IF I'M LUCKY, I can reach the post, find my cell phone, call Mrs. Tafa, and get back to Tiro before dark.

The empty highway makes me shiver. Why? I'm better off than I was yesterday. No cars or trucks means no one to take advantage of me. That calms me down for a few minutes. Then I round a bend, go down a small hill, and Tiro's out of sight. Walking through silence, my mind plays games. I imagine eyes peering from the brush. Men following me behind the grasses.

I spot a movement in the ditch reeds up ahead. I freeze. A hare pokes its nose through a sedge patch. It hops out of the ditch and onto the shoulder of the highway. Sits on its haunches. Sniffs the air. The still of the road must be strange for it, too. I relax. The hare catches the shift of my shoulders and bounds across the potted pavement to the reeds opposite.

What a baby I am. Even the lieutenant thinks we're safe until dark. I don't know if he's right, but it makes sense. Bandits and rebels have to sleep too. Better for them to hide by day, attack and escape by night.

All the same, I see a sharp rock at the side of the road. I pick it up, clutch it tight. Not that it'll help if I run into Mandiki, but it makes me feel safe. Safer anyway.

An army patrol jeep heads down the road toward me. A soldier's at the wheel, a civilian in the passenger seat. The civilian keeps his head burrowed in his jacket, as if he's afraid he might be recognized. Is he under arrest? Or is he helping the soldier? The jeep slows as it passes, then turns around, and pulls up beside me. The civilian shrinks down until he's practically under the dashboard.

I nod at the soldier and keep walking, as if nothing's the matter. Nothing *is* the matter, is it? The soldier lets the jeep idle forward. He's older than the troops in town, and rougher. A homemade tattoo snakes up his neck from under his collar. Or maybe it's the tip of a birthmark. Or an AIDS sarcoma.

I walk a bit faster, eyes straight ahead. The jeep keeps pace, then brakes. The soldier watches as I walk away. And watches. And watches. I start to feel nervous. Please let him drive off. Instead:

"You," he barks.

I stop.

"Yes you. Come here, where we can see you."

I walk back to the jeep, my eyes on the gravel.

"Turn around," he says. "Let's get a good look at you."

I turn. Once. Twice.

"Raise your arms."

I raise them.

"Why do you have that rock in your hand?"

"No reason."

"*Sir,*" he corrects me. "No reason, *sir.*"

"No reason, sir." I let the rock drop.

His eyes narrow. He looks me up and down, slowly. I feel naked.

"Sir, can I put my arms down. Please?"

"No." He stares at my breasts. A long pause. "What are you doing out here?"

"Heading to my family's cattle post."

"Who's your family?"

"The Thelas."

"Who's on your post?"

"My uncles Enoch and Chisulo, and their herd boys."

The civilian eyes me from inside his jacket. He mutters something to the soldier.

"My friend here's never seen you before," says the soldier. "He says the Thela boys have one grown niece. Lily."

"That's my sister, sir. I'm Chanda Kabelo, visiting from Bonang."

The soldier keeps staring. The tattoo on his neck is pulsing.

I choke. "Is there a problem, sir?" He keeps staring. I start to perspire. "My uncles are expecting me. I'm already late. They've probably sent people out to find me."

The soldier considers this. He shifts in his seat. "You know about the curfew?"

"Yes, sir."

He presses a finger against his left nostril, and snorts a wad of snot onto the highway. Then, without a word, he presses his foot on the accelerator, wheels the jeep around, and takes off toward Tiro.

The moment the jeep rounds the bend, I start to shake. I drop to my knees, pick up my rock, squeeze it to steady myself. If that's how I faced a government soldier, how would I face Mandiki? I can't think about that. I've lost time. I better hurry.

A few minutes later, I'm going so fast, I almost don't notice the boy ahead of me. He's about Soly's age, standing at the entrance to a path coming out of the bush, unwashed, in his underpants, a tear in the shoulder of his thin short-sleeved shirt. Three older boys hide in the shadows of the brush behind him, gazing out with hooded eyes.

Normally I'd ignore them. Not today. Today, I imagine the blank faces in the photographs of the child soldiers from Ngala.

I cross the road. The boys come off the path onto the highway. I move past them. Slowly. Carefully. Check the weight of the rock in my hand. Turn it so the sharp edge faces out. Grab it so I can gouge and slash.

The hairs on the back of my neck tingle. I feel the boys' eyes on my back. Are there more of them? How many? Are they following me? Do I run? Do I attack? I glance over my shoulder. But they aren't after me. They're just ordinary kids off to Tiro, looking back at me fearfully over *their* shoulders.

The heat of the afternoon sun is going down. I should be at the post by now. I walk faster. Ahead, more children appear on the highway: six fairly close up, ten in the distance. A few may be herd boys, but most are too young, and some are girls. They're farmers' children who stay on the posts, most likely. So why are they going to Tiro?

Two girls, hand in hand, straggle behind. "What's going on?" I ask. They look up, startled. At the sight of me, they scream and race to catch up with their friends. Who do they think I am? *What* do they think I am?

My heart pounds. By the time I get to the turnoff leading to the posts of my family and the Malungas, the road is alive with children. They dot the highway, ahead and behind, all of them heading to Tiro.

It's my dream come to life. No. That's crazy. It's *not*. There's no storm, no mud, no magic grass. Mama isn't a bird. And Soly and Iris are safe with Granny.

I dart up the path to the cattle post. I reach the ghost trail to the old compound. Take two swift steps into the bush. There's movement behind me. I crouch down. A dozen young men peel by, Uncle Enoch and Uncle Chisulo rattling after them on their mule cart; they're herd boys and cousins from my family's post, I'll bet. Word must have spread about curfew. They're afraid they'll miss it.

I'll miss it too, if I don't hurry up. To speed things, I follow my route from yesterday. The grasses are still slightly bent from where I pushed through. It was a lazy, old trail to begin with. Add all my zigs and zags around stumps and thornbushes, and the way I flounced on my way home, my path could've been made by an old cow. Nelson would have a laugh. "Did I call you cow child?" I hear him tease. "I should have called you Granny Cow!" Ha ha. Very funny.

What's not funny is the time. The sun is orange and heavy. It's just above the trees. I should head back. No. I've come too far to go back empty-handed. Who cares if I miss curfew, anyway? I can sleep out here. No one wants me in town. No one'll miss me. At least with my cell, I'll have Mrs. Tafa and Esther.

Two shots ring out in the near distance. Silence. If it was anything serious, there'd be more than just two, wouldn't there? It was probably a farmer shooting at scrub hares. Or a jeep backfiring on the highway. Maybe, I laugh dryly, Mr. Kamwendo's bicycled out to clear the brush of owls.

I press on. It's heavy going, the vegetation up to my waist, sometimes over. At last, I come around a cluster of thornbushes. I halt in my tracks. Take a deep breath.

I've reached the dead land.

22

I GO TO the crumbled ruin where I found Mama, and start to retrace my steps. I face the termite mound. That's where I was when I started to run backward. The grasses are almost upright from yesterday, but if I look closely I can see they're still slightly tipped.

The trees are casting shadows. I move about twenty feet back through the blades to around where I fell. I lost my cell by an anthill. Where is it? What was the last thing I saw? I turn around to get my bearings.

Suddenly Nelson bursts out of the bush on the other side of the clearing. I almost don't recognize him. He looks crazed like his brothers. Shirt gone, chest streaked with dirt, sweat, and blood.

"What's going on?"

"Get down."

"Nelson?"

"I said get down!" He thrashes through the thick grass, eyes blazing.

"Stay back!" I raise the rock.

Too late. Nelson jumps on a stump, leaps like a wild cat, grabs my wrist. The rock flies loose. He falls on top of me, hard, my right arm wrenched behind my back. I hit him with my free hand. Punch him in the head. He grips my hand tight. Smothers it to my mouth.

"I'll only say this once," he pants. "Stay down. Shut up. Or you're dead. We'll both be dead."

I stare up, terrified.

"Promise you won't scream?" he asks. "Promise you'll stay down?"

I nod as well as I can with my head pressed in the dirt.

He lets me go. "You were right."

"About what? Nelson. Tell me!"

"Mandiki. He crossed the border days ago. The rebels have been at my cattle post. They could be anywhere. We have to stay still." He takes a furtive glimpse over the grasses and falls back beside me, gulping air.

"After I saw the bodies in town," he gasps, "I went to my cattle post to clear my head. Word's been spreading south, post to post: Send your kids to Tiro, the rebels are all around. Our herd boys were scared. My brothers were drunk. They said it was a joke, that they'd whip any boy who left. I gave the kids a wink and started to pen the cattle early. A cow was missing. I climbed a tree to try and spot her. That's when Pako showed up. Yes, Pako. He was leading a man with a necklace of bones."

"Mandiki?"

Nelson nods. "My brothers were too drunk to know who he was. Runako gave Pako a swat and spat on the general's boots. Samson demanded his name. 'You don't know me?' Mandiki asked. Samson said the last time he'd seen a face like Mandiki's, it was on the ass end of one of his cows. Mandiki tilted his jaw and a circle of men and children rose from the grasses outside our fence. Runako and Samson suddenly understood. They fell to their knees and blubbered. Mandiki put his gun in Pako's hand. He planted the muzzle on Runako's forehead. 'Say goodbye to your brother,' he said, and squeezed Pako's finger. Runako flew backward. Then Mandiki aimed the gun at Samson. 'Last time I saw a face like yours,' he said, 'it was exploding.' He squeezed Pako's finger again. And that was that."

"Oh, Nelson." I touch his hand. "How did you get away?"

"Luck." He trembles. "Some of the rebels went to the main path. The rest tied the herd boys' hands. While they were busy, I leapt from the tree and ran low through the grass. I made it to your uncles' post—they'd already left—and now I'm here."

My throat tightens. "Tiro. We have to get back to Tiro."

"We can't. It's too late. We'll have missed curfew. If the soldiers spot us, they'll shoot us on sight. Worse, if we're wandering through the brush, we could bump into Mandiki."

"But Tiro's in danger. Our families—"

"Tiro is safe," Nelson says. "It's guarded by soldiers. They control the highway. Why would Mandiki attack a place that's protected when he can steal from the farms?"

"So what do we do?"

"Nothing. We wait here till morning."

Twenty minutes ago, an overnight in the bush seemed like an adventure. Now that it's real, I feel sick. I bunch my knees under my chin and rock.

"You really are a city girl," Nelson says. He's not being mean this time, just honest. "Don't worry." He puts a hand on my foot to calm me. "I've camped around here since I was little. It's nothing special."

"But what if the rebels don't stick to the paths? What if they come this way, cross-country like you did, to stay out of sight?"

"We hide in the grasses. They're up to our waists, don't forget. We just have to stay low. Make sure they don't see any movement. We'll be as hard to spot as buttons in a cotton field."

"What about our trails?"

For a second, Nelson's hand tightens on my foot. "Cows graze all over the bush. The rebels won't give the trails a thought. Even if they did, it's too dark for them to see prints."

"Unless they use flashlights."

"They won't. In the bush, what lets you see, lets you be seen. Once the rebels set camp, they may light a fire; there's campfires all over cattle country; that wouldn't arouse suspicion. But traveling with lights? No. If they come through here, they'll move by the stars, like me. Anyway, let's not think about that. Let's think about the morning. Mandiki will have passed through. It'll be safe to go home."

I get a chill. "What about Pako?"

Nelson sucks in his breath. "Pako is gone," he says,

voice flat. "He's gone and he's never coming back." He chokes. "How do I tell Mama? How do I tell her about Pako, Runako, Samson? How do I tell her I watched and did nothing?"

Nelson's face turns into a scream, but no sound comes out. He rolls away, body heaving, cut by thorns, slick with sweat. I take my kerchief and wipe his back. He winces. A few thorns are stuck in his flesh. I pick them out. It's hard to see. While we've been talking, the sun's gone down behind the brush. Slivers of sunset blaze through the branches. Shadows melt into the grass.

A branch snaps behind the nearby thornbushes.

A man's voice cuts through the air: "You said there was a clearing. Is my little scout telling tales?"

Mandiki.

23

WE PRESS OURSELVES against the ground.

"The clearing's just ahead. I promise." It's Pako. His voice is hoarse and frightened. "There's an old ruins in the center. Nobody's ever there. Not ever."

The high grass rustles. We cower like ground swallows hiding from hunters. I have a desperate urge to run. Nelson knows it. He grips my shoulder. I close my eyes and pray to disappear. To vanish into the air.

"There it is! The dead land," Pako says. "Straight ahead. See?"

They're on top of us now, so near we could trip them. Boots crunch a few feet to my right. I look up. Out of the heavy dusk, a line of men rises above the stalks. As it forges forward, the thick blades bend over us.

Mixed in with the men, I see the bobbing heads and

shoulders of children, some with automatic rifles, others loaded down with sacks and crates. They focus ahead, faces hard. After them comes a man yanking a line of boys tied to a length of rope. Burlap bags hang over their heads. As they pass, Nelson shudders like he knows them. His herd boys? Another man brings up the rear, shoving the last one forward with the muzzle of his automatic rifle.

They move into the compound ahead. I peek through the row of bent stalks beside my head, and up the newly trampled path. I can't see to the sides, but I have a view straight in front of me. My heart flutters, but not like before; buried in deep grass, we're far enough back not to be seen, so long as we don't move.

In the deepening gloom, I see the men, maybe fifteen or twenty, toting machine guns and rifles. Twice as many children—girls and boys both—setting down their burdens. Directly ahead, Nelson's herd boys huddled together in front of a man with a little boy: Mandiki and Pako.

Bird whistles echo from all sides of the compound. At the sound of the all-clear, Mandiki claps his hands. "Build me a fire. Make an altar beside it." He points to my family's old resting place at the back of the compound. "Use that waste of rocks."

"No, don't take those," Pako cries out. "They're Thela burial stones. They've been there since forever. Since before the village cemetery even. They belong to the ancestors. We'll be haunted."

"You'll be haunted, little scout, not me." Mandiki laughs. "I own the dead."

A handful of rebels yank the hooded line of herd boys over to my family's graves. They hoist the rocks into the boys' arms, destroying the resting place of my Auntie Amanthe, my great-grandparents, and generations of Thelas before them. I struggle to see.

Nelson touches my shoulder. I keep down and watch as the boys stagger back with their load, suffocating under the burlap hoods. They heave my family's burial stones into a pile. The men drag them back to the graves for a second load, a third, while other men shape the pile into a pyramid.

Meanwhile, children Pako's age, weapons hanging from their waists, collect sticks, kindling, and broken mopane poles from the edges of the compound. They stack them beside the altar of burial stones, next to Mandiki. The fire is lit. In the flickering glow, shadows float over the ruins like spirits.

The rebels open their sacks and crates. Liquor bottles are pulled from the crates; from the sacks, slabs of freshly slaughtered meat. Nelson's lost cow, I'll bet. The raw stench of it fills the air. The rebels feed. It's like they haven't eaten in days. Some cook skewers of beef over the fire; others swallow strips raw. The blood on their hands glistens in the firelight.

What time is it? I don't know. Minutes could be hours; hours, minutes. I've stepped out of time. Hypnotized by fear, like a mouse in front of a snake.

Every so often, children with machetes add new wood to the fire. Their eyes are sunken, as if peering from tiny caves. Their hair is matted with mud and straw. Mostly, they're dressed in rags, some of the girls in burlap maize sacks, seams split for arms and heads. Only a few have shoes. Others have sandals made of rubber tires, tied to their feet I'm not sure how. By sapling strips? Nylon cord? The rest are barefoot. A lot of them hobble about on swollen feet.

Mandiki downs the end of a bottle. A boy takes it away, while a girl wipes his mouth with a cloth. He gives her bottom a slap, rises, and claps his hands. The group falls silent. Mandiki takes a cattle brand and sticks it in the fire.

He grins through his mouth of dead men's teeth. "It's time to meet the new recruits."

The rebels, both adults and child soldiers, force the bound herd boys onto their knees in front of the flames. The child soldiers pull off the hoods, while the adults plant the barrels of their automatic rifles at the base of the herd boys' heads. The herd boys' faces are frozen in terror. Pako is thrown down beside them.

Mandiki stares into their eyes. "Don't think you can escape," he says quietly. "Don't think you can run home to your mama and papa. You have no home. I am your home. If you ever try to leave my protection, you will be caught. And do you know what will happen then? You'll be held to the ground and chopped into bits. Your families, too."

Silence except for the crackling of the burning wood.

An older child soldier drops on one knee in front of Mandiki. He holds up an ebony box. Mandiki reaches inside and takes out a skull wrapped in a monkey skin. The skull is missing its lower jaw. Is it one of the jaws in the necklace around Mandiki's neck? Are some of its teeth imbedded in his mouth?

Mandiki puts his right hand into the cavity of the skull, letting the monkey skin hang from his wrist as if it was the skull's shawl. "These are my new recruits," he whispers into the skull's ear hole, his voice as dead and dry as maize husks. He looks at the boys. "This is my special friend. Once, he was the most powerful spirit doctor in Mozambique. Now he guides me, stealing the spirits of my enemies while they sleep."

Mandiki extends his arm and parades the boney hand puppet in front of his captives. "My friend knows who you are," he continues. "He knows what you think. What you dream." The skull nods, gleefully twisting its gaze from one to the other. It nuzzles into Pako's neck.

Nelson stiffens as Pako recoils. Mandiki smiles and kisses the skull's forehead. He drapes the monkey skin over the altar of burial stones, places the skull on top, and falls facedown on the ground before it. In the flashes of light cast by the flames, the skull glares, mocks, and threatens.

The rebels chant, the children among them beating their chests, while their elders rhythmically strop their machetes. As they chant, Mandiki prays words I've never heard. He growls and grunts sounds I imagine might come from the animals in the park, or from somewhere deep inside the earth.

He rises. Rolls back his head. Splays his arms wide. His eyes and cheeks have disappeared. His face is like the skull. He moves as if its spirit lives in his body. He lifts the branding iron from the fire. The brand glows red-hot from the blaze. Mandiki stabs it into a metal pot and pulls it out, a wad of flaming batten twisted on its tip. He raises the iron above his head and lowers the burning end into his mouth. A jet of fire shoots from his lips.

The herd boys wail. A good thing too, or the rebels would've heard Nelson yelp. This time, I'm the one who calms us down. "It's an old fire-eater's trick," I whisper. "My teacher told me how it's done." I pray that Mr. Selalame's right. Here, at night in the dead land, I can believe that demons rule the earth.

Mandiki enjoys the herd boys' fear. He juts his jaw and winks at his troops. Taking their cue, the older child soldiers drop behind Pako and the herd boys, rip open their shirts, and pin them tight. Mandiki steps up to the first in line. He holds up the glowing brand. "With this brand, the world will know you are mine. No one—not even your mama or papa—will ever take you back. If they try to, they will die."

The child whimpers.

"My soldiers don't cry," Mandiki warns. "Cry, and I'll burn a hole down your throat." He raises the brand. I turn my head. I hear the hiss as it sears into flesh, the sound of feet kicking against the ground. But no screams.

When it's over, I look back. The skull is grinning.

"Well done," Mandiki says. "My friend approves."

As the boys nurse their blistered chests, Mandiki throws aside the brand and steps beside Pako. He squats on his haunches, his boney legs folded up like a giant locust's. Without flinching, he reaches into the flames and takes out a glowing shard of mopane pole. He holds it out to Pako. "Now then, my little scout, draw me your town."

Pako cringes.

"Draw me a map of your town now," Mandiki says, "or I'll hunt down your mama. When I find her, I'll make you do to her what you did to your brothers."

Pako shakes. He grips the smoking pole-end with both hands and drags it back and forth, up and down, over the dry earth. When he's done, he drops the shard and cradles his burned hands to his mouth. "Where's the general dealer's?" Mandiki says.

"Here," Pako says softly.

"And the clinic?"

Pako points at the dirt drawing.

"Across the street from each other. Good," Mandiki says. "That's where the soldiers will be, controlling the highway, gas tanks, and medicine . . . And what's that mark, away from the highway, back of the town?"

Pako pauses. "The Tiro cemetery."

"Is that so?" Mandiki laughs. "We'll make sure it gets some new business." He claps his hands. "Hyenas, load up. Take everything. We won't be back."

The child soldiers pack. Mandiki stands in profile, Pako and the herd boys cowering at his feet, the men in a double line in front of him. "Micah's in position for the diversion," he says. "He'll rocket the Shawshe gas tanks within the quarter hour. My cousin's scouting in the reeds by the Tiro cutoff. He'll radio when the Tiro squad pulls out to reinforce Shawshe. We'll wait half an hour till the army's far off. Then attack at will."

The men nod. "Where do we cache our gear?"

Mandiki taps his toe on the map. "Here, out of sight, in the cemetery. I'll wait there with the patrol till you're done." He points to the men on his right. "You three, take the kids from Ngala. Shoot a smoke bomb into the clinic to clear any troops left behind. Load up the boys with guns and ammo. Load the girls with the clinic's drugs."

He nods to the rebels on his left. "These herd boys are your new pack mules. Weigh them with goods from the general dealer's. The rest of you, storm the village outskirts with my little scout. He'll show you where the children live. Bind as many as you can, their families, too. They can carry our cemetery cache till we're far away in new brush."

Pako covers his face.

Mandiki kicks him. "Stay alert, boy. You've already betrayed your village. There's no turning back."

24

Soon the rebels are packed and ready. As they wait for the order to move out, some guard the herd boys, kicking them at random. Others bunch in small circles and smoke. Their chatter rises and falls. Mandiki wraps the skull in its monkey skin and puts it back in the ebony box. He sits on the altar of burial stones, stroking the box, his dead eyes lost in the coals.

My joints are as stiff as Granny's. How long have we been stuck here? I don't know. But we have to escape. We have to warn Tiro—we have to save Soly, Iris, our families.

The fire is dying. Ash drifts through the air. No one's paying attention. I tap Nelson's elbow. "Now's our chance. Let's go."

He shakes his head.

I ignore him, and inch back alongside the trampled path.

"Stop." His eyes widen in panic. "You'll make a noise. We'll get caught."

The rebels fall silent. Did they hear us? A crackle of embers from the fire. A log collapses. The talk bubbles back. We're safe.

"Do what you want," I say softly. "I'm off." Where, I don't know. Once out of this place, I'll be lost in the night. But I have to do something. Anything.

I wriggle back a bit more. Nelson sees I'm serious. He hesitates, then follows. We slide back slowly, slowly. Freeze. Slide back slowly, slowly. Freeze.

My legs rub over coarse sand. Something tickles. Ants. I've backed beside the anthill. They're crawling all over.

Out of the blue, a loud stream of water hits the grass at the top of the trail. One of the rebels is peeing into the dirt at the edge of the compound. It's so dark we didn't see him coming. He inhales. His face glows from the end of a lit cigarette.

The ants start biting my legs. The itch is driving me crazy. I want to scratch, to roll around, to get up and run.

The rebel finishes his business. Leave, leave. But he doesn't. He stands stock still, staring down the trampled path in our direction. He turns to the group and snaps his fingers. A man in one of the circles gets up and comes over. A few other rebels rouse to join him. Mandiki looks up.

The man who was peeing mumbles something and points in our direction. His friend turns on a flashlight. Its beam shoots down the trampled path. The tips of the high grass flash yellow and green in the night air. A row of blades is all that separates us from discovery. I steel myself for the end. And then—

A faint thump in the air. A blush of orange in the sky, far, far to the south.

"Fall in," Mandiki barks.

The flashlight is turned off. The man who was peeing takes a step toward us, stops, and stares into the dark.

"Come on," his friend says. "It's only bush rats." The two of them hurry back and into formation, a long single column. It's faced at a right angle to us, heading cross-country toward the highway.

"Fire and death," Mandiki growls. "Fire and death."

The rebels move out, slow but sure. Like Nelson said, they see by starlight. In seconds, they've vanished into the night. Silence.

The coast clear, I brush the ants off my arms, my neck, my face. Some have crawled up my skirt. I plant a hand on the earth, to stand up and get rid of them. As my hand pushes off the ground, my little finger taps against something hard. My heart skips.

"You almost got us killed," Nelson hisses.

But I'm not listening. I'm back on my knees. Yesterday. The ants. I fell on the ants. Fell here. What did I touch? Just now. What did I touch? Please, let it not be a rock. Please, please. Please let it be what I came for. Please. I run my hands frantically over the ground. Where is it? Where? It's got to be here. I felt it. I just felt it. Where?

"Are you listening to me?" Nelson demands.

"No."

"What do you mean, 'no'?"

My hand brushes into the object. I race my fingers up its sides. Wrap my palm around it. Yes. I feel the ridge of sticky tape.

"Nelson," I say. "My cell. I found my cell!"

"Your what?"

"Back home, my neighbor gave me a cell phone. It fell out of my pocket yesterday when you tripped me."

"I never tripped you."

"Who cares? I have it. We can warn the soldiers in Tiro. They can set a trap." I flip open the cell. It lights up. "My friend Esther programmed the general dealer's. The troops are at the clinic. Mr. Kamwendo is just across the road."

Nelson grabs my wrist. "No. Pako. The army'll shoot Pako."

"Not for certain," I say. "If the rebels are ambushed, Pako can run, fall on the ground, maybe escape. Your herd boys too. But one thing's sure. If the army goes to Shawshe, it won't be just Pako in danger. It'll be Soly, Iris, my family, your mama, the whole of Tiro."

He lets me go. I get Mr. Kamwendo's number, press Talk. I shove the cell at Nelson. "You speak to him," I say. "If Mr. Kamwendo hears my voice, he'll hang up."

Nelson holds the phone awkwardly to his ear. I press my head next to his to listen in. The phone rings forever. Finally—"Hello?"

"Sam, it's Nelson."

"Who?"

"Nelson!"

"Nelson? What are you doing on a phone? "

"Never mind. Mandiki's about to attack Tiro."

"What?"

"Mandiki, he—"

"Nelson, I can't hear a damn thing. There's a lotta commotion. The soldiers are heading out. Shawshe's under attack. Big fireball. Can't you see it?"

"Shawshe's a diversion, Sam."

"What?"

"A diversion. Sam, turn up your hearing aid."

"Sorry, Nelson, can't talk. There's soldiers at the door. Both of the jeeps need gas." He hangs up.

I grab the phone out of Nelson's hand. Press Redial. It rings and rings. "He's got to pick up sometime."

"After the soldiers have left," Nelson says. "Once it's too late."

I have a flash. "Mrs. Tafa!"

"Who?"

"The neighbor who gave me the cell." I find her number, press Talk. Mrs. Tafa answers in the middle of the first ring. I used to joke she sat by her phone like a hen on her eggs. I'll never do that again. "Mrs. Tafa—Auntie Rose. It's Chanda."

"Chanda? What time is it? Why aren't you in bed?"

"I'm in trouble. Big trouble. You've got to help."

"Of course. Is it about your granny?"

"No. Mandiki. General Mandiki."

"Mandiki?"

"He's about to attack Tiro."

"Dear lord. Get Iris and Soly. Run."

"I can't. I'm at the old camp. Mandiki was here. I heard the orders."

"Ohmygod ohmygod ohmygod ohmygod—"

"Don't panic. Are soldiers still down the road at the Lesoles'?"

"There's a guard there, yes."

"Run as fast as you can. Tell him to phone his commander. Radio word to the jeeps heading from Tiro to Shawshe. Shawshe's a diversion. The target is Tiro. If they're lucky, they can catch Mandiki in the Tiro cemetery."

"What if he doesn't believe me?"

"Have him call me."

"You're hanging up?" Mrs. Tafa wails. "Chanda, no! Don't hang up!"

"I have to. I don't know what's left on the time card. We may need it."

"Ohmygod ohmygod ohmygod! Leo, grab your shotgun! Guard my tail!" I hear her screen door banging shut.

"Run, Mrs. Tafa. Run."

"I'm running, child," she pants. "Thank heavens, my nightie's clean."

25

I PUT THE cell in my pocket and shake my hands over my head. "ABCDEFG, ABCDEFG."

"What are you doing?"

"Chanting, do you mind?" I spot a branch in a pile of unused wood next to the fire, strip the side shoots, and break it over my knee. With a piece in each hand, I head for the rebel path leading to the highway, using one piece as a cane to feel the ground, the other to sweep in front of my face. "I'm going to Tiro."

Nelson blocks me. "No. You don't know the night. The shapes in the dark. What they mean."

"So lead me."

"Are you crazy?" His eyes are wide with terror. "The rebels are between us and the village. How do we get through?"

"You want to just sit here?"

He grabs my elbows. "Your neighbor's talking to an army guard. Word'll get to the jeeps by cell or satellite phone."

"Not if the guard won't believe her."

"Then she'll call you. Or *he'll* call you."

"By the time everyone's called everyone, it'll be too late. Our families will be dead. Iris, Soly, and Pako will be lost forever."

"Not if the warning works." He grips his shoulders. "Besides, what if we're killed? How does my mama survive with no one to tend our cattle? What happens to your brother and sister?"

"Stop it! That's just an excuse to stay safe!"

"So what?" He shifts nervously. "It's the truth."

He may be scared, but he's right. I slump to the ground. Doubts run through my head like mice in a nest. What should I do? What? What? Seconds turn to minutes, turn to I don't know how long.

Nelson breathes deep. "Let's try Sam again." We try. There's no answer. "He's probably with the soldiers."

Probably? I hate probably. I need to know things for certain. Like, why hasn't Mrs. Tafa called back? She was going to call if there was a problem. So the fact that she hasn't is good, right? Probably. But she'd call either way. So the fact that she hasn't is bad, right? Probably. Well which is it? Are things good or bad?

The more I worry, the more my finger gets itchy. I ring Mrs. Tafa. No answer. I wait. Ring again. Again no answer. I'd call every minute if I could—only what if the battery wears down? I decide to wait a few hours. It's torture.

Nelson lowers himself cross-legged beside me. "The one thing for sure is, Mandiki's not coming back. He said so before he left. We've seen the last of him. That's good news, right?"

"For us, I guess."

He goes quiet. Time takes forever in the dark. It crawls so slowly I can feel my fingernails grow. Why isn't it morning?

Nelson sits closer. His arm presses against mine. We haven't said a word in ages. It's as if, if we break the silence, we'll miss something, or something will happen, or I don't know what. But we're both dying to talk, I can tell. I've started to say something half a dozen times, Nelson too, but each time we've stopped.

Nelson breaks the spell. "For what it's worth, they haven't blown up Sam's gas tanks," he says hopefully. "If they had, we'd have heard it. Maybe it's a sign the soldiers scared them off."

"Maybe," I say. "Or maybe Mandiki wanted to be quiet, so the army wouldn't race back from Shawshe."

It's like I've hit him. "Why think the worst?" he demands.

"Because that's usually what happens."

"Who cares? We won't know what's gone on till we're home. Let's hope for the best."

"Dreaming a lie makes the truth hurt more," I say quietly.

Nelson pushes away from me. "Fine. Think what you want. Me, I've had enough truth for a lifetime."

Silence. I reach out my hand, touch the curve of his back. He's shaking. "I'm sorry," I say.

"Leave me alone."

My cell phone rings.

I blink. I don't remember drifting off, but I must have. There's a dark velvet haze in the air. It's almost dawn. I fumble the cell from my pocket. "Mrs. Tafa?"

"Chanda! You're alive! And Soly and Iris?"

"I don't know. I'm still at the post. You told the guard?"

"Yes. But Chanda, he didn't believe me. He laughed. 'Some kid hears Mandiki's plans and lives to tell the tale?' I told him to call you. He said I was drunk. Me? Drunk?"

"What did you do?"

"I slapped him!"

"You slapped a guard?"

"Chanda, I got arrested! Thrown behind bars with thieves and whores. They took my cell phone!"

"The warning never got through?"

"I yelled. I begged. They told me to sleep it off, went outside and played cards. A few minutes ago, they got a call. They took me to a little room. Said they'd let me go, if I'd forget I told them about Tiro. Otherwise, they'd put me away for a long time: assaulting an officer, resisting arrest."

"So it's happened," I whisper. "They don't want to be blamed."

Mrs. Tafa sobs. "Chanda, I failed. I'm sorry. I'm so sorry. You're in my prayers, the little ones too. Pray god, your family's all right."

We say our goodbyes and hang up. I turn off the cell.

Nelson sees by my face what's wrong. He opens his arms. We hold each other tight. Light lifts the morning. Curfew is broken.

We head to Tiro.

26

"Aiiii . . . Aiiii . . ."

Granny's voice is a moan—an endless moan that rises and falls as she tells her story, rocking on a stool, supported on either side by my uncles. Her dress is ripped; she's bundled in her shawl. Lily and my aunties, Agnes and Ontibile, wipe the blood from her legs with rags dipped in a pail of warm water. Granny shudders when the rags brush the places where the flesh is scraped raw.

Other relatives fill the yard. My male cousins—the ones I saw returning from the post with my uncles—have come from the rest house on the far side of the village, where they spent last night drinking with old friends. By the time they smelled fire, Mandiki had already gone. My female cousins, who left the family compound years ago to marry, have come from their in-laws with husbands, babies, spare clothes, blankets, and food. Lily's husband, Mopati, is here too, along with their little boy; they got back to Lily's as dusk fell. All of them have gathered together to witness. To grieve.

I wish Nelson was here, but he has heartaches of his own. He's carrying his mama's body to the undertaker's. Then he's going to his cattle post to bring back his brothers' remains.

Me, I'm kneeling at Granny's feet. As she keens, my eyes drift over the other homes at the edge of the village. What's left of them. Some of the outer thatching lies scattered around the yards. It must have fallen away when the roofs collapsed in the flames. Mud walls are standing, but shutters and doors are shattered and charred. Wisps of smoke curl up from the insides.

"Aiiii . . . Aiiii . . . ," Granny moans. "Soly . . . Iris . . . your Auntie Lizbet . . ."

Soly and Iris were inside, asleep, when the rebels came. The rest of my family was sitting around the firepit. It had died out hours before, but they'd stayed there in the dark, worrying about the rumors my uncles had heard on the post and wondering where I was and if I was all right.

Granny remembers the sound of a pail being knocked over on the Malungas' property and the sight of Mrs. Malunga standing in her doorway with an oil lamp. "Who's there?" Mrs. Malunga called. Pako's voice came out of the dark: "Hush, Mama. Go back inside, and you won't get hurt." Mrs. Malunga raised her lamp and ran into her yard. "Pako, where are you? What's going on?"

That's when my relatives saw the shapes creeping up from the cemetery. "What are you doing with my boy?" Mrs. Malunga cried. "Give me my child! I won't let you take my baby!" She grabbed hold of Pako. A machete flashed, and she fell to the ground.

My uncles grabbed their wives and ran into the night. Granny and Auntie Lizbet raced inside for Grampa, Iris, and Soly. The rebels found them in the back room. They bound them together, except for Grampa, stuck in his bed. Poor Grampa, he thought the rebels were guests come for Mama's wedding. Granny begged the rebels to let her die with him, but they dragged her away: her, Iris, Soly, and Auntie Lizbet. As they left, they threw a torch on the thatched roof.

"Aiiii . . . Mashudu, my Mashudu," Granny moans. "What did they do to you? . . . Aiiii . . . Aiiii . . ."

Six of the neighbors' compounds were also attacked. Granny tells how all the families were hauled to the cemetery, greeted by Mandiki, and forced to lie facedown at his feet. Rebels moved among them, stroking their cheeks with gun muzzles, telling them that if they cried out or looked to their husbands and wives, their mamas and papas, their children, they'd be killed.

Soon other rebels joined them, child soldiers, with weapons and crates of dried goods from raids at the clinic and general dealer's. They laughed about the soldier who'd been left behind when the jeeps left for Shawshe; how he'd run choking from the smoke bomb fired into the clinic, his gas mask all back to front; how they'd thrown him to the ground and crushed him with sandbags. "The general dealer was asleep when we broke in," one said. "He thought we were bandits, came after us with a rake. We showed him what to do with a rake."

"Aiiii . . . Sam . . ." Granny keens. "Sam . . . Aiiii . . . Aiiii . . ."

She tells how Mandiki boasted that his cousin had radioed from Shawshe; he'd fired rocket-propelled grenades at the jeeps as they approached from Tiro, and escaped into the brush. "Survivors will be hiding all night," Mandiki taunted them. "Abandon hope. There's no one to save you."

Mandiki had the families tied in a row, loaded with sacks, and led single file up a trail at the far end of the cemetery. They marched north, parallel to the highway, for a long time. One of the neighbors, Mr. Bakwanga, collapsed. Mandiki cut his hands from the line and left him to die.

They turned inland. After a while, they reached a stretch of rock in the middle of nowhere. Mandiki lit a torch. The rebels formed a circle. They put the families in the middle. One of the rebels poked Auntie Lizbet with a stick: "This one can't keep up, with that foot of hers."

Granny says how Iris suddenly spoke up, too frightened to know better: "I can take Auntie's load," she said. "I'll carry her sack on top of my own."

Mandiki laughed. He had Auntie untied, made her stand apart from the others, and told her to dance. Auntie tried. The rebels pelted her with stones. She fell. Mandiki ordered the herd boys to kick her until she was dead. Iris screamed and screamed. Mandiki said if Iris didn't stop, she'd be killed too. "Hush, my sweet," Auntie Lizbet called to her, as the herd boys swarmed. "Don't cry. Be happy for me. Rejoice. Tonight, I shall be with the ancestors."

Granny's eyes fill with light. "It was then, my Lizbet began to sing," she says. "She sang a harvest song, a song of thanksgiving. She sang with joy to the very end. Not a single cry of pain. Just joy. Joy, to keep the little one quiet. Joy, to keep her safe. Oh, Lizbet, my Lizbet, she died a saint . . . Aiiii . . . Aiiii . . ."

After Auntie passed, the rebels did things to the other adults. Granny doesn't say what. I don't ask. It's written in the blood on her legs and carved in her neighbors' faces. When the rebels were done, the adults were set free.

"Crawl back to the village with your dead," Mandiki taunted. "Crawl back, you men who can't protect your women. You women who can't protect your children. Let your neighbors see what Mandiki has wrought. If you speak to the army, if these children are seen in your homes again, I will be revenged. I will come in the night when you least expect me. And when I do, I will bring such fire and death that you will remember tonight as a time of celebration."

With that, Granny tells us, the rebels took the bound children and marched them off into the dark.

Soly. Iris. Pako. Aiii. Aiii. I rock with my family, wild with grief.

Three army jeeps rumble slowly up the road, soldiers with semiautomatic rifles stationed in their open backs. They scope the horizon on all sides. Do they think Mandiki's lurking in our yards? I want to throw things at them. I want to scream: Why weren't you here last night? Why didn't you save my family?

The jeeps brake in front of our compounds. An officer blares into a megaphone: "We're here from Rombala. Know this: The bandits will be brought to justice."

Bandits? They're not bandits. They're the rebels of Ngala. The army must know that. We all do. Why are they lying? Who are they trying to fool?

As the jeeps idle, soldiers fan up and down the road to families like ours. Everyone turns away. Two officers approach us: an older man with a notepad and a walkie-talkie, accompanied by a young man barely old enough to have pimples. My relatives open a wide path to Granny, my aunts and uncles. The soldiers keep a respectful distance.

"We need your help," the older one says. "What can you tell us about last night?"

Granny squeezes Uncle Chisulo's hand and presses her face into his side. He cradles her.

"Why talk to you?" Uncle Chisulo murmurs to the soldiers. "You can't protect us. You can't even say the name of who did this. If we talk, he'll return. You'll be back in Rombala. Why risk our lives for nothing?"

There's a pause. The soldiers stand awkwardly. "We'll be sending patrols throughout the afternoon. If you think of anything . . ." He puts his notepad back in his pocket. They turn and go.

I run after them to the road. "Are you going to track them down?"

"We're waiting for orders."

"That means no, doesn't it?"

"It means, for now, we're here to secure the village."

I gulp back a cry. "My little brother and sister have been kidnapped. They can't be more than twenty miles away. You could still find them."

The soldier bristles. "Two villages have been attacked. There are bodies in the streets. We'll look for the bandits when we can." The soldiers get into their jeep.

"Cowards!" I yell. "Cowards!"

I race into what's left of the house, into the bedroom I shared with Soly and Iris. Above me, the open sky. Stray bits of blackened thatching hang from collapsed roof poles. I lean against a wall. The mud is scorched, cracked; the dirt floor, warm. Everything's covered in soot and ash. Our mats are singed. Our belongings, burned. All that's left are Soly and Iris's metal lunch boxes, their little treasure chests.

I see Mama in my dream: She's alive and well, watching Soly and Iris play. "I'm so proud of you," she says. "You've kept them safe like you promised." My eyes fill with tears. Why did I come to Tiro? Why? If only, if only, if only—

Wait. The treasure chests.

I squat down. The morning air has cooled the metal. I open the first. It's Iris's. Her torn mosquito net's stuffed in with her combs and costume jewelry. I shake it out. Mr. Lesole's tiny binoculars fall to the floor. She swiped them from my bag. Never mind, right now I could hug her for keeping them safe.

I dive into Soly's. On top of his old sock puppet and special stones—the map of Mfuala Park, protected in the lunch box thermos. I pull it out, unfold it, touch the pictures of the animals on the back, the inset map of our country on the front.

My forehead tingles. There's a fluttering in my ears. A power surges through my body. I raise my arms to the open roof, the sky. Stretch my fingers to the sun. "Rest easy, Mama," I say. "Soly. Iris. Wherever you are, I'm with you, you hear? I'm coming to get you. I'm going to bring you home."

Part Four

27

IF I'M GOING to do this, I can't make a mistake. I clutch Soly's sock puppet, shut my eyes tight, and try to work out a plan.

Starting out will be easy. According to Granny, the rebels marched the captives single file, north, from the cemetery. There'll be a well-beaten path as far as the stretch of rock where Auntie Lizbet was killed. But where did they go then? I'll have to figure that out when I get there.

One thing I know is, I better move fast. If I don't catch up with the rebels soon, I never will. Under the midday sun, the trampled grasses will rise back up. The trail will vanish. A tracker would know other signs to follow, but I'm not a tracker.

Nelson. He'd know. Would he join me? Who am I fooling? He'd find excuses. I can just hear him: "Suppose you catch up to the rebels. What then? How do you keep from being captured? Killed? How do you rescue anybody? How do you escape?"

Well, how? What if he's right? Stop. If I think like Nelson, I'll give up before I start. I can't. I won't.

I shake out my legs and prepare to say goodbye to my family. First though, I phone my other family. Esther and Mrs. Tafa. They'll be worried sick, wondering what's happened. I picture them slapping their thighs, pacing back and forth beside our cactus hedge since dawn. Bad news is awful, but not knowing anything is even worse.

Mrs. Tafa picks up in the flick of an eyelash; I hear Esther a heartbeat later. The two of them listen in together. They're horrified by news of the attack and kidnapping, but even more horrified by my plans.

"Don't you dare go after the rebels," Esther pleads. "There's no shame in saving your life."

"I don't have a choice," I say. "If Soly and Iris disappear, they're as good as dead. Then how do I live?"

"You'll live because you'll live!" Mrs. Tafa sputters. "When my son, my blessèd Emanuel, passed, I prayed for the end. But I survived. You will too."

"No. I'll blame myself. The rebels came here because

they captured Pako, because he ran away, because I shamed his papa. It's all my fault. Always and forever. If it wasn't for me, Soly and Iris would be safe."

"That's crazy talk," Mrs. Tafa explodes. "Why not blame me and your family? If it wasn't for us, you'd never have gone to Tiro in the first place. Things happen in life, Chanda. There's twists and turns we can't foresee. All we can do is our best, and hope the stars are smiling."

"Then hope they're smiling now. Auntie, Esther—I love you both so much."

I turn off the cell, before I lose my courage. Have I talked to them for the last time? Don't think like that, don't. I take a deep breath, and step outside to say goodbye to Granny.

My relatives have laid her in the shade of a mule cart, on one of the blankets my cousins brought. She's sitting up, propped against a sack of maize. My cousins brought that, too, along with vegetables and strips of dried chicken and beef, so we'd have something to eat. They're seated around her, rocking and moaning. When Granny sees me approach, she waves them away.

I kneel in front of her. "Granny . . . Granny . . ." My mouth bobs open and shut, but nothing comes out.

Granny puts her finger to my lips. "You're going after them, aren't you?"

I look at her, bewildered. "How did you know?"

"You're your mama's daughter." I search her face for judgment. There is none. Just a deep ache.

"Don't worry about Mandiki's threat," I say quickly. "I won't put anyone in danger. If I get Soly and Iris, I'll take them straight to Bonang. We'll never be seen here again."

"I'm not thinking about Mandiki's threats," Granny says. "I'm thinking about you. What we did to you. What you're about to do to yourself." Her cheeks sag with weariness. "I can't stop you leaving, any more than I can stop the rains in rainy season. But I can beg. Chanda. Please. Don't go. Stay."

I look around the yard. Relatives mutter in small groups, glancing in my direction. "Granny, I can't. Soly and Iris need me. Besides, like you, there's things I know in my bones. Our family says Mama was cursed. They think I carry that curse. No matter what, the other relatives don't want me. They'll be glad to see me go."

Granny sighs. Her eyes are as deep as wells. "Forgive us."

I kiss the hem of her dress.

She pats the blanket beside her. I crawl up and nestle at

her shoulder. She strokes the side of my head. Out of the stillness, she whispers in my ear: "I believe in the power of the ancestors. They speak to me. I always try to do what they say. But sometimes, I think what they say and what I hear are two different things. I think, maybe, sometimes I've heard what I wanted to hear. I'm old now. Soon, I'll join the ancestors. When that time comes, I'll ask them what they really wanted me to do, and I'll ask myself why I didn't listen more carefully."

A silence, then Granny waves Lily over. I tell her my plan. From her face, I know she's relieved I won't be back. She offers me her baby's sling as a knapsack. I pack it with things from my cousins—a small box of matches and a bag of dried chicken and maize bread—along with my torn mosquito net, map, binoculars, and thermos of water. Uncle Chisulo wanders by with a thin blanket, a small ball of fishing line, and a machete. "From your Uncle Enoch and me," he says, looking off in the distance. He lays the gifts at my feet and hurries away before people see us talking.

Soon, I'm bundled up, the machete at my side, the sling over my shoulder. Lily carries Granny to the edge of the Malungas' compound, so she can wave me off as far as the cemetery. Everyone else pretends not to notice. Good. The less they know, the better.

Granny asks Lily to set her down, and steadies herself on Lily's arm. I bow. Granny kisses my forehead. "Bless you," she says. "Whatever may lie ahead, I pray that the ancestors bring you peace."

28

I PASS THROUGH the Tiro cemetery.

A handful of village elders wander the grounds in shock, grieving the desecration by the rebels. Wooden crosses have been broken. Moritis have been ripped from the ground. Brick markers have been tossed in all directions. The burial site of the ancestral chiefs has been fouled with human waste.

I pause at the far side of the cemetery. For a second, I want to turn around and run back to Granny. But that would betray the most important people in the world: Soly. Iris. Mama.

Five trails lead from the cemetery through the waist-high grasses in the fields beyond. Granny said the captives marched north for a long time, veering inland "at the place Mr. Bakwanga lost his hands." That rules out three of the trails: the two that swing west to the highway and the one that heads inland within a stone's throw. The other two fit Granny's description, going north till they disappear into a valley near the horizon. The first starts at the cemetery's left corner. The second starts two thirds of the way across.

I close my eyes and try to imagine I'm General Mandiki planning my escape. Granny said he didn't expect to be followed: The Tiro soldiers were blown up in Shawshe, and villagers were hiding or running for their lives. Still, if I'm Mandiki, I'll be careful. I'll confuse my enemy about my route by keeping my path as undisturbed as possible.

Suddenly things make sense. Mandiki tied his captives in a line. I'll bet it was to keep them from wandering off the path and trampling the tall grass. It also made them walk in one another's footsteps to hide their numbers.

I check the two trails heading north. The one at the left is rough, with crushed patches at the side where folks have passed each other; they clearly weren't tied together. And the stalks lean *toward* the cemetery, bent by people coming in to pay their respects—the elders, maybe?—or taking a shortcut from the posts to pick up supplies.

The second trail is different. There are footprints on footprints. Even up the trail, the grasses are barely disturbed.

There's just an occasional lilt of stalks pressing *away* from the cemetery, as if gently grazed by departing shawls. I think of Granny, Auntie Lizbet, and the mamas.

This is it. I bite my lip and begin. One step leads to another. Soon I'm clipping along, certainly faster than captives could travel at night. Especially with gear. It's only late morning, not too hot yet; I'll catch up in no time. Who needs Nelson? Tracking's not hard. All I have to do is think.

The trail dips into the valley. The cemetery disappears behind me. I don't care. I'll be safe till I get to the stretch of rock where Auntie was murdered. I can't imagine the rebels doubling back; they'd know the army's had time to regroup.

At the bottom of the valley, the trail winds through a stretch of brush. It ends at a cart lane. The footprints turn right, onto the lane. That's strange. Granny never mentioned a lane. And she said they went inland only after Mr. Bakwanga's hands were chopped. So where's the blood?

Details. Granny could have been confused by the night, the shock, or the horror. The tracks are the most important thing. The earth around here is damp because of the shade and runoff from the hill. The footprints are clear.

They go along both of the lane's broad cart grooves. Hidden from the town, Mandiki had time to separate his captives into two groups so they could escape faster. I decide to hurry up myself.

I follow the tracks through another quarter mile or so of twists and bends. Then the brush opens up, and the lane leads into a dirt yard with five thatched mud houses, a nearby shed, and a reed outhouse. To the right, there's a post fence lined with barbed wire penning a herd of cattle taking shade from the late-morning sun under a row of broad-branched acacias.

A post compound? Granny didn't mention this, either.

"That's far enough." The man's voice comes from behind me. "Arms up, turn around."

I do as I'm told, and find myself looking down the barrel of an old shotgun.

"She's alone, far as I can tell," yells another man. He's calling from on top of a baobab. Immediately, young men emerge from the brush on all sides, guns and machetes drawn. So that's it. Mandiki overran this post and left scouts to trap pursuers. Less than an hour from the village, and I've been caught.

I'm such a fool. Who did I think I was?

The man with the gun is old, in dirty coveralls, a dark plaid shirt, and a gray bandanna. He sees my machete. "What are you doing here?"

If I'm going to die, I won't be a coward. "I've come for my brother and sister. Give them to me."

The men give me an odd look. "What?"

"Leave her be." A young woman in a yellow shawl comes out of the shed. She's my age, maybe. A baby's slung from her shoulder. At the sound of her voice, other women and children emerge from all the homes on the compound. "I saw her in Tiro," the mama continues. "She's nothing to worry about. She's not with them."

The men put down their weapons.

"So what's she doing here?" asks the old man.

"She told you," the mama says. "She wants her brother and sister."

"They're not here."

The mama sighs like he's simple, and gives me a tilt of her head: "Care for some tea and biscuits?"

I'm about to say no when it hits me: These people were here when Mandiki passed through. They'll have information that can help me. "Yes. Thank you," I say. "But I'm in a hurry."

We pull up benches, stools, and upturned pails into a circle. The women rock their babies on one side, the men smoke on the other, while the children play tag beyond the row of acacias. In no time, I discover they're a family living full-time on the post: a widower, his six sons, their wives and children. Yesterday, with rumors on the wind, the women took the kids to folks in Tiro. The men stayed behind to guard, taking cover in the trees and outlying brush. The women and kids returned this morning. Tebogoc, the young mama, was the last in. She walked the road by Granny's, before taking the shortcut here from the cemetery. She remembers me yelling at the soldiers, and how she laughed at my nerve.

This is all very nice, but it's wasting time. "Tell me about the rebels," I say.

The men shift in their seats. "Nothing to tell."

"But you must have seen them."

"Didn't see nothing."

"Heard something, though," says the young man who scouted me from the baobab. "Middle of the night, off that way." He points west up the lane.

The old man shoots him a look. "You didn't hear nothing, neither. Nothing."

The young man scratches his ear. "Guess that's so. If I heard something, it was only bush rats."

"Bush rats?" I say. I look the men hard in the eyes. They concentrate on the curls of smoke from their cigarettes. They're scared.

I take another glance around the compound. The thatching on the houses is intact. Nothing's been burned. No one's been cut or maimed.

Cold sweat seeps across my forehead. I've been on the wrong trail. The rebels didn't come by here. The grasses from the cemetery weren't bent by captives. They were bent by Tebogoc and her sisters-in-law. The footprints on footprints were made by them and their kids.

But what other route could Mandiki have taken?

The answer hits me hard. Mandiki led everyone off single-file. But once he separated the children, the villagers scrambled home in the dark. I was so busy thinking about their leaving, I forgot about their return. They'd have retraced their steps, coming back on the same route as they left. I should have chosen the grasses bending *toward* Tiro.

Idiot! I'm an idiot!

The trail at the left of the cemetery, that's the one the

rebels used. Those grasses weren't trampled by people passing each other to pay respects or pick up supplies. They were crushed by survivors racing home in fear of their lives.

I clutch my knees. What do I do now? How do I get to the right trail? How do I make up the lost time?

I thank Tebogoc and the others for the tea and biscuits and stand up. My legs wobble. As I walk away, I stumble. The young man who said he heard something helps me to my feet.

"About those bush rats," he mutters, "there were dozens of 'em. They were heading north. You'll spot their trail twenty minutes up the lane, past the heavy brush."

29

I GO UP the lane to where the bad trail ended. Do I take it back to the cemetery and start over? Or do I keep going and hope Mr. Bush Rat is right? I left Granny's almost an hour-and-a-half ago. If I go back, I'll have wasted the whole morning. I'll be walking in the heat of the afternoon sun. Signs of the rebels will be disappearing.

But what if Mr. Bush Rat really didn't hear anything? What if the rebels went inland before they got this far? Granny said they marched north for a long time, but in the dark a few minutes can seem like forever.

Breathe. Don't panic. Breathe. ABCDEFG, ABCDEFG.

I close my eyes. I picture I'm back at the cemetery looking over the fields. In my mind, the good trail—the one I should have taken—is seventy yards to my left. If the rebels went inland before they got this far, their path would've had to cross mine. It didn't. So it must still be on my left, up the lane, like the man said.

I cross my fingers and run. Sure enough, past some heavy brush, a path cuts across the lane. There're streaks of blood on the crushed grass. Blood from Mr. Bakwanga, dragged home by his legs, his severed wrists smearing the trail. Did he have AIDS? What if I'm cut? Since Mama passed, I act like all blood's infected. It's the only way to stay safe. Safe? I'm following murderers, and I think about "safe"?

I rattle some sense into my head. The blood's been exposed for hours. Any virus will be dead.

I step on the bloody trail. The farther I go, the slipperier it gets. I keep my eyes up, off the gore. Soon, a fresh path veers to my right, the tall blades packed down by dozens of pairs of feet. At the divide, there's been a whirlwind of motion, as if people didn't know where to move and tried to move everywhere at once.

A rusty ring circles the edge of the trampled patch, turning a brackish red as it reaches the patch's core. More blood. Blood sprayed far and wide. Dried brown on the outer stalks and bushes. Still thick and wet at the center, clotting on the inner grasses, puddling in the hardened groove of the footpath.

The stench is overpowering: the vegetation alive, crawling with insects come to feed on the sticky sweet. Flies buzz around my eyes. I brush them away from my face, take the kerchief off my head, and cover my mouth and nose. The tea and biscuits lurch at the base of my throat. I swallow hard.

So this is it—the place where Mr. Bakwanga was murdered. When I started my trek, Granny's story was like a tale. But here, now, the shock of the killing is real.

I imagine myself tied to that line of prisoners, pulled back and forth by family, neighbors—struggling to escape the hot blood, the horror, fearing for our lives and the lives of the children. Iris, Soly, Granny, Auntie Lizbet—I see them, shapes in the night, masks of terror, tripping over the body, pressing their cargo tight between wrists and bellies—can't let it fall, or Mandiki's machete will find them next.

Yes, this is the place where Mr. Bakwanga was murdered. And this is the path the rebels took inland, like Granny said. The path that leads to where Auntie died. Where the mamas and papas were abused. Where the children—Iris, Soly, Pako, and the others—vanished.

Where were they taken? To do what? To become what? I

don't want to know. All I want to know—*do* know—is this:

This is the place where Mr. Bakwanga was murdered. And this is the path where the rebels went inland. Soly. Iris. Hang on.

In a quarter mile, the landscape changes. The grasses thin, their stalks shorten, their color drains. The tips tickle my thighs. It's dry here, not much for them to grow on, not much for them to drink, as the dirt grows spare, giving way to stone plates breaking through the earth's surface.

I have a sip of water from my thermos. It's hot. Pretty soon, I'll need to find some shade, or I'll dry out like an old bone.

As I walk, I think about Mama. Mama and me, when I was little. How she stood pounding maize with that heavy wooden mallet that was taller than her; or sat on her mat, legs to the side, rolling her wicker pan to separate the husks. The whole time, she sang songs, and I danced around her, clapping, and falling on my bum.

I remember the first time Mama let me toss feed to the chickens, and how they came at me flapping and squawking. I was so scared. Even scareder than when I'd see their feet floating in the soup pot.

And I remember how I'd go with her to the standpipe, and touch the sides of the bucket as she pumped it full of water, and listen as she'd tell the women behind her what a big help I was. They must've been winking at each other. Especially when Mama'd fill my little plastic cup and have me hold it on top of my head, like she did her bucket. When we'd get home, I'd pour my cup over a few bean plants in our garden, and Mama would say, "Well done, my little bee catcher. Because of you, we'll have food." She made me feel like the most important person in the world.

Oh, and then, then there was the time I had that fever. I'd have been about Soly's age. It's mainly a fog, but I remember Mama sitting with me, telling me stories, patting my forehead with a damp rag, fanning my face with a piece of cardboard. They say I nearly died. But I didn't. Mama wouldn't let me.

Mama. Mama.

I freeze. Without realizing it, I've stepped out of the grasses. I've reached the stretch of rock where the children were taken away.

I'm not sure what I was expecting when Granny talked about "a stretch of rock." Something about the size of my yard, maybe. But this is as big as the soccer field beside my old high school. It tilts up to a low ridge at the far end. Cracks rut the gray surface like wrinkles. Sow thistles have taken root in the deep seams.

Where did the rebels go from here? A little dirt's been kicked onto the rock from where they left the grasses, and a couple of the weeds have been stomped on, but the stone floor hides its secrets. Under the midday sun, it's hot to walk on, even in my shoes. I decide to go around the outside of it. The rebels had to step off somewhere. I just have to find the spot.

About twenty yards up the left side, I spot a cluster of stones on the rock. They must be the ones that pelted Auntie Lizbet. When they hit her, they dropped to her feet. Beyond the cluster, on either side, there's a stone starburst: the ones thrown wide.

In my mind, I hear Auntie Lizbet singing the harvest song. Her song will live in these rocks forever. Poor Auntie. She was a demon to Mama, a saint to Iris. How can one person be so different? I'm sorry I hated her. I pray she forgives me. And I pray that somewhere, she and Mama have made peace. They loved my little sister. Love can heal a lot. I hope Auntie has some left over for me.

I reach the end of the stretch of stone. The ridge is

about eight feet high. The rise drops back to the ground. The slope is shaded. Cool to the touch. I scramble up to the top to get a better view.

Yellow grasses flow from the rock to a broken wall of thornbushes. But when I look for Mandiki's trail, my stomach seizes. The rebels have split up. Instead of one path, more than a dozen lead from the stone. Soly and Iris could've gone down any of them.

What do I do? Which path do I take? Think. Why? It's hopeless. They could be anywhere.

I sink to the ground, too hot and tired to cry. Waves of heat ripple the air. The paths vibrate. My forehead tingles. I shade my eyes with my hands and count them.

It doesn't make sense. There are fifteen paths. But I saw fewer than twenty adult rebels. That's barely one adult for each path. How can one adult and a few kids attack a village? They can't. Besides, this isn't Ngala. The rebels don't know our land or our people. Alone, they'd be easy to pick off, and the children hard to control.

Mandiki knows that. He may be insane, but he's not stupid. *Ergo*, as Mr. Selalame would say, Mandiki *hasn't* divided his men. These paths are a trick to confuse people. Maybe to make it look like there're more rebels than there really are. Or maybe to make people like me give up.

Well, whatever the trick is, it won't work! If the rebels haven't split up, I can choose whichever path I want. Sooner or later, they'll all come together.

A voice in my head says, "What if you're wrong?" I tell it to shut up.

I pick the farthest path on my far left. It takes me out deep, then arcs wide, spiraling off through the bushes. It loops around one jackalberry after another, before returning to the ridge, where it divides in two. I take the right fork.

It's hot, but I'm not sweating. I'm too dry. My lips. They're parched. I should drink some more water. Not yet. I don't want to run out. Still, I should get some shade. I will. Once I get somewhere.

My trail zigzags like a drunk on shake-shake. I stare at the ground so I won't lose my way. Suddenly it dawns on me—I'm wandering around in large figure eights. Mandiki's trails are a trick all right. They're a giant maze. I stagger off the path. Where *is* the path? It's so bright. So hard to see. There's so much light. So many prints. So much . . . so many . . .

What am I thinking? What am I trying to think?

The air is smothering. I see dots. Is it the sun? The

heat? A vision?

Yes, I'm having a vision. On top of the ridge, I think I see Nelson. He's waving. Calling my name. "Chanda! Chanda, over here!" I go to call back. I can't. My throat's too dry. I need some shade. I need some—

"Chanda!"

The air rolls up in hot waves. Everything blurs.

"Chanda!"

My vision swims through the air.

I think I'm smiling.

I think I'm—

I think—

I—

30

I'M ON MY back in the shade of the ridge, my feet raised on a rock. There's a wet bandanna on my forehead. Nelson has my head in his lap. He's pouring water down my throat. I wave the canteen away, gulp for air.

"What's your name?" he says.

I blink. "You know my name."

"Answer the question."

"Chanda Kabelo."

He puts a hand in front of my face. "How many fingers am I holding up?"

"Three."

"Where are you?"

"At the stretch of rock where Auntie died."

"Good. You're not as far gone as I thought." He takes his bandanna from my forehead, presses it under my neck, and rests my head in his palm. The cool damp of the cloth feels good. "What were you thinking, trekking at midday?" he mutters. "You're not even wearing a kerchief."

"I am too." I reach up. My hand grazes hair. He's right. Where did it go? I suddenly remember using it to cover my nose from the smell of Mr. Bakwanga's blood. With all the shock, I must have let it drop. How stupid. How careless. How—

I roll off Nelson's lap, wobble to my knees. My stomach feels like it's full of bad soup.

"Lie down," he snaps. "Feet back up on the rock, higher than your head."

"I'm fine."

"You're dehydrated. If I hadn't come along, you'd be passed out in the sun, frying. By day's end, you could've been dying."

"Hah!" Determined to look strong, I toss my chin like Iris. My head explodes with pain. I crumple back to the ground. Nelson doesn't say anything; he doesn't have to. "You've come to bring me home, haven't you?"

"Who says I'm here for you at all?"

"You aren't?"

"No," he snorts. "The whole world doesn't revolve around you, you know."

That shuts me up. I look off at one of the thornbushes,

clear my throat. "If you're not here for me, then why are you here?"

"Pako."

"I don't believe you. Yesterday when you found me at the ruin on my family's post, you acted like he was already dead. You wouldn't follow him, and he was right there."

Nelson's eyes narrow. "Things have changed."

"How?"

"You ask too many questions." He rips a blade of grass, shoves it between his teeth, and sprints over the top of the ridge. There's a strange sound, as if he's struggling for air. At last he comes back down. He sits on his haunches and stares at the horizon, idly fiddling with the chewed stalk like nothing's happened. A silence grows so big I can't stand it.

"If you find him . . . Pako . . . what are you going to do?" I say.

Nelson gives me a funny look. "Bring him home. What else?"

I choose my words carefully. "Mandiki's threatened to attack Tiro if any of the kids are seen again."

Nelson shrugs. "I'll hide him on the post till things cool down. But who says Mandiki can come back? He can pull those threats in Ngala. He knows his country's villages and posts like the back of his hand. Here is different. This time, he got us by surprise. Next time, our army will be ready."

"In case it's not," I say quietly, "you could come with us to Bonang. It's an eight-hour drive away. No one would ever find you."

"What would I do in Bonang? Who'd look after my family's cattle?"

"I just thought . . ."

"Yeah, well, it's an idea," he says, his voice all cramped up. "Thanks. But no."

A hum of bush crickets rises and falls. I wrestle myself onto my elbows. "So . . . what do we do now?"

He stretches. "Nothing. Not in this heat. In a few hours, when the sun's lower and it's cooled down, I'll take up the hunt. Your uncles said they'd tend my herd while I'm gone. Mama and the others will be at the morgue for three days, to let folks from away have time to come to the funerals, what with the highway delay. By then, I'll either have Pako, or be dead myself."

"What about me?"

Nelson tosses the stalk aside. "In a few hours, you'll be cooled down enough to return to the village. You know the route. You'll be there by sundown."

I shake my head. "I'm not going back."

"What?"

"You heard me."

Nelson pauses. "Chanda, if you go home, I'll save your brother and sister too."

"No. If I give up and you fail, I'll never forgive myself."

Nelson leaps to his feet. He twists in a circle, kicking at the dirt. "I don't have time for babysitting," he yells. "You got this far. Great. But you're not a tracker. You'll slow me down."

"I won't. If I do, leave me behind."

"In the middle of nowhere?"

"Yes. Why not?"

"Because you're a girl, that's why not."

"Look, Nelson, if you want to get Pako on your own, fine. But we could help each other. You decide. Either way, I'm going after Soly and Iris."

He waves his arms, stomps his foot, and puffs his cheeks like a blowfish. Despite myself, I burst out laughing.

"What's so funny?" he glares.

"You're like Soly having a tantrum." I mean Iris, but that would really make him mad. "Come, sit, save your energy. The air will be cool in no time."

31

NELSON STAYS UPSET till I offer him lunch. A little of my chicken and maize bread and he settles down. I think he's even impressed when I tell him how I figure the trails from the rock will eventually hook up. At least he doesn't roll his eyes.

I watch him eat. I've never seen anyone do it like him before. I'm glad. He's kind of disgusting. He holds his food to his mouth with both hands and nibbles away like a rodent. Crumbs stick to the down over his lip. Every so often he flicks his tongue up to lasso them. He practically licks his nose. Not that I care. I'm too busy staring at his eyelashes. And the dimple in his chin.

I have to admit, he's pretty good looking. Smart, too. He's right about not trekking in the heat. Still, the longer we wait, the more I fidget.

Nelson watches me wriggle. "What's the matter?" he says. "You got fleas?"

"Very funny. I'm thinking about Mandiki. Every minute we're here, he's getting farther away."

"I doubt it." He wipes his mouth with the back of his hand. "He's been on the move since yesterday afternoon. Attacked a town. Escaped with kids and loot. He'll be resting."

"Then now's the time to catch up."

"Don't worry. We'll catch up easy."

"How?"

A chicken fiber's stuck between his molars. He tries to suck it loose while he talks. "What's the key to Mandiki's success? He's traveling with a small raiding party. That gives him speed and surprise. He can move faster than an army, because his unit is small. It can attack and escape at will. Come out of nowhere, like a gang of cattle thieves."

The fiber's still stuck. He covers his mouth and turns away. I watch his elbow move up and down as he pries at it with a fingernail. "Mandiki's advantage against the army is our advantage against him," he continues, mouth full of finger. "He's slowed by kids carrying weapons and crates, traveling by night. All we've got is our knapsacks, and we

travel by day. As for surprise? He doesn't expect to be followed: the army's off-guard, the people are scared. So he's
in no rush. He'll take his time, save his strength till he
needs it."

The thread of chicken pulls loose. I watch from behind
as he inspects it. "When I was little, our post got robbed by
cattle thieves," he says casually. "Papa tracked 'em down.
Killed 'em with his slingshot. Stones to the temple. They
never knew what hit 'em."

"You're planning to kill Mandiki with a slingshot?"

Nelson turns back to me, popping the chicken bit in his
mouth. "Who knows?" he chews thoughtfully. "But I
brought one with me." He fishes it out of his knapsack.
"Made it myself. Like it?" I nod. He's stitched a leather
pouch around a strip of inner tube, and tied the tube's rubber ends to a forked piece of mopane wood. "If we run out
of food, I can pick off a bird or a lizard, like I do at the post.
If we run into the General, well . . ."

I search his face. He said things had changed. But more
than "things" have changed. He's changed too. This isn't
the Nelson who ran terrified across the dead land. The one
afraid to follow the rebels to Tiro. This Nelson is fearless.
Reckless even. What's happened? What's he hiding?

* * *

A few hours later, my nausea's gone. My body's cooled. So has the air. Before we leave, I look for a head cover. Nelson needs his bandanna for himself. I take Iris's swath of mosquito net, fold it four times, and tie it under my chin.

Nelson laughs. "Some kerchief. Is mosquito net the new fashion in Bonang?"

"What do you suggest?" I joke back. "My underwear?"

We skip up the ridge to get a better view of things. I sweep my hand across the trails. "How do we solve the maze?"

"Same way I do when a cow wanders off in a field full of spoor."

"Spoor?"

"Spoor are tracks," he sighs. "Anyway, if a cow wanders off, I walk in a wide circle beyond the grazing field. If my cow's truly gone, somewhere her spoor will cross my arc. That's where I pick up the hunt."

"You always find her?"

"Sooner or later. She'll be chewing her cud, looking up at me with her big, stupid eyes as if to say, 'Oh, hello. What took you so long?' Sort of like you this afternoon."

"Ha ha. So how far out do you think the maze goes?"

"About where you got to, I'm guessing." He scratches the back of his neck. "Mandiki'd want to pitch camp by dawn. He wouldn't have had much time. Certainly not enough to mess around in a patch of thornbushes in the dark."

"So, then . . . we make a big arc beyond those bushes?"

"We would, if I didn't already know where the paths end up." He points to a massive boulder breaking the wall of bushes. "The rebels went through there."

"How do you know?"

Nelson's throat catches. "Mandiki's got Pako as his guide. Except for the flatbed, this is Pako's route when he runs away."

"Then why did you waste time telling me about cows?"

Nelson pauses. "We probably won't survive this. You know that, don't you?"

A chill goes up my spine. "I try not to think about it."

"Well, think about it. " He squeezes my hand. "You shouldn't be here. You really shouldn't. But you are, and I can't stop you. What I *can* do, is teach you my bush tricks, so you can carry on when they kill me."

"If."

"When." He pauses. "Do you understand?"

I nod. But inside, it's like the earth's giving way. I'm falling. Before I crash, I grab hold of my knapsack. "Right. Let's go."

32

"So where's Pako taking the rebels?" I ask as we go around the boulder, through the wall of bushes.

"A waterhole straight north of here. It's pretty much his private place. Least, I've never seen anyone else there."

"How far?"

"Maybe three hours," he shrugs. "Three and a half."

We don't say much at first, then Nelson starts going on about Pako's hideaway. I'm not sure if it's for my benefit, or to keep himself from being bored.

"Pako's waterhole's a good size," he says. "It must've been made twenty, thirty years ago, before the elephants and hippos got hunted out. Back then, it would've been just a small depression on some flatland. But by the time the animals disappeared, they'd rolled, stomped, and mucked about in it so much, they'd made it into this huge pond. Nice and deep. The water that collects in rainy season stays for months."

According to Nelson, there's only a few active posts in the area. Over the last ten years, everyone else has passed away. Whole families. "A lot of pneumonia," he says. But we both know what he means. "That's why this place makes a great stopover for the rebels. They can stock up on water, and there's nobody to report them."

I'm glad Nelson knows the way. Following the rebels' path is getting hard. Since the stretch of rock, the grasses barely come to our knees. Without the thickness and height to weigh them down, they've been able to right themselves in the sun.

Nelson doesn't care. He shows me other signs of rebel movement. Here and there, blades broken mid-stalk: "Folks pick grass as they walk, without even thinking." We come to a place full of flies and stink: "They shit, too," he grins.

The vegetation thins. I see spots where people have stepped outside the narrow path. The prints aren't as clear as the ones I saw this morning. "When the sun dries the dirt, the edges of the spoor crumble," Nelson explains. Something catches his eye. He squats. "See the wavy line across that one?"

I nod. It's the trail of a small snake.

"Watch for anything crossing the spoor. Grass snakes like that one come out early, find a rock, and bake all day. What does that tell us?"

"Well, that print was here before the snake, and the snake was here early morning. So that print was made by dawn."

Nelson nods and winks. It's like being in class with Mr. Selalame. There's so much I don't know, but the way he acts when I get something right, I want to learn more.

The sun begins to drop. Even with less light, the prints are suddenly easier to spot. Are my eyes adjusting to this new world? Am I turning into a tracker? I grab Nelson's arm. "It's like I have new eyes," I say, all excited. "The spoor are lifting off the ground!"

He laughs. "When the sun's low, the rim around the track casts a shadow. Every mark—claw, hoof, or boot—looks underlined. That's why tracking's best just after dawn and before dusk."

My shoulders slump. "Oh."

"Cheer up. At least you're not hallucinating."

There's a haze on the horizon. "It'll be dark soon," I say. "How far to the mudhole?"

"Under a mile. We'll have time to make camp, wash up."

"What if the rebels are still there?"

Nelson frowns. "Good question."

The waterhole is in the middle of a tract of land, maybe a quarter of a mile across, sunk into the landscape. It's as if a giant has pressed a shallow baking pan into the earth; the mudhole is a biscuit at the center. We approach the edge of the high ground on our knees. Nelson holds up his hand for silence. He listens hard, scans the sky, and motions me to lie flat. We crawl up to the rim on our bellies and peer down the rugged slope to the land below.

The animals that made the mudhole were pretty smart. The area around the water is flat as a pancake. Predators could be spotted with ease, or smelled, depending on the wind. In case of attack, there's a sweep of thornbushes for escape. Back then, this would've been like the pictures Mr. Lesole has of mudholes in Mfuala Park: the nearby trees stunted, dead or dying, their leaves devoured, their bark ringed by elephant tusks; the vegetation by the water trampled to bare mud.

Today, free of elephants, it's a lush oasis. The circle of high ground we're on has sent down enough runoff to create a woodland. I see acacia and baobab trees. Sedges and reeds line the mudhole's banks; algae blooms green the surface. It's become a place where people can hide, shielded from view by thick branches and broad-leafed undergrowth.

Nelson scouts with his eyes. Me, I need the binoculars from Mr. Lesole.

"See all the birds?" he says. "The egrets on that candelabra tree? The water-walkers off the far bank of the mudhole? Nobody's squawking. Good sign. I'll crawl down, get a better look. Keep your eyes peeled. If you spot anyone, back away. I'll see that you're not here, and retreat. If everything's fine, I'll wave an all-clear."

He slithers down the slope. I watch him zigzag from a termite mound to a sausage tree to an acacia. He's amazing. Even though I know where he is, half the time I can't see him. It's as if he decides to be invisible.

Now he's beside a date palm. They're mainly up in the park around the river. Way back, an animal must have wandered down with dates in its poop and dropped them here by the waterhole. My god, the park. Traveling north all day, we must be halfway there.

I scan the high ground for rebels. Nothing. I look back

for Nelson. Where did he go? I swear at my binoculars. With a cracked lens, it's hard to focus.

Oh, there he is. On the top of the date palm. He must be scanning the rebels' spoor. There's spoor everywhere. No surprise. The rebels arrived, made camp, and moved around before leaving. I see breaks in the sedges where they broke through to get water.

I zoom in on his face and adjust the lenses. He looks up at me and grins. Can he tell I'm staring at him? He waves the all-clear.

By the time I join him, Nelson's sitting on a hollow tree that's fallen near the mudhole. A candelabra tree grows through the heavy mulch at the far end.

"They camped here last night," he says, pointing at the ashen remains of a campfire. "But here's the best news. We've almost caught up. They only left within the hour."

"How do you know?"

"The earth has a thin, dry crust. When it's disturbed, the damp underneath shows up darker. The tracks we saw today were made last night. The sun had dried them out. But look . . ." He points to the spoor in front of us. "Those tracks are darker than the ground around. The moisture hasn't had time to evaporate."

"Which means . . . they're new."

"Well done, O wise one." I know he's being sarcastic, but he's smiling. I smile back.

The shadow from the high ground rolls over the woodland. Puffs of tiny insects float into the dusky air. I get a mouthful, spit them out. "With the rebels so close, we should get a move-on."

Nelson shakes his head. "I wouldn't know where to go. Pako never went much farther than this, and we can't see tracks in the dark. We'd lose them easy."

I turn away in frustration.

"Look, with the kids and the dark, the rebels are slower than us, remember? If we head out at first light, we'll catch up by tomorrow night. That's a promise."

We spread our blankets by the thornbushes, then Nelson washes up in the waterhole. When he comes back, I take my turn, and he makes supper. He's the sort to sneak a peek, so I wait till I'm past the sedges to take off my clothes. On my way across the bank, I notice something odd. There are dozens of tracks in the mud, but all of them go into the water. How can that be? Didn't the rebels come out?

I smile with the answer: When they left, Mandiki made them walk backward. It's a trick to confuse people about the direction you're headed.

I remember this from a game of hide-and-seek when I was little, before we moved to Bonang. My older cousins had entered a stream and retraced their steps backward. I saw footprints heading into the water and none leaving. I thought they'd drowned. After Mama calmed me down, she showed me how to tell the trick. "When people move forward," she said, "they hit the ground with their heels; the heels press deeper. Going backward, they walk on their toes; the toes press deeper." I tried it. It was true.

Both kind of prints are at the mudhole. Heels-deeper, as the rebels marched forward into formation, then toes-deeper as they headed away. Follow the toe prints, we'll have their route. Tomorrow morning, I'll shock Nelson with what I know. I can't wait to see his face.

By the time I've cleaned up, Nelson's laid out our meal: some biltong and biscuits from his food stash. The biltong's tastier than the beef jerky we get in Bonang.

"Papa loved extra coriander," Nelson smiles. "Pepper, too."

The sun's gone down behind the high ground. The sky's a dusty gray. A few minutes later, a sheet of stars. All I see are the silhouettes of treetops, and a few silver streaks—

the moon's reflection peeking through the cracks in the reed curtain around the waterhole. I lie on my blanket, my knapsack under my head as a pillow. "Good night."

"'Night," Nelson says back. There's a pause, then he adds: "You should shake out that 'kerchief' of yours. Use it to keep the mosquitoes off."

I chuckle. "Too many holes. That netting's only good to make me look like an idiot."

"You aren't an idiot," Nelson says quietly. "You don't look like one either."

Does he mean it? I look over. How I wish I could see in the dark.

33

I WAKE UP in the middle of the night shivering, probably from all the sun I got midday.

My old dream flashes through my mind: the road to Tiro; Soly and Iris taken away. Was it a warning? Is this my punishment for not listening? No, don't think like that. Dreams can mean anything. Mrs. Tafa thought it meant I *had* to go to Tiro. If I'd stayed home and something bad had happened, would I have tortured myself for that instead?

I wrap my blanket around me and stare at the moon. Soly. Iris. Where are you? What are you doing? Are you looking at the moon too?

A faint moan rises from the direction of the hollowed log. I'm not the only one awake. I feel for my shoes, slip them on, and walk gingerly toward the sound. As I get close, it stops.

"Nelson?"

Silence.

"Nelson, tell me it's you."

"It's me."

"Nelson, keep talking. Please. Guide me to where you are."

"Go back to your blanket. Go to sleep. Leave me alone."

My foot taps into the log. I reach down, touch it, edge along it, till I sense his presence. I sit. The skin on my arm tingles. I feel his heat beside me.

We stay like that for a long time. Then out of the hush, Nelson's voice, so delicate it's like he's talking to himself:

"I remember the first time I tracked him here," he says. "Pako'd been running away from home for years. Every few months, since he was four. When things got rough, he'd take off. Like me. He didn't go far, at first. He'd just walk till he got lost, or tired, or scared. Then he'd sit and wait for someone to find him. It was always me, went after him. I'd get mad. He'd wasted my day. But one look at him all slumped over, I'd hug him and hug him. We'd talk a bit, then I'd carry him home. I'd tell him it would be okay, he wasn't in trouble anymore. I'd pray I was right. I usually was."

Nelson gulps for air. I stare at the ground.

"Pako always took the same route," he says at last. "I figure it's because deep down he wanted me to find him. Only each time he'd go farther. When he was five, he started taking food and water. 'When I'm big,' he'd say, 'I'm going to walk around the world. I'm going to walk so far, I'll disappear.' Two years ago, I thought he had. He ran away early, when I was at the post. By the time I got back, it was too late to see anything. Next day, I tracked him for what seemed like forever. I ended up here. Poor Pako. He must've been so scared when I didn't come that first day. Maybe he thought Mama and me, we didn't love him anymore. Maybe he thought we didn't care."

He chokes. Then his voice goes quiet as a baby's breath: "I remember I followed his trail to this log. Pako was hiding inside. I pretended I didn't know. I knelt on the ground. 'Dear god, and all the ancestors,' I said, 'I'm looking for my little brother. His name is Pako. I miss him so much. But I don't know where he is. Please help me find him.' A few minutes later, he crawled out and snuggled next to me."

Silence. Nelson begins rocking slowly.

"For the last two years, this is where Pako'd run," he says. "It's his special place. He's made up stories about it:

'This log belongs to the god of the mudhole. Anyone who goes inside it is safe. Even Papa's spirit can't get in.' Sometimes Pako asked if he can stay by himself a day or two. I bring provisions, camp up on the high ground, stay hidden, so he'll feel grown up." Nelson throws back his head. "I'm a coward. A coward."

"That isn't true!"

"It is!"

I hear him wiping his eyes with his shirtsleeve. I find his hand.

"I never faced them," he weeps. "I never stood up to Papa, Runako, Samson. On the post, when I was little, Mama hid me in the granary bin when they'd get drinking. Later, when we moved to town, I'd hide in your granny's outhouse. They'd pound on your granny and grampa's door. Your family pretended they hadn't seen me. Your grampa and uncles would get them home."

"That doesn't make you a coward. You were only a kid."

A roar rips from his throat. "I wasn't a kid when Pako was growing up. Or my other little brothers. First sign of trouble, I'd be gone. Anything to make the shouting go away. In the morning, I'd see the bruises. 'They fell,' Mama'd say. 'Yeah, Mama,' I yelled, 'well they fall a lot when

Papa's drinking.' I never did anything though. Just yelled and left her with everything. I'm so ashamed! If I'd stood up to them, this would never have happened. Pako wouldn't have run off. He wouldn't have been captured. Mama would still be alive."

"You're not to blame. Especially not for Mandiki."

"What do you know? Mama died to save Pako from the rebels. It should have been me who died." He sinks to the ground.

I kneel beside him, feel for his shoulders. He quivers into a ball. I hold him tight.

"I swear to god," he says, "I won't let Mama down again. I'm going to find my brother. I'm going to bring him home, like I did when he ran away. I won't be a coward. Not ever again. I'm going to be like you."

I rock him and rock him and rock him. His body goes limp. Asleep in my arms, he's a little boy like Soly. My lips brush his forehead. I roll him gently onto his side, faced away from me, and press my back against his.

I'm not sure if this is a good idea, sleeping next to each other. Mrs. Tafa would say I was looking for trouble. I don't care. Nelson's warmth feels good. I wish I could throw one of our blankets over us, but I'm afraid to crawl around in the pitch black trying to find them.

Nelson shifts like crazy all night. Every so often, a shiver ripples across his shoulders or his legs twitch. It's like he's trying to run in his dreams. "It's okay," I whisper. "It's okay." He doesn't hear me.

I don't sleep. Nelson. What does he mean, he wants to be like me? I'm not brave. I'm scared to death. Are my babies alive? Last time I saw them, they hated me. Do they still hate me? Do they blame me? Please god, let them forgive me. For shaming them. For being away when they needed me most. Let Mama forgive me too.

Oh, Mama, I want to get them back. But I don't know if I can. I'm so afraid. I'm so . . .

It's first light. My back feels cold. Where's Nelson? I roll over. He's gone. I sit up in a panic. Then I see him near the mudhole with his knapsack, surveying the ground. I lie back down and pretend to sleep, half-closing my eyes so I can watch him without him knowing it. He heads into a thicket. Doing his morning business, I figure.

Silence.

I hear a bird, a few more. In minutes, there's squawking all around. The world is waking up. I stretch. Nelson should be back by now. Oh well. I take care of my own affairs and wash up at the mudhole. Nelson still hasn't come back.

I suddenly get it. He's taken off without me!

I grab my things and run up the trail. What with the great lord having just gone through, the path's easy to follow. The brush clears. I see Nelson in the distance, getting ready to scale the high ground to the north. I run to within shouting distance.

"Stop!" I holler. "Where do you think you're going?"

He pretends not to hear me.

"Are you deaf? I said, stop!"

He keeps going.

I scramble after him. "Have the guts to face me. You think you can leave me without a word?"

His voice comes low, hard: "You know the way back."

"I told you, I'm not giving up."

"Fine. Just go by yourself. Leave me alone."

"Nelson?"

He whirls on me. "Papa was Papa. My papa. He wasn't a monster. He fed me. Clothed me. Gave me a roof. He's dead. I owe him respect. I mustn't shame him. I mustn't dishonor his memory. Not ever. No matter what."

I raise my hand to touch him. He waves me off. "Get away." All at once, I understand. In the dark, you can say things, and it's like there's no one there. But in the morning . . . in the light . . .

We stand there, staring at each other, breathing hard. I step back. Let the air fill my lungs slowly. Once, twice, three times. "Nelson," I say, "about last night. You didn't say anything. I didn't hear anything."

A butterfly floats up from the grass, circles my head, and flutters off. Nelson follows it with his eyes. He swallows. "Okay, then." He rubs his nose. "Make sure you keep up."

I adjust my knapsack. "Worry about yourself."

We walk in silence.

Midmorning, we spot the vultures.

34

THE BIRDS CIRCLE slowly, black specks in the distance.

"They're a quarter mile ahead," Nelson says. "Something's got their attention."

It could be anything. A dead hare. A dead warthog. A dead cow. All the same, the hairs on my neck tingle. There's evil around. I close my eyes. I see the skull puppet twisting on Mandiki's fist, his necklace of bones, the long fungal nails, that grin of dead men's teeth.

I check the horizon with my binoculars. Beyond the vultures, a thin wisp of smoke rises from behind a thicket. Nelson's already seen it. "It could be a family on some compound," he says. "Maybe they're getting ready to cook seswa."

"Or maybe it's the rebels cooking."

We move quickly but cautiously. In no time, we're

underneath the raptors. They're circling lower now, ebony wings glinting in the sun. Talons and beaks etched sharp against the sky.

Nelson stays me with a finger. We stand stalk still. Just ahead, something's moved off the main trail. Its path is fresh. It goes maybe twenty feet into the savannah and stops. Whoever, or whatever, made this path is still out there.

For a moment, everything's still. Then a rustle. We crouch down. Have we been seen? Is this an ambush? We take off our knapsacks. Unsheath our machetes. Nelson motions me to circle out below where the path ends, while he circles above.

I crawl slowly, pulling myself forward on my elbows, gripping my machete by the handle, blade out. My hands are wet. My heart pounds. I stop. Whatever's there is only a few feet away. I listen hard. Nothing. Then a sudden whoosh of air above me to my left. I look up. A flash of feathers. A vulture lights down.

Nelson and I leap to our feet. We pounce toward the end of the path. Two vultures rise from the flattened patch of grass, beating their wings. We fall back. They settle, twist their necks, and stare, feathers raised, daring us to approach. There's a terrible stench. It's lunchtime.

Nelson's closer to the raptors than me. He gasps. "Don't look," he says. He retreats to the trail.

"What's there? What did you see? What?"

"You don't want to know."

It's true. I don't. But the way he says it, I have to.

I raise my machete across my body, shielding my head with my forearm in case the vultures try to drive me off. I inch forward. They make a low, grating hiss, but instead of attacking, they hop off a few steps. I glimpse their meal.

At first, I'm not sure what it is. I take a step closer. Look harder. I cover my mouth. It's a child. He's maybe twelve, sprawled facedown, naked. His calves are as puffed as balloons, the gangrenous flesh blistered to bursting. Above the knees, though, he's scrawny, bruised skin stuck tight to his ribs and skull, arms all tendon and bone.

I run in a circle, swinging my machete. "Aiii! Aiii!" The vultures fly up. They fake attacks, dipping and diving, trying to force me to leave. I don't. I kneel at the boy's side. He doesn't move. I roll him over to check for life. His chest lies flat, no sign of a breath. His eyes are turned into his head. The lids are caked. His hair crawls with lice.

"Nelson," I cry out. I try to say more, but words fail. "Nelson. Nelson. Nelson."

"Chanda, come away."

"Nelson—he's one of the soldiers—one of the child soldiers we saw hobbling at the post."

"I know. Chanda, come away."

"I can see the sores on his toes and ankles. It's chiggers. He's lousy with chiggers. The ticks have burrowed into his feet. He must have had them for months. Nelson. He's been rotting alive."

Nelson comes up behind me. He puts his hands on my shoulders.

"They took his clothes. Nelson. They left him naked." I think of Soly and Iris and all of the other children stolen in the night. I think of them dragged away with what they had on, Iris in her nightie, Soly in that green feedbag. Think of them given the clothes of the dead. Wearing the pants and shirts of boys like this.

A sound as delicate as a tuft of milkpod rises from the ground: "Ma . . . ma . . . ma . . ."

I look down. Nelson and I were wrong. The boy isn't dead. His eyes roll forward. He doesn't see me. Doesn't see anything. But somehow he knows we're here. Or someone's here.

"Ma . . . ma . . . ma . . ."

Nelson leans in close. "We have to go," he whispers.

"No. He's alive. We can't leave him to the vultures."

"It's too late, no matter what we do. Look at him. The poison's through his body. It's into his brain. He can't even feel anything anymore."

"Nelson, this child could be Pako. Soly. Iris. If it was one of them, what would you want a stranger to do?"

"I don't know," he shouts back. "All I know is, we have to find them soon, before they turn into him."

"Ma . . . ma. Ma . . . ma."

I look down at the boy's blank face. I take his hand in mine. "Yes," I say. "It's me. I'm here."

There's a flicker around his mouth. "Ma . . . ma . . ."

"Shh. It's all right. I'm here."

The child's eyes slide back in his head. Has he passed? I don't know.

I've been wearing the mosquito net as a shawl this morning. I take it off my shoulders and unfold it. Nelson and I wrap it gently around the boy's body.

"We can carry him as far as the compound up ahead," Nelson says. "Check your hands for nicks. Chiggers can get in anywhere."

We each take an end of netting and carry our load toward the smoke.

35

THE SMOKE'S DIED down by the time we reach the compound.

Mandiki's paid a visit. There's a smell of burned flesh coming from the main house. Its thatched roof was set on fire and fell into the center. The charred door is blocked shut by a wagon, planted sideways, wheels locked by rocks. The wooden shutters have been pushed out by people struggling to escape. Their bodies, riddled with bullets, plug the two mud frames.

Nelson and I toss the rocks off the wheels and roll away the wagon. Inside the house, we find more bodies, some collapsed by the entrance, others huddled at the far end of the main room.

We stagger out of the place and vomit. I spit the smoke and bile out of my mouth. "Mandiki rounded up the whole family. He trapped them inside."

"Except for the children," Nelson whispers on his knees. "The kids who'd know the hiding places north of here, like Pako knew the mudhole."

When we can breathe again, we go back into the house. We bring the bodies into the yard and lay them together. The boy in the mosquito net is dead beyond certainty. I nestle him beside one of the mamas. Then we rock the wagon on its side and turn it over the remains. It'll keep out the scavengers. That will have to do for now.

It's midday. We rest through the worst of the heat in the shade of an outbuilding. Neither of us can eat. Iris. Soly. Pako. What did they see? I won't think about that. I can't. I busy myself making a new knapsack out of my blanket; I wrap Lily's sling around my head for sun cover.

"I can't stay here any longer," I say. "There's nothing but death. We have to go."

Nelson has the same sick feeling. We fill our canteens with water from the compound's well and force down a few bites of my maize bread. There's not much left. Nelson still has a stock of biltong, but our food's running low. Another day and I'll be digging for kasaba roots, while Nelson hunts lizards and bush rats with his slingshot.

We go north all afternoon, through savannah, scrub,

and now a mixed woodland. I look up as we walk under the sausage trees; if their heavy fruit falls on us, it'll crack our heads open. I'm careful near the marulas, too; bees hum around their sweet-laden branches.

We've traveled far. Twenty miles to Pako's mudhole. Ten or twelve this morning to the compound. Another ten since then. That's at least forty miles in total. I should know what that means. All the same, it's a shock when Nelson says: "Listen."

I hear a delicate lapping of water, catch a faint smell of fish. We emerge from the woodland at a broad, muddy river. It's the east fork of the Kenje. It has to be; that's the only river up here. I climb onto a large flat rock and look over the reeds.

Fifty yards away, on the far bank, I see elephants—three females and a baby—grazing in the sedges, their thick trunks curling around bunches of reeds, ripping them up by the roots. A colony of cormorants roosts on a stand of yellow fever trees near the water's edge. It's just like in Mr. Lesole's pictures. I start to tremble.

"Nelson," I say, "it's the park."

36

Mandiki's trail heads into the reeds at the water. Nelson climbs a tree to scout. For a moment, I stare in awe at the elephants. Then, filled with fear and excitement, I sit on the rock and pull out Mr. Lesole's map.

Mfuala National Park. It stretches two hundred miles, east to west; fifty miles, north to south. The Kenje River starts in the mountains at the border with Ngala and flows south. Safari camps are marked along its tributaries. Above the entrance to the park at Mfualatown, the Kenje forks in two. The west fork cuts across our country on a diagonal. The other fork, the one Nelson and I are beside, goes sharp east and marks the park's south boundary.

My eyes drift back to the elephants. There aren't any fences, but according to Mr. Lesole, the animals usually stay on the park side of the river. West of Mfualatown, the land is cleared, and there's a long strip of towns, roads, warehouses, and other things they don't like. East of Mfualatown, there's this river. Some of the animals can cross it, but except for a few bachelor elephants they usually don't. Over here, there're poachers everywhere. Mr. Lesole says they sense it.

Nelson swings down from a lower branch. "Chanda, we're in trouble."

"Mandiki?"

"Worse."

"What?"

He squats, as if dizzy. "I've looked up and down the river. There's no sign of the rebels coming out, on this side or the other."

I stop breathing. "You mean . . ."

"We've lost them. They could be walking along the water's edge in either direction. Or they could have crossed over miles away. There's no way to tell."

"What if we split up? You go along the river one way, I go along the other?"

"For how long? They could have walked for hours. If we're on the wrong track, how do we know when to turn around and come back? And what if they've crossed into the park? Where did they do it? We don't even know where to look!" He flings himself into the air. "We were so close! If only we hadn't wasted time with that kid."

"Nelson—"

"I never should have let you follow me!" He spins in a circle and storms off into the woods.

I slump down, eyes fixed blankly at the color drawing of the park and the inset diagram of the country. It's over. Over, over, over.

Nelson returns. If he yells at me again, I'll smack him. But the woods have calmed him.

"We have an outside chance to figure this out," Nelson says.

"What? How?"

He collects himself. "Here's one of the first things I learned about hunting," he says quietly. "Know your prey. If you know your prey, you'll know what it's likely to do. Where it's likely to go. That'll help you catch it."

"I don't understand."

He sits beside me on the rock. "Mandiki thinks everyone's his prey. He's wrong. You and me, we're hunters. He's *our* prey."

I'd never thought of it like that. My spine tingles.

"So," Nelson continues, "what do we know about Mandiki?"

"Well," I clear my throat, "we know he's traveling light, maybe twenty men and a few dozen kids. That means he can't fight a major battle. He has to be able to hit and run."

"What else?"

I smooth out the map and sketch Mandiki's route on the inset drawing of the country. "Mandiki came over the mountains, raided Mr. Lesole's camp in the foothills, and made his way through the park," I say. "Then he swept down alongside the highway, striking Tiro and Shawshe. Since then he's headed north and inland. The army's got patrols along the highway. He's been trying hard to avoid them."

"But will he *keep* heading north?" Nelson asks, rubbing his ear. "Maybe he'll double back south to surprise people."

"I don't think so," I say. "With dry season starting, the high grasses are dying. Every day, he'd be more exposed. Why risk it? Especially with Tiro and Shawshe getting reinforced. And below them there's the army base at Rombala."

"So Mandiki gets to this river. He's not going south," Nelson says. "Where then?"

I think hard, every fiber focused, clear. "Not west. That gets him near Mfualatown. It's big and heavily armed. We saw lots of tanks going there from Tiro."

"Then east?"

"Why? There's nothing east but a few family compounds."

"He hit a family compound last night," Nelson shrugs.

"Yes," I nod. "But that wasn't part of a plan. It just happened to be on his way."

"Where?"

My brain whirs: "Home!"

Nelson shakes his head. "Mandiki can't go home. He's on the run. The Ngala army found his main camp."

"So what?" I say, nerves sparking. "He's dodged the army there for six years. If he really had to escape, the rest of his troops would have followed him. They didn't. Mandiki came with a small brigade. He's been on a mission."

"What mission?"

"To punish us. Why? For signing the friendship treaty!" I'm on fire now, the words tumbling from my tongue. "In less than a week, he's proved he can take our kids, murder our families, and nothing can stop him. That's not all. He's pushed our country toward ruin."

"How?"

"Think, Nelson, think! Our government knew Mandiki was here. It sent tanks to Tiro. So why did it blame his attacks on poachers and bandits?"

"To keep us calm."

"No," I jump up. "To calm investors. Tourists."

Nelson frowns. "If Mandiki wanted to scare *them*, he would've murdered the guests at the safari camp."

"And risked his own future? If he killed foreigners, who knows what their governments might have done."

"Fine." Nelson swats a mosquito. "But why should investors or tourists worry about Mandiki now? As far as they know, he isn't even here."

"The official lie won't last."

"Why not?"

I take a deep breath. "Back in Bonang, I have a teacher, Mr. Selalame. I know what he'd say. 'Satellites track government armies. Rumors circulate in embassies.' One way or another, the truth will get out. When it does our economy will get hammered."

"Not if Mandiki's gone home."

I throw up my arms. "Wake up. Once the world knows Mandiki's been here, it'll know he can come again. Any time. What then? Investors fear instability more than death. Mandiki's job is done. That's why he's off to regroup at a new camp in Ngala."

Nelson exhales slowly. "They teach you a lot in Bonang."

"Mr. Selalame's very special," I say grimly. "Anyway, if what I've said is right, we have another problem. It's just fifty miles to the mountains. Once Mandiki crosses the border, rescuing Soly, Iris, and Pako will be impossible."

Nelson bites his lip. "We better move fast." He scans the river. "Where do you think he crossed?"

"Someplace shallow enough for children. Look for sandbars, ripples in the water running shore to shore."

Nelson's eyebrows lift off his forehead. "Mr. Selalame taught you that, too?"

"No, I got that from my neighbor, Mr. Lesole."

"Between the two of them, you know everything."

"Not tracking," I smile. "That's your department. You're King of the Spoor."

He shuffles, embarrassed.

I look east. "Let's scout down there, away from Mfualatown. My bet is, Mandiki took the first sandbar he could find. There'd be light. He'd want to take cover as soon as he could."

"Wait," Nelson says. "What if he crossed at night? He

had the kids from the last compound. They could have led him to the shallows in the dark."

"Even so, he wouldn't have crossed then," I say. "At night, it would've been hard to spot the crocodiles."

Nelson's eyes twitch. "Crocodiles?"

"Of course, crocodiles. The north Kenje River's full of them. What did you think?"

"I didn't think anything." He struggles to calm his voice. "I mean, of course there's crocodiles. I know that, sure. It's just, they live up here, I live down there. I don't think about them. I—well—What do we do?"

"Relax." I wish I was as confident as I sound. "The river's slow, but crocodiles like it slower. Like it says on the back of my map: 'They like to bake on the banks of a lazy oxbow.'"

"Well, they also like to eat. What if they're underwater at the edge of the reeds? The water's too muddy to tell."

My heart flips. "Look for little bubbles," I say. "Check for the tip of a snout. Anyway, crocs can only stay under for five minutes. We've been here longer than that and nothing's surfaced."

I march along the riverbank. Nelson holds back. I turn and put my hands on my hips: "Look, Nelson, don't be a baby. According to Mr. Lesole, crocodiles go for weeks between feedings. There were rebels in the water this morning. Any hungry crocs have already eaten."

Nelson steps toward me gingerly. "That's not too reassuring."

"Sorry," I say, "that's as good as you get."

A half mile downstream, we spot a series of sandbars. We take off our shoes, step into the water, and push through the reeds lining the shore.

I always took notes in school, but never at the Lesoles'. How much do I remember? How much am I jumbling? How much did Mr. Lesole make up for the sake of a good story? I guess I'm about to find out.

37

WE EDGE OUR way through the reeds. The muddy water's halfway up our calves. We part the last sedges. There's a ripple straight ahead. Is it a ridge of silt or a crocodile? I don't see any bubbles. It's too late to run anyway. I step forward. The ripple shifts. Please let it be the current. My toe bumps into it. It's not silt. It's hard. Slippery. It's—it's—

"Careful," I call to Nelson. "There's a half-sunk log or something. Don't cut your feet."

Near the shore, the river's shallow. We tread knee-deep, talking to keep our minds off what's scaring us.

"On the other side, there's all these trails leading from the river," Nelson says. "They're bare to the ground. From the safari camps?"

"No. Hippo highways."

"Hippo highways?"

"Yes." I give him a smug look. After all his teasing it feels good to know more than he does. "Hippos come to the water at dawn to stay cool. At night, they go inland, maybe ten miles, to graze on sweet grass. Each family makes its own path. They always follow the same route, wearing the trails to bare dirt."

Nelson considers this. "The hippos are a good sign, right?" he says. "They wouldn't be in the water if there were crocodiles, would they?"

I pretend not to hear. If that fantasy makes him feel better, good. The truth is, crocs leave hippos alone. "The hippopotamus is one dumb, ugly sonovabitch," Mr. Lesole told us. "Mean, too, if you're not careful. Those jaws can crush a croc in half. And lord, can they run—run faster than a sprinter. Get between a hippo and water, it'll trample you to death. Folks don't believe it, but hippos kill more people than anything else in the bush. More than lions, leopards, elephants, you name it."

We're almost halfway across. The water's deeper, the current stronger. Nelson's up to his waist; I'm up to my chest. We hold our knapsacks over our heads. This would come up to the children's necks. How did they make it? Maybe they didn't. Maybe we're at the wrong place. Or maybe the men stretched a line across, a rope maybe. How did they carry their gear? Do crates float? Did they make a raft? They would have had time. Not like us.

Something catches my eye. It's barely breaking the surface, heading our way from upstream. It's hard to make out what it is, with the sun in our eyes and the light bouncing off the water. But it's dark brown. I think I can see holes in it. Nostrils? A snout!

"Nelson! To the west! It's coming toward us! Hurry!"

He sees it too. We churn through the water. Struggle to get to the other side. The croc's getting closer. I lurch forward. There's a break in the sandbar. Nothing under my feet. I can't touch bottom. I'm underwater, except for my arms and knapsack. My legs flail. I burst through the surface. "Help!"

Nelson thrashes toward me. "Chanda!"

"I can't swim!"

"Neither can I! Float!"

"How?"

The river pours down my throat. I choke. Need my arms. Go to pitch my knapsack. Can't. Hands locked. Have to keep it dry. Under again. Kick like crazy. Break the surface. Nelson. Can't see him. "Nelson?" Has the croc—?

Nelson surges up from the water. He's over his head too. "Cha—" He sinks back under. So do I. This is it. We're going to drown or be eaten.

My heels hit mud. I'm pulled by the current up the side of the next sandbar. Somehow, I find myself on my knees. It's shallow, the mud floor pale under the water. I stand up. "Nelson?" He surfaces nearby. Staggers to his feet coughing.

The crocodile. Where is it? Frantic, I search the surface. I see the brown snout. It's ten feet away, coming fast, spinning in the current. Spinning? I look hard. It's not a snout at all. It's the rosettes of a rotting water hyacinth. It floats by harmlessly.

The two of us stand apart, shaking, gasping for breath.

"You!" Nelson explodes. "You almost got us killed!"

"I didn't make the gap in the sandbar!"

"Well, you—you—"

I raise a hand. There's a pod of hippos standing in the water just downstream. I count twelve animals in the family, their dark ears, snouts, and backs barely breaking the water. The current's brought us toward them. Our commotion's got their attention. I can hear Mr. Lesole's voice: "Those bastards are sneaky. Mean, too. They can stay submerged for six minutes, walk on the riverbed, then charge to the surface. They tipped a motorboat at one of the camps a few years back."

"Nelson," I say quietly. "Be very still."

"What?"

"We have company."

Nelson takes note.

"Avoid their eyes," I whisper. "Look off to the side." He does as he's told.

After a few minutes, the hippos get tired of watching us. A few make a hoarse honking sound. Silence. A shake of the head from some, the massive jowls spluttering in the water. One of them rests its chin on another's rump. They go still. It's like they're posing for tourists on a photo safari.

Nelson and I inch slowly along the sandbar. We reach the far bank.

"We're alive," Nelson says. He sounds surprised.

So am I. But there's no time for celebration. There's only a few hours before dusk, and so much to do.

"After he crossed, I'll bet Mandiki took one of the hippo highways," Nelson says. "It'd be a clear route, he could move fast, and once the hippos stomped over his tracks, his trail would be gone for good."

I nod. "Mandiki's lived in the bush for six years. He'd know not to go up a hippo path until the hippos had come into the water. Who wants to get trampled?"

"That fits with your idea that he crossed in the light."

"It also means that his tracks will be there till sundown, when the hippos leave."

I untie my knapsack. The blanket's damp from splashes of water, but thank god I kept my hands out of the river; things inside are pretty dry. I take out my binoculars. We walk out twenty feet on the sandbar and scan the shoreline. There are hippo highways up and down the river. I give the glasses to Nelson. "Here, you see better than me."

He takes a look. "From here, I can't tell if any of the tracks are human," he says. "But there's a bit of garbage in the reeds down there. I've never heard of a hippo carrying a feed sack."

My heart skips. "What kind of feed sack?" I grab the glasses, focus the lens. The bag's barely visible, dark green among the reeds. I run to the bank, snatch my things, and race downstream, nicking my legs on thorns. I leap over a hippo highway full of footprints heading inland.

"Stop," Nelson says. "This is it. The rebels' trail. You've passed it."

"I know," I say. The bag in the reeds is just ahead. I pull it from the water. There's a draw string, snagged to a sedge root. At the bottom, two leg holes.

Nelson catches up. "What is it?"

"Soly's diaper. It fit over his towel. He must have used it as pants. But now he's left it." I rip it from the water. "It's a sign. A sign to guide us."

Nelson pauses. "Your little brother would think to plant a marker?"

"Maybe not. But Iris would."

"Why here?" he asks gently. "Why not before?"

"I don't know. Maybe he's got proper pants now. It doesn't matter. The point is, he left us a sign. It drifted a bit. But we found it. Nelson, they're alive. They haven't given up."

"Chanda . . ." Nelson's face is pained. He might as well have kicked me in the gut.

"What?" I yell. "Why are you being like this?"

"It's just . . ." He hesitates. "Chanda . . . you know what we've seen."

"Yes, I know what we've seen," I say, hurt and mad. "I know exactly what we've seen. I know what else this bag could mean too. But don't you dare say it. Or even think it. Don't you dare—dare—take away my hope!"

"When Mandiki first came through, you told me: 'Dreaming a lie makes the truth hurt more.'"

· I can't speak. I can't breathe. I clutch the feed sack to my chest and sob. "Soly. Soly."

Nelson goes to say something. He can't. He stares at his feet. "I'm sorry," he whispers at last.

"Never mind." I wipe my face with my arm, bury my heart. "Let's get up that trail before the hippos destroy Mandiki's tracks."

I throw my things together. I swear, before I sleep tonight, I'm going to reach the rebel camp. Whether Soly and Iris are dead or alive, I'm going to know the truth.

38

In no time, the hippo highway takes us far from the river. The weight of the beasts has made deep grooves on either side of the path. The rebels' prints stand out in the loose soil kicked to the center.

We trek through scattered woodland. Clusters of dead and dying trees, the bark of their trunks gouged and ringed, tell tales of passing elephants. Old baobabs invite us to cool off in their hollow cores. But who knows what's lurking inside?

We're making good time, gaining confidence, when a twig snaps behind a thicket. We freeze. Is it rebels? Before we can breathe, an antelope bounds in front of us. Nelson yelps and scrambles up a tree. The antelope leaps into the air, kicking its heels, wiggling its rump, and disappears into the brush.

"It could have been a *leopard!*" Nelson exclaims.

My heart's in my mouth, but I pretend I'm Mr. Lesole. "If it'd been a leopard," I say, "you'd have been in real trouble. Leopards are climbers. They leave carcasses hanging from the branches."

"Don't talk down to me." Nelson drops to the ground. "In the old days, predators came through the posts. Grampa went on hunting parties. He killed a lion once."

"I'm sure he did. Once. In the old days."

Nelson kicks the dirt. "I'm just saying, there's predators in the park. Anything can happen."

I picture the children sitting on Mr. Lesole. "Leopards wouldn't go after the two of us," I say gently. "Lions might, but not likely, unless they're sick. And hyenas are scavengers. They attack if you sleep unprotected."

"Right. Then they'll rip off a chunk of your face."

"That's why you make yourself a little hyena hideaway. A circle of thorn branches, and you're fine." I'm not sure why, but saying out loud what I've learned from Mr. Lesole seems to relax Nelson. It's almost as if he thinks I really *am* an expert. Who knows, if I can fool him, maybe I can fool myself.

We carry on. As we walk under a marula tree, a family of

baboons pelts us with fruit pits. For a second, we're ready to dive to the ground. But we catch ourselves.

"Baboons," Nelson says sheepishly.

"Well done."

The hippo highway bends right, toward the scent of sweetgrass, but the rebels' tracks continue north. Something's new along the path. Tufts of fur. Blood. My insides tighten. Blood. That *will* attract predators.

"The rebels must've killed something in the grasses back there," Nelson whispers. "They're dragging the carcass to their campsite. We must be close."

He's right. Soon footprints fan out from the main route. The trail breaks up. The air fills with the smell of roast game and a ripple of voices. To our left, a fig tree towers over an ancient baobab. Their massive ground roots intertwine. Aerial roots from a baby fig, growing in the rotted crown of the baobab tree, hang to the ground, some strangling the baobab's bulbous trunk. We take cover.

"Mandiki's near enough to touch," Nelson whispers. "If we're not careful, we'll stumble right onto him."

"How could we be so careless? If we'd looked to the sky, we'd have seen smoke from their firepit."

Nelson shakes his head. "I doubt it. They're probably

waving palm leaves to break it up. That's what cattle rustlers do." He grabs hold of a thick aerial root. "I'm going to climb up, see what I can see."

"Wait!" I say quietly. "You'll be in the open. Check for a way into the baobab."

We circle around it. Like the others we've passed, the baobab tree's over twelve feet across, with an opening near the base of its trunk. We look through the narrow entrance. A shaft of light beams down from above; the core is hollow from top to bottom. "Climb up from the inside," I say. "You'll be invisible."

Before we enter, I toss handfuls of dirt into the opening and step aside. If there're animals in there, better to find out now. The earth sprays against the far sides of the hollow. Silence. The baobab's empty.

Nelson squeezes inside. I follow. The sky is visible through the rotten treetop. Three aerial roots, tough as vines, dangle down from the hole. Nelson tests his weight on the thickest. It holds. He's about to climb, when I grab his arm. "Nelson, above us!" High over the baobab, a giant beehive hangs from a branch of the neighboring fig tree.

"Who cares?" he says. "It's getting dark. The bees'll be settling in for the night."

I shiver all the same. I hate bees. I hate something else, too. As my eyes adjust to the shadows, I see a colony of bats, hanging upside down in the gloomy upper crevasses of our hollow. If only I'd thrown the dirt higher. "Bats," I whisper. "Dozens and dozens of bats. What'll we do?"

Nelson snorts. "Are you an insect?"

"No."

"Then relax. At least I worry about things that can eat me."

He hoists himself up, one hand over the other, his feet pressed into the thick aerial root, securing his weight. His head comes level with the bats. The hollow is six feet across. Nelson passes up the middle between them. They stay sleeping. He pokes his head through the rotted hole, gives a quick look around, and slides back in a rush.

"We got inside just in time," he says. "The camp's only fifty yards away, behind the next row of thornbushes. Most of the men are resting; that's why we didn't hear much."

"What about the children?"

He motions me to the ground. Outside, a crunch of twigs. And another. We lie on either side of the baobab's opening and peer out. Child soldiers are all around, collecting kindling. I see a girl hunched over in a soiled nightie. She turns my way. It's Iris. I almost don't recognize her. Her face is puffed. Her beautiful hair dirty, matted, the braids undone, the beads stripped away. But she's alive.

My eyes race for Soly. Where is he? Is he alive too? I spot Pako, just off the path. There beside him, nursing a stubbed toe—it's Soly. He lifts his head. Looks around. Can he tell I'm here? Or is he just scared of the bush?

"Keep moving." An older boy gives Iris a shove with the end of his rifle.

Iris trips face-first into the dirt. Scrambling at ground level, she glances in our direction. She opens her mouth as if to cry out. Nelson seizes. I put my finger to my lips.

The older boy gives her a kick. "I told you to move it."

"I'm moving, I'm moving," she says. She gets up with her kindling and disappears with the other children behind the thornbushes.

"Can your sister keep a secret?" Nelson asks nervously.

"When she wants to."

"Meaning?

"We're safe."

Together, we guard the opening. Mandiki must be proud, I think. After weeks of marches and raids, he's escaped to the wild with child slaves and plunder, far from even the nearest safari camp. No wonder he's having a feast. All at once, I'm hit with an idea. Mandiki thinks he's escaped? Well, he's in for a surprise. I burrow into my knapsack, fish out my map and cell phone.

Nelson cranes his neck. "What are you doing?"

"Getting the army. We've found Mandiki's camp. I'm calling in his position."

"What?" he says in disbelief. "They won't believe you."

"So? I can try."

He rolls his eyes. "Your phone won't work anyway. We're in the wilderness."

"Let me tell you something," I say evenly. "Safari camps like Mr. Lesole's need mobiles for their customers. They've got transmission towers all through the mountains. There's better reception here than on the cattle posts."

I turn on the cell. I press Talk. Then a horrible thought. I turn it off fast.

"What?"

"Nelson—if I get word to the army, if they listen—they'll attack with mortars, missiles, and grenades. It won't just be Mandiki who's hit, it'll be the children, too. Before I call, we have to free them."

39

I'M NOT SURE if my plan will work, but it's the only one we have.

Nelson's idea was crazy. "I'll use my slingshot," he said. "A rock to Mandiki's temple, and he's dead."

"Then what?" I demanded. "There'll still be all the rebels with machine guns and machetes. We'll be caught and tortured to death. Brilliant."

Nelson thinks my plan will end up the same. Maybe. But at least it gives us a chance.

We lie on the ground, looking up through the baobab's core to the branches of the fig tree and the sky beyond. Dusk hangs in the air. The shadows of our hollow deepen. The bats rouse in a whisper of flight. I cover my face as they swoosh down around us, some flying out from the baobab's base, most funneling up through the hole at the top, a tornado of wings.

The sky turns navy velvet. There's a full moon to the west. Overhead, the branches of the fig tree are silhouetted against the stars.

From the campsite, sounds of a party. The rebels are getting drunk. Good.

We wait. And wait.

Finally, a sharp hand clap. The carousing stops. Mandiki's voice pierces the night air. "Gather the new recruits. Fetch me my ebony box. My friend, the Skull, has greetings from the dead."

I wish I could see what's happening. Ah well, I'll see soon enough. Nelson squeezes my hand in the dark. I squeeze back.

"Now?" he whispers.

"Now."

Nelson wriggles out of the baobab. In a few seconds, I hear him murmur, "All's clear." He stays outside, guarding in case of patrols.

I take my cell phone, fumble it open. I haven't used it much; it should be fine. Still, the way Mrs. Tafa used to bang it off her tree, who knows? I feel the sticky tape, press down on the buttons.

There's a crackle in the connection, but Mrs. Tafa's voice comes through loud and clear: "Who, in the name of the saints and ancestors, is calling at this ungodly hour?"

"It's me, Chanda."

"Chanda! Where are you? I've phoned a million times. We're worried sick."

"Shh, please, Mandiki's only a few hundred feet away."

"Lord Almighty!" Mrs. Tafa whispers hoarsely.

"I need you to do something," I say. "I'm going to hang up. When I do, wait ten minutes, then call me. I won't be picking up, so don't worry. Just let the phone ring. Let it ring and ring and ring."

"What are you up to?"

"I don't have time to explain. Just do as I say. All right?"

"Whatever you want." Mrs. Tafa's voice chokes. "We love you."

"I love you too." I hang up and stick my head out of the tree's entrance. "Okay, Nelson. We've got ten minutes."

He slips inside, puts the cell between his teeth, and zips up the aerial root to the top of the baobab. He rests the phone on the lip of the rotten hollow and slides back down.

I check that the park map's in my skirt pocket, then go over the plans for the last time. How I wish we could use the hippo highway, but it'll be full of beasts and rebels. "Mfuala Lodge is the nearest safari camp. It's twenty miles due west," I whisper. "Once I get the kids—*if*—that's where we'll go."

"Right," he nods. "Aim for the jackalberry. It's the tallest tree around, past the campsite. I'll have caught up by then. If not, keep going, I'm dead."

I seize up. "Don't be dead. I'm not like you. I can't travel far in the dark."

He hugs me. "With the full moon, you'll be surprised. Anyway, no more talk. We have to get into position."

I'm about to say something stupid, but I can't. His mouth's on top of mine. We kiss. And he's gone.

I'm off in the other direction. I stay crouched down, moving stealthily from tree to thicket. Nelson's right. It's amazing what I can see. Not just by the moon, but by the flickers of campfire glowing through the thornbushes. I move faster. Too fast. I trip over a stump. Pride, pride. Am I hurt? I can't tell. Every inch of my skin is electric.

I'm at the end of the thornbushes. I peak through the branches. Mandiki's pitched camp in a small clearing. There's a firepit at the center, the low flames shielded from above by a canopy of acacia boughs. Two girls on their knees fan away whatever smoke remains; the skin and skeleton of an impala have been tossed to the side. Rebels are scattered throughout. Some of the men have passed out on the ground, empty bottles in hand. Others lounge against the tree trunks circling the clearing, stropping machetes or picking lice from each other's scalps. I see an older boy, lifting a swollen foot to the light of the flames. It looks like he's digging out chiggers with a penknife.

I spot Iris, Soly, and Pako among the newest and youngest recruits on the other side of the firepit with Mandiki. Mandiki's in a loincloth, his body slick with the blood of the impala. At least I hope it's from the impala. The spirit doctor's skull is twisting on his outstretched fist, its shadow snaking up a backdrop of vines and creepers.

I circle wide, careful to stay hidden.

"Tonight we celebrate victory, my little friends," Mandiki swaggers. "Tomorrow we'll be in Ngala." He wiggles two long fungal nails through the skull's eye sockets. The children cower. Soly clings to Iris. Mandiki snuggles the bony puppet against Soly's cheek. "Missing your family?" he smiles.

Soly sniffles.

"Uh-uh-uh," Mandiki whispers. "Remember what happens to soldiers who cry?"

A flash of rage surges through me. Hurt my Soly, I'll

kill you, I think. No. Don't lose control. Don't. I race the alphabet through my head, and crawl through the night.

I reach the far side of the clearing. Slip through the vines. I'm behind Mandiki; he faces the children. I slide forward. As close as I can get. When the time comes, I'll have to act fast. Closer, closer. Nothing between them and me now but a stretch of weeds and a fallen tree.

Something slithers in front of me. I rear back on my hands. For a second, my head's above the tree trunk.

A child sees me through the weeds. "Ah! What's there? Something's there!"

Mandiki whirls around. I duck down. I feel his eyes read the bush. Hear his skeletal legs step toward me. Closer. Closer. Any second he'll be on top of me.

Iris distracts him. "General!" she pipes up. "It's a ghost crocodile, isn't it, sir?"

Mandiki stops. His feet turn in the weeds. "Who said that?"

"Me," Iris says. "I'm right, aren't I, sir? It's a ghost crocodile."

Mandiki pauses. "Yes, my girl." The words hiss through his teeth. "It's a ghost crocodile. One of my spirit friends." He chuckles. "What's your name, girl?"

"Iris, sir."

"Iris." He makes a gurgling sound. "What makes you so brave, Iris?"

"I'm a soldier, sir."

"A special soldier. I like special soldiers." He squats to the ground and pats his knee.

Before I can think what he'll do next—what *I'll* do next—a stir from across the clearing.

"General!" a rebel shouts. "There's something at the baobab."

The camp falls silent. Then, cutting the night air, a ring.

"What the hell?" Mandiki leaps to his feet. "Who lost their goddam cell?"

Ring.

"It doesn't sound like ours," the rebel says.

"Then whose is it?"

Ring.

Mandiki waves the skull in the children's faces. "Did that phone come from the dealer's in Tiro? Did one of you steal it? Did you call out when you were getting kindling?"

Ring.

"Answer me! Who's been playing with things they shouldn't? Whoever it is, I'll chop off your arms and legs. I'll toss your stump to the hyenas."

Ring.

"Don't just stand there," Mandiki yells to his troops. "Get it."

Five armed rebels, two with flashlights, run behind the thornbushes to the baobab. In seconds, flashlight beams run up the baobab's trunk. They're guiding a rebel climbing an outside aerial root. He's high above the bushes.

Ring. Ring. Yes, Mrs. Tafa! Keep ringing!

Mandiki whispers in the skull's ear, "Who's the traitor? Hmm? Who do we kill?"

The climber gets to the top of the baobab. The spill from the flashlights lights up the fig branch above. The giant bees nest.

Nelson fires a rock from the dark with his slingshot. The rock breaks a huge hole in the nest. Bees everywhere.

The climber swats at his face. He falls to the ground screaming.

"What's going on?" Mandiki yells.

The hive swarms the flashlights. The rebels holding them holler in pain. The beams flash in all directions. The rebels throw them high in the air. They hit the ground. The bush goes black. Stung in the dark, panicked, the rebels fire their automatic rifles into the air.

"Who's out there?" Mandiki shouts. "How many are there?"

The men at the baobab don't hear him. They're too busy screaming, firing. "Help! Save us! Help!"

Everybody dives for their weapons.

The men from the baobab run around the bushes into the clearing, the hive on their tail. Firebursts.

"Attack! We're under attack!"

Bullets fly through the air. The children at the firepit press themselves to the ground. The bees swarm toward them, but swing away when they get near the smoke.

Some circle wild, striking anything in their path. Others regroup, a deadly mass of stingers. They have a target: Mandiki—slick with the sticky sweet blood of impala. The hive dives at his head.

"AAA!!!" Mandiki shrieks. "AAA!!!" He lurches in circles. Bodyguards throw him a blanket. But he can't see. His face is covered in bees. His neck puffs up. His eyes swell shut. He swings at his head with the Skull. "AAA!!!" Midscream, he coughs. Chokes. Claws at his throat. He can't breathe. Can't even gasp. He staggers blind. Drops to the earth. Convulses. Bodyguards drag him to the bush. His head bounces off rocks.

Now everyone's running, howling, from the camp. The rebels shoot at god-knows-what. The children cling to their friends.

I look to the firepit. Iris has Soly and Pako by the hand. She's nodding in my direction. The boys' eyes bulge. It's as if they're living a dream. They scramble toward me, keeping low with the smoke. I wave them through the curtain of vines. We flee toward the jackalberry, the shouts and screams of the rebels disappearing in the bush behind us.

Nelson's waiting for us when we arrive. But he was right. We don't need him to see. The moon is large and luminous. It lights a thin cloud floating across it. Against the night sky, the cloud looks like the outstretched wings of a giant stork.

We rush toward the moon. The stork. Mama.

Part Five

40

It's dawn. We've run all night, scared to death, no time to think. Now we're far, far from the rebels, at the edge of a large floodplain. In the distance to our right, a herd of Cape buffalo, still as statues; to our left, a makeshift road. According to the park map, that road should take us to Mfuala Lodge.

We stagger to a halt. The children drop to the ground. Nelson, too. They roll on their backs and gasp the clear morning air. Me, I throw my arms to the sky and laugh for joy. "Hello world, we're alive! We're alive!"

The others look at me like I'm crazy, then start to laugh too at the sheer wonder of it. I flop down beside them and hug Iris. "You were so brave," I say. "When the General came toward me, I thought I'd die. Then you spoke up. You saved my life." Iris grins so wide I think my heart'll break.

"As for you boys," I continue, "who knew you could run so fast? And you!" I give Nelson a playful poke in the ribs. "That shot of yours was amazing. Bees everywhere. I never guessed there'd be so many."

"But Chanda," Soly whispers, "what if the General finds us? He'll chop us into bits."

"The General can't find us now," I whoop. "He and his men ran all over the place. By the time they get back together, they won't know who's gone where."

"The owls know," Pako murmurs. "The night things. They'll tell."

Nelson cradles his brother in his arms. "The night things are in bed now. They can't hurt you. And when the sun goes down again, I promise, I'll be there. I'll be there forever and ever. You're safe."

Pako looks away. "I'll never be safe."

Something flashes through the far brush: the sun off a windshield. At first I think it's tourists on a morning game drive. I wave.

"On your knees, hands in the air," a voice booms over a megaphone.

"They must be rangers," I say. "Maybe they think we're poachers."

But they're not rangers either. They're soldiers in a jeep. As they approach, more troops emerge from the bush around the plain. The government's not just guarding the highway and northern villages. It's protecting the safari camps as well.

The children are scared. I tell them not to worry. "For all these soldiers know, we're rebel scouts from Mandiki. After all, we sure don't look like tourists."

I tell our story to the officer in charge. At first, he's suspicious. But when I show him the rebels' position on the park map and give him Mrs. Tafa's cell number in Bonang, he pays attention. As final proof, Nelson takes off his shirt: He doesn't have a brand. The officer radios the rebels' coordinates to his commander and orders reinforcements for the lodges and camps in the immediate area.

We're piled into the rear of the jeep and driven toward the army base in Mfualatown. As we exit the park through the heavily guarded gate, a surveillance plane and two Apache helicopters roar toward Mandiki's encampment. Moments later, we hear the sounds of heavy bombardment.

Mfualatown is an old trading post that's become a major center thanks to the tourist trade. In addition to its bus depot, there's a regional airport a few minutes past the outskirts. Gas stations, restaurants, discos, hotels, bars, rental stores, and souvenir shops stretch out in all directions along broad, unpaved streets. Our jeep meanders through an open-air farmer's market, avoiding bicycles, stray chickens, and potholes deep enough to drown a goat.

The children press against me. "Are the soldiers going to kill us?" Soly whispers.

"Of course not."

Iris digs her fingers into my arm. "The General said if we were caught, we'd be shot by a firing squad."

"He was just trying to scare you. Firing squads are for bad people."

"I know," Iris says, "I know." She clings even tighter.

"Soly, Iris, you haven't done anything wrong. You're fine. You're with me. Forget the General."

The three-story district hospital is the tallest building in sight. As we approach, I notice four rocket launchers on its rooftop. Across the road is a trailer park and campgrounds. Normally it'd be used by budget tourists taking day safaris into the park by minibus. Now it's commandeered for a tented barracks; soldiers with machine guns patrol the perimeter. Our jeep navigates through a wall of tanks into the hospital's parking lot.

How does the government explain this to the world? I wonder. Training exercises?

At a desk inside the main doors, a sergeant in shirt-sleeves fills out an identification card for each of us. He reeks of cigars; there are sweat stains around his armpits.

"Is there a phone?" I ask. "We have people in Bonang and Tiro worried sick about us."

"The phone's for official calls only," he mutters, swatting at a fly that keeps landing on his forehead. "You can find one in town when we're through with you."

He waves us off to a pair of hospital attendants. They take us to men's and women's shower rooms to get cleaned up. Nelson stays with the boys; I stay with my sister.

Iris looks scared when she's asked to take off her clothes. Our attendant, an older woman, smiles and promises not to look. Iris has never been shy around older women before. What's happened? From the corner of my eye, I watch as she scrubs herself. Even faced to the wall, she keeps one hand planted firmly over the left side of her chest.

All of a sudden I understand. Mandiki branded her. She's ashamed. How do I tell her I know? How do I tell her it's all right? How do I tell myself that?

I dry off and step into a coarse cotton hospital gown smelling of bleach. Our own clothes have been taken away for incineration. The attendant leads us to a small examination room. We sit on a pair of metal folding chairs opposite a table cluttered with boxes of medical supplies.

"The doctor won't be long," the attendant says. "Before he gets here, let's deal with those lice."

Lice? I don't have lice, do I? But it's not me she's talking about. It's Iris. With the shock of things, I hadn't noticed before. But under the bright fluorescents, I see them clearly, little parasites wriggling through her hair, hopping around her ears.

The attendant puts on rubber gloves and hands a pair to me along with a plastic bag. "Hold this open, tight under the hairline," she says, and pulls an electric clipper and a straight razor from a drawer. Iris's eyes go wide.

"Please," I say. "Can't you just rub in Kwellada?"

"Not with matts like that," she says. "I'd never find the nits in a month of Sundays. That head's got to be clipped and shaved."

"My hair," Iris says in a small voice. "My hair."

The attendant turns on the clipper. The buzz is hard. Cold. Iris's fingers tremble over her knotted clumps. Tears spill down her cheeks.

I touch the attendant's arm. "Wait. Before you shave my sister's head, shave mine." I take Iris's hand. "There's nothing to it," I say gently. "You'll see. We'll be like twins. Okay?"

The doctor arrives shortly after. Iris has drifted into another world. When he lowers her hospital gown from her shoulders, she covers her brand wound with a hand. But she offers no resistance when he moves the hand away. Instead, she hums vacantly, gazing at the ceiling with empty eyes.

Iris, where are you? What's happening in your mind?

After the doctor treats the wound and completes the examination, he takes me aside. "Her chest will be scarred," he says. "Apart from that and a few bruises, she's fine. You'll be relieved to know, there's no genital trauma."

My head swims. "She's only six."

"It happens."

We're given new clothes and head kerchiefs donated by an overseas relief group. Then we're brought to a holding room, where we're reunited with Nelson and the boys. They look at our scarves, wrapped tight to our scalps; they can tell what's happened, but they're too kind to say anything. Soly and Pako had lice too, but their hair was short enough that it didn't need to be shaved. As with Iris, they'll be left with a nasty scar on their chests, but nothing more.

We barely have time to exchange the news before we're separated once more, this time for questioning. The army needs to hear our stories individually to make sure we're telling the truth. The children hang on to us in a panic. Nelson and I promise them we'll be together again in a few minutes.

I'm taken to a makeshift interrogation room that's actually one of the hospital's walk-in linen closets, and made to sit on the edge of a lower shelf, while two soldiers stand over me firing questions. I tell them exactly what I told the officer in the park this morning. They seem to be deaf or simple, because they keep asking me to repeat myself. It's like they're waiting for me to trip up.

At one point, they pause to compare notes. "Excuse me," I say. "Mandiki had dozens of child soldiers. Have they been rescued too?"

The soldiers look up sternly. "We ask the questions."

Down the hall I hear young voices, voices I don't recognize. Could they be some of those kids? I tell myself Mandiki stole the children from cattle posts and small villages here and in Ngala. They'll know the bush. It may take days, but they'll get out safe and sound. Won't they? I hope so.

There's a guard watching an old TV in a lounge opposite my interrogation room. The television gets a shaky signal from the government station in Bonang. During breaks in the questioning, I watch through the open closet doors. I keep expecting a report about this morning's bombardment, but there's nothing. Just cooking shows, old cartoons, and interviews with local mayors. Finally, late afternoon, programming's interrupted for a special bulletin from Ngala.

"Ngala officials have confirmed the death of General Charles Joseph Mandiki," the announcer says. My heart stops. "The remains of the rebel leader were found earlier today by the Ngala army during its continuing sweep of Ngala National Park. It is believed he was killed by his own troops. Dental records were used to identify the corpse. It had been torn apart by hyenas." We see close-ups of half-eaten bones.

I call to the guard. "The news is wrong. The General wasn't in Ngala. He was here."

The guard stares at me. "Mandiki was never here."

"He was. Everyone knows it."

The guard crosses his arms. "That's not what the television says. Is it?"

I fiddle with the hem of my skirt. "I guess not," I say quietly.

So . . . did Mandiki make it over the mountains? Or was his body dumped across the border to protect the official lie? For once, I stop asking questions. Mandiki is dead. That's all I need to know.

41

AFTER THE GRILLING, Nelson and I are brought back to the holding room and told to wait for the children; the soldiers aren't through with them.

I get more and more anxious as the hours pass. Finally, near dusk, Soly is led in, followed by Iris and, a while later, Pako. I don't know what they've been asked, but they're quiet, withdrawn. When Nelson and I cuddle them, they hug us tight like they're afraid we'll disappear.

The army's made arrangements for us to stay overnight with Mrs. Rachel Jaworka, a local widow who runs a center for orphans out of her home. A large frothy woman, she bounces in jangling bracelets and beads. At the sight of the glitter, Iris's eyes flicker.

The desk sergeant stops us on the way out. "Everything you saw in the bush is classified. Say anything, there'll be trouble. Understood?"

"Yes." Who'd listen to us anyway?

Mrs. Jaworka waltzes us to the street, flashing a toothy grin and waving at everyone in sight. I follow a step back, Soly and Iris on either hand; Nelson carries Pako on his shoulders. "I left the car at the center," Mrs. Jaworka calls over her shoulder. "With crowds and the goat carts, it's faster to walk."

The air is alive with excitement. Since the announcement of Mandiki's death, the curfew's been lifted and the road south is being reopened. Everyone's buzzing with plans. "I have a daughter in Rombala, holding her water for days," Mrs. Jaworka says. "I'm driving down at dawn, middle of the night if she goes into labor."

"Could you take us as far as Tiro?" I ask. "We have relatives killed in the attack three nights ago. Our family was planning funerals for tomorrow."

She stops. "Oh, you poor things, of course. I'm sorry for your loss."

Soly tugs my hand. "Who all is alive then?"

"Almost everyone," I say. "Granny, Lily, Uncle Chisulo, Auntie Agnes, Uncle Enoch, Auntie Ontibile, your cousins—"

"Auntie Lizbet?" Iris asks. "They hit her with rocks. She fell down. Did she get back up?"

"No," I say softly. "I'm afraid Auntie Lizbet passed. Grampa too. They're the ones being buried. We'll have a chance to say goodbye."

Iris's lip quivers. I go to wrap my arms around her, but she pushes me away. Mrs. Jaworka gives a knowing look and I back off. Iris walks the rest of the way on her own, off to the side, staring ahead. Every so often, she slaps her thigh.

At last we reach Mrs. Jaworka's. It's a good-sized property with a large, cinder-block house, a garden, and a rusty Corolla by the toolshed. The yard is full of children waiting in line for soup ladled out by volunteer neighbor ladies. "A lot of the kids have grannies to go to at night," Mrs. Jaworka says. "For those that don't, we lay out ground-sheets under the tree."

"Their parents . . . did they die of AIDS?"

"Yes, most of them," Mrs. Jaworka nods, "but nobody calls it that here."

"My mama passed of AIDS."

"Ah." She gives my shoulder a squeeze.

Thanks to public donations and church groups, the center has electricity, running water, a large gas stove, and a phone. I use the phone to call Mrs. Tafa and Esther. "We're safe," I tell them. "We'll be back the day after tomorrow." I don't know who to call in Tiro now that Mr. Kamwendo's passed, but Nelson thinks to phone the rest house. The hotel owner knows our families; he promises to send a runner over to Granny's and Nelson's sisters-in-law to say we're fine and will be there for the burials.

After we've eaten, Nelson tells stories to the kids while I help Mrs. Jaworka wash the soup bowls in the kitchen. I tell her about my dreams for an AIDS center in Mama's memory, something like she's got here, and ask her how she got started. She fills me up with ideas, then says: "I wish you the best. But maybe you should wait a few years."

"Why?"

She lowers her voice. "Your little ones have been with Mandiki. I have a cousin in Ngala. She's seen kids who've escaped. They're a handful."

"Ours were only with him a few days."

"It doesn't take long." Mrs. Jaworka puts down her dishrag. "The thing is, you don't know what they've seen. You don't know what they've done."

My mouth goes dry. "What do you mean, 'what they've done'? Soly and Iris haven't done anything."

"I'm not saying they have, but . . ." Mrs. Jaworka cups her hand to my ear.

A voice from the kitchen doorway: "What are you talking about?"

I turn with a start. It's Iris. "Nothing," I say. "We're not talking about anything."

"Then why are you whispering?"

"Private things, that's all. Grownup things."

Her eyes are a volcano. How much did she hear?

"It's time for bed," I say. I bring her back to the living room and get us organized, rolling out spare mats next to the couch. Iris nods at Soly and Pako; they nod back. It's like they share a silent language. What are they thinking? What do they suspect?

We wake to the smell of fresh biscuits being lifted from the oven. "Thought I'd leave a batch for the morning volunteers to pass around," Mrs. Jaworka smiles. She has us in her Corolla before the first rooster crow.

The car is an old standard. Pako sits on Nelson's lap in the passenger seat, while I sit on the bump in back, Iris and Soly under my arms. The streets are empty, except for the odd cart coming to market from the country. By the time the air turns pinky-blue we're on the highway.

The whole drive, we keep telling the kids that the

General's dead and any surviving rebels are running back to Ngala. All the same, they sit low in their seats, barely daring to peek out the windows at the countryside. We slow down approaching the place where the flatbed truck was ambushed. Pako slides into the space under the dashboard to hide, gripping Nelson's calves. The flatbed's hulk has been moved to the side, but the sun glints off shards of metal and glass littering the road. Two drivers have pulled over: one to patch a flat tire punctured by the debris, the other to rummage around the hulk for scrap.

The sun's hot by the time we near Tiro. "Granny and the others will be so glad to see you," I say, squeezing Soly and Iris's shoulders. Soly is soft and pliable; Iris is hard as carved rock. "It didn't hurt," she murmurs to herself. "It didn't hurt."

"What didn't hurt?"

She gives me a frightened look, hunches her shoulders, and shrinks inside her dress.

We leave the highway and enter Tiro. The smell of smoke and explosives lingers in the air. The windows of Mr. Kamwendo's store have been boarded shut; a couple of soldiers lean against the crumbling stucco. Across the road, a tent's been set up next to the empty clinic.

Nelson directs Mrs. Jaworka to our families' compounds. Last night, the bodies of the dead were returned from the morgue for the laying over. Friends and relatives who slept in our yards are readying themselves for the services. Mrs. Malunga, Runako, and Samson are being buried in the Tiro cemetery. My Auntie Lizbet and Grampa will be laid to rest with the ancestors on the cattle post.

Mrs. Jaworka brakes in front of Granny's place. The children cringe at the sight of our family's homes. The collapsed roof beams have been cleared to the junk piles back by the outhouse, but the blackened shells are still full of rubble and ash, visible through the charred window and door frames. The plywood coffins are visible too, resting across sawhorses inside the ruins.

Soly sees Granny and runs to her, burying himself in her skirts. Iris marches after him, arms rigid at her sides, staring away from the devastation. The rest of us leave the car too. Except Pako. He stays pressed under the dashboard.

"You don't have to see Runako or Samson," Nelson whispers in Pako's ear. "I'll make sure their coffin lids are closed."

"But I see them already, every night," Pako whispers

back. "They come for me in dreams, like Papa. Get the spirit doctor. Put a spike through their skulls, and magic. Nail their spirits in the ground."

Mrs. Jaworka and I pretend not to hear. While Nelson coaxes his brother from the car, I take her over and introduce her to my family. They embrace me like I've risen from the dead. "I promised we'd stay away," I say. "But with Mandiki dead I hoped it'd be okay. We needed to say good-bye to Auntie Lizbet. To Grampa, too."

Granny's eyes glisten. "They'd want you here. We all do. You're family."

Mrs. Jaworka says her goodbyes. She accepts our thanks, but refuses the offer of gas money. We wave as her car putters down the road. I'll probably never see her again.

I look over at Nelson's yard. He's talking with his sisters-in-law, a firm grip on Pako's arm, as if he's afraid his brother will run off. I long to be with him; strain to hear the flavor of his voice. Will he disappear from my life like Mrs. Jaworka?

There's no more time to think. A handful of pickup trucks arrive to take us to our family's funerals. I pay attention as Uncle Chisulo organizes us into groups.

We drive up the highway to the cutoff for our cattle post.

Someone's scythed the grasses over the old cart trail. My uncles and male cousins carry the coffins, while the rest of us walk behind, clapping and singing prayers. Before it seems possible, we're at the abandoned ruin. Soly and Iris have never been here before. At first, they cling tight: Soly cowering, Iris with clenched fists. But soon the light and the crowd take away the scariness.

I'm relieved too. I'd been afraid the place would bring back memories of the rebels, but all trace of them has vanished. The grasses have righted themselves, and Mandiki's altar of family burial stones has been dismantled. Uncle Chisulo and Uncle Enoch know which stone belongs to which ancestor going back to the first generation, and have returned each marker to its proper place.

"The air feels clean," I say to Uncle Chisulo, as we gather in a circle for the funeral.

"Thank our local spirit doctor," my uncle whispers. "He did a ritual yesterday so the ancestors could sleep again. See him over there with the priest? They're cousins. They like to stay up all night arguing about whose prayers are stronger."

The services are filled with stories and song. Granny talks about Grampa on their wedding day, his tenderness, and how lucky they were to have had so many years together. My uncles tell tales of his bravery in the bush. My aunties remember his practical jokes. Grampa just passed a few days ago, but in so many ways he's been gone for years. Here, today, he lives as bright and alive as in the days of his youth.

Auntie Lizbet is remembered too, for the tireless way she worked about the compound, the pride she took in her biscuits, and for her love and devotion to family. There's a moment of silence. Then Granny tells the story of Auntie's death, and of the heroism of her end. As her coffin lowers into the ground, Soly holds my hand. Not Iris. She stands apart, in her own little world, and sings the harvest song.

I talk to Granny at the burial feast. "If staying in Tiro is ever too hard," I say, "come live with us in Bonang. The aunties and uncles are welcome too."

"Bless you," Granny smiles, "but this is our home. Tiro is where we belong."

That's pretty much what Nelson tells me too. The next morning, he waits with my family for the new flatbed that'll take Soly, Iris, and me back home. My relatives fuss over the kids, while the two of us walk up the road apiece.

After all we've been through, I'm not sure what I'm expecting. But it's not this. Nelson keeps his hands in his pockets the whole time. He hardly looks at me.

"You don't have to go," he says.

"I do. I have people waiting. Come with us. You and Pako. There's room."

"What would we do in Bonang? I have my sisters-in-law to take care of. Their babies. The cattle. It's only me at the post now. Well, Pako too, but . . ." His voice trails into silence.

"I'll be back," I say quietly.

He looks off. "Sure."

"I will."

"Sure."

The truck arrives. I go to hug Nelson. Instead, he sticks out his hand. We shake awkwardly. Uncle Chisulo hoists Soly and Iris onto the flatbed. I follow. The truck pulls out. Everyone waves, except Nelson. He won't even look up. Maybe he can't. Before we hit the bend at the highway, he's turned to go.

42

THE FLATBED'S PACKED. With the highway closed the past few days, people have things to catch up on. Family affairs, trips to trading posts. We get stuck between a man with three goats and a couple with live chickens hanging upside down from a pole.

We approach Bonang. The children get anxious. Their feet tap the flatbed floor like elephant shrews.

"What's the matter?" I ask. "You're going home."

"No one'll want us," Soly says.

"Of course they will," I laugh. "Why wouldn't they? Our relatives did."

"They had to. Granny was in the bush too."

Iris crosses her arms. "What did you tell Mrs. Tafa and Esther?"

"That you were kidnapped. That you're safe."

344

"What else?"

"Nothing else."

"Oh?" she challenges. "What did you say to that lady in the kitchen? What did she whisper to you?"

Soly rocks back and forth. "Did you talk about the night people?"

"Shut up, Soly." Iris punches him.

I grab her arms. "Stop that!"

"Make me!" She spits in my face. Kicks and hollers. The man with the goats tries to hold her down. She bites him. The couple on the other side protect their chickens. Then, out of nowhere, Iris lets out a bloodcurdling scream and goes limp. The man with the goats wipes his forehead. "That girl's possessed." He makes the crazy sign.

"Don't you talk about my sister!" I raise a fist. He backs off as if I'm possessed too. I lean over Iris. "Shh," I soothe. "It's all right."

She trembles. "It's not all right. It's not."

Mrs. Tafa and Esther have been busy. Our house, shed, and garden are festooned with bright strips of colorful rag. Mrs. Tafa's hung her Christmas ornaments on the quills of the cactus hedge. As the truck pulls over, they run up to greet us, along with Mr. Tafa, Sammy and Magda, Mr. Selalame and his wife, and neighbors from around.

Iris frowns. "What do they want?"

I give her a friendly nudge. "They've missed you, just like I said."

"Tell them to go away."

"I can't. Be nice."

Greetings and hugs as we get off the truck. Esther twirls me in a circle. "Thank god you're home!" She kisses me on both cheeks.

Mrs. Tafa throws her arms wide and wobbles the flab. "You've grown so big!" she teases the children. She tries to give them a peck on the cheek. They turn away. I'm embarrassed, but Mrs. Tafa just laughs. "The poor things are tired. They need a treat." She claps her hands. "Leo!"

As Esther leads us to benches and stools, the Tafas scurry next door. They return with two large pitchers of lemonade, a chocolate cake, and Mrs. Tafa's lawn chair. Mrs. Tafa pours the lemonade into her best teacups and settles her rump.

"A toast!" she says. "To the children's safe return!"

Everyone toasts and talks, except for Iris and Soly. They press together, holding their drinks between their knees.

Mrs. Tafa cuts the cake. "It's store-bought," she beams.

"Full price, too. I couldn't resist." She winks at the kids. "Would you like a corner piece?"

"I don't want any," Iris says flatly.

"Me neither," Soly echoes.

"But I got it specially for you," Mrs. Tafa coaxes.

"We said no!" Iris glares.

"But—"

"No!" Iris leaps to her feet. She throws her lemonade at Mrs. Tafa.

"Iris!" I gasp. "Apologize!"

Iris whips up her stool. "What do you *know*?" she yells at the circle. "What do you want?"

Mrs. Tafa's hankie flutters to her eyes. "We want for you to be happy."

"Then why are you staring?"

"We aren't."

"You are. Since we got off the truck."

"She's right," Soly says. "All of you. Staring. Staring. Stop it!"

"Yes, stop!" Iris cries. "Leave us alone!" She throws her stool to the ground and races into the house with Soly.

"Auntie Rose, Esther, everyone," I sputter. "I'm sorry. Forgive us, please."

I run inside too. Soly and Iris are huddled in their

room. I bang my hand on the door frame. "What's going on? Those are our friends. Our neighbors. Esther. The Tafas. The Selalames. They're all here. They love you. You know that."

"We don't know anything," Iris says. "You're the ones who know things. Like those soldiers. Like that lady. She told you, didn't she? You know. You act like you don't, but you do. What did you tell Mrs. Tafa on the phone? What did you tell Esther? What are they saying about us? Why are they staring?"

"Iris, you're talking crazy."

"She's not," Soly gulps. "Where's Mr. Lesole?"

"Pardon?"

"You heard him," Iris demands. "Where's Mr. Lesole? Why isn't he here?"

"I don't know."

"You do too!" she says. "You know, but you won't say."

"Like with us," Soly echoes. "You know, but you won't say."

"Know what?"

"Mr. Lesole is dead," he exclaims. "He's dead!"

"Who told you that?"

"The boys from Ngala. They attacked a camp in the foothills. There was a scout with a boom box. They did things to him. It was Mr. Lesole, wasn't it?"

"He was attacked, yes," I say. "But he's alive."

"Liar!" Iris rages. "We saw what they do to people. To people like Mr. Lesole."

"We did more than just see," Soly weeps. "The night people. The night people."

"Who?"

Iris doubles over. "You know, don't you?"

"All I know is I love you. I always will, no matter what."

"You won't," Soly weeps, voice lighter than air. "You can't."

Esther appears in the doorway. "Everyone's gone. It's our fault. We shouldn't have done anything till you were settled."

"Never mind." I run my hands over my face. "The children think Mr. Lesole is dead. They have to see him. Now."

Esther lowers her eyes. "They can't."

"What? Why not?"

"Two days ago . . . his mouth . . . it got infected bad. The safari company got him into the hospital. It's serious. No visitors except for Mrs. Lesole. She's staying on a cot beside his bed."

"He's going to die," Soly whispers. "He's going to die like the night people."

43

BEDTIME COMES AND goes. The children won't sleep. I tell them over and over that Mr. Lesole will be all right, but they don't believe me. Iris covers her ears and wails, and Soly keeps moaning about "the night people." Only he won't say who they are—or what. Just howls and beats his head with his fists.

By morning, they've exhausted themselves. While Sammy and Magda leave for school and Esther heads to the Welcome Center, they lie passed out on a corner of their mat, tangled up in their sheet. I let them rest.

Mrs. Tafa drops by on her tour of the neighborhood. I motion to her that the kids are sleeping, and she invites me over to her place for a lemonade. I only mean to be away a few minutes, but before I know it I'm pouring out my heart about the last few days. When I get home, the children are gone.

Mrs. Tafa and I search everywhere. Outhouses, chicken coops, and dry cisterns up and down the road, the rocks around the sandlot, and the junkyard with its abandoned well and piles of truck tires, ovens, iceboxes, sinks, and washtubs. Nothing. We return hours later to find Soly and Iris in their room, cut and bruised.

Esther's standing guard. "I passed them, biking back from the Center," she says. "They were a mile off at the riverbed, throwing stones at each other. One at a time, in turns, like it was a game."

I whirl on the children in disbelief. "What kind of craziness is this?"

Soly covers his head and trembles. Iris looks up at me, helpless, dried blood on her cheek.

I try to calm down. "For now, just play in the yard. And no more stones. All right?" I edge out of their room, pretending everything's fine.

I pretend for the rest of the day. And the next day, too, when I take them to school. I have a word with the principal about starting back to work in a few weeks. Then I peek into their classrooms. They've run off. I find them at the Sibandas' shabeen, shoving Ezekiel Sibanda's head in a pail of shake-shake. The drunks are laughing. I grab my babies and drag them home.

I give them a talking-to, then rake the yard to calm my nerves. Mrs. Tafa waves me over to the hedge. "Soly and Iris. They're not right," she mutters darkly. "You should take them to Mrs. Gulubane."

"Why? Her spells didn't help Mr. Lesole."

"They most certainly did," Mrs. Tafa huffs, scratching her back with a lemonade straw. "He may have lost his tongue, but without that magic pouch he'd have been killed."

I keep the children inside all afternoon. Their eyes light up when Esther brings news from the hospital that Mr. Lesole's out of danger; he'll be released in a day or two. Apart from that, they brood. Every so often Soly bursts into tears about the mysterious night people. Each time he does, Iris flies into a rage and screams, "Shut up, Soly. It didn't hurt."

I can't breathe. I'm losing them. Not to Mandiki, but to the demons he's unleashed. There's only one place I can go for help. "Esther, keep the children close," I say. I run to my bike and pedal hard to the high school.

Mr. Selalame is alone in his classroom, hunched over a pile of marking. He barely has time to say hello before I'm rocking at my desk, pacing the aisles—babbling, babbling. Now I'm leaned out the window, banging his blackboard erasers. I look like a fool. I don't care.

"Something happened in the bush. Something worse than anything I know about. Soly and Iris, they won't say what. I'm afraid they're going to hurt themselves. *Really* hurt themselves. Or hurt somebody else. They need help. But who? I don't trust Mrs. Gulubane, and I can't afford a psychiatrist. I'm scared. What do I do? How can I find out what's wrong?"

My arms are too tired to whack anymore. Mr. Selalame takes the erasers and returns them to the ledge under the blackboard. He gives me a tissue to wipe the chalk dust from my hands, and another to wipe the tears from my eyes. Then he thinks a bit, clicking his tongue against the back of his teeth.

"Whenever I've been to your house," he says slowly, "I've noticed you've put the children's drawings on the walls."

I nod. "Mama taped up everything they brought home from school. I've done the same."

Mr. Selalame goes to his filing cabinet and pulls out a stack of blank paper. He gets a box of colored chalk ends from beside the old globe in the corner, and a rainbow of pencils from the top left drawer of his desk. "Give these to the children. See what happens."

"I don't understand."

He winks knowingly. "Soly and Iris have a lot on their minds. They won't talk. But they love to draw."

By the time I get home, everyone's eaten. Esther's sitting by the cistern watching Sammy and Magda play in the twilight. Iris and Soly are inside on their mat whispering. Strange, they used to like to play apart; now they're inseparable. I set the paper, colored chalk, and pencils on the floor against the side wall of their room and leave without saying a word.

"What's that for?" Iris calls after me.

"Whatever you want," I shrug. "I thought you'd be bored."

"We're not."

"Then they can just sit there. I don't care."

I go outside and have a bowl of seswa left warming over the firepit. Esther puts Sammy and Magda to sleep, then the two of us talk. And talk. Finally Esther heads to bed. I stay propped against the cistern, looking up at the stars, thinking of Mama, Nelson, Granny, and above all, the children.

I drift to sleep. When I wake up, it's the middle of the night, but there's light coming from the main room. I peek between the window slats. Inside, Iris and Soly are sitting at the table, coloring furiously, drawings scattered at their feet. The oil lamp glows between them.

I open the door. The flame flickers. The children look up, startled. At the sight of me, Iris grabs her work, crumples it into a ball, and runs into their bedroom. Soly stays at the table. I move toward him slowly. When I reach his chair, I kneel down. His arms are over his paper. He stares at the red pencil in his hands.

"Can I see what you were drawing?" I ask quietly. He doesn't answer. I stay very still. "You're such a good drawer. I'd really like to see."

Soly hesitates. He moves his arms off the paper. It's a mass of scribbled color. Red, orange, and black.

"That's a lot of orange," I say simply.

Soly rolls the pencil between his fingers. "It's fire."

"Fire?"

He nods. "They put the night people in the house. It's all on fire."

"Of course. Yes." I pause. "And those red parts on the sides?"

"Blood." He looks anxiously at the bedroom and whispers in my ear. "When the night people come out the windows, the men shoot them."

"Why do the night people use the windows?"

"Because." His face crinkles up with pain. "Because."

And suddenly I understand. I was there the next morning, after the waterhole. "There's a wagon in front of the door, isn't there?"

Iris comes out of their room, the crumpled drawings hanging from her hand. "The General, he made us put rocks on the wheels," she says. "Rocks, so it wouldn't move. That's when he set the roof on fire."

"The night people screamed," Soly cries. "They wouldn't stop screaming."

Iris beats her chest with the drawings. "They burned to death. They hurt so bad. We killed them."

"No," I say. "Whatever happened out there, it wasn't your fault. It was the General. You couldn't stop him. You know that."

"Don't tell us what we know, what we saw, what we heard," Iris wails. She hurls the drawings into a corner and runs into the night.

I race after her with the oil lamp. "Iris?" I hear her

whimpering behind the chicken coop. "I have a little sister," I call gently. "I love her very much." Silence. I set the lamp on an upturned pail and sit on a nearby chair. "Iris? I'm here. Whenever you need me, I'm right here."

Soly comes outside. He curls up by my feet. Iris remains hidden behind the coop. We stay like that all night.

44

At DAWN, I collect Iris. She's curled up, deep asleep. Her arms wrap around my neck as I lift her up and carry her inside to her mat. I tuck her sheet around her, smooth the kerchief over her shaved head, and tiptoe to the counter to make breakfast. All the while, Soly follows me like my shadow. As I cut the maize bread, I feel his fingers on the back of my dress. His touch is cautious, like he's making sure I'm really here. I glance down. He runs to his room.

Esther arrives with Sammy and Magda for breakfast. They eat in the yard while I scatter feed for the chickens and check their nests for stray eggs. Then Sammy and Magda go to school and Esther bikes to the Welcome Center. I go back inside, intending to lie down in my room.

I don't get past the doorway. Iris's crumpled pictures stare at me from the shadows in the corner. It's like they're calling to me: *We've waited here all night, waited for you to pick us up. To look at us. Now you're alone. What are you going to do?*

I'm afraid. Soly just scribbles colors; Iris draws images. I've seen enough. I don't want to know any more. I want to rip the pictures up. To throw them away. But I can't. The children's lives are on those pages. I need to be in the drawings with them.

The air around me disappears. Nothing exists but that ball of paper. I bring it to the table and separate the sheets, slowly, slowly, chanting the alphabet as I smooth each one flat in front of me.

From the corner of my eye, I catch Soly and Iris in the doorway. They stare at me, shy, defiant, and awkward, all at once.

"I'd like to tape these up in my room," I say.

Iris frowns. "Why?"

"I want to understand."

A pause. "Do what you want," she says, and closes their curtain.

In the afternoon I fix up the garden, clean around the out-house, and have Mrs. Tafa watch the yard while I get a sack of chicken seed at the feed lot. When I return, I go to my room to lie down. There's a dozen new drawings on my mat.

After the sun's gone down, Esther and I put the kids to bed and talk outside in the low glow of the firepit. Around midnight, she nudges my toe and nods toward the over-turned wheelbarrow. Soly and Iris are peeking out from behind it.

"I know you're hiding." I wave them over.

Iris approaches warily, then plunks herself down between us. When Soly sees everything's all right, he comes and snuggles beside me. We sit in silence. After a while, I realize Soly and Iris aren't staring at the logs. They're staring at Esther. The flickering light plays tricks across the scars on her face, the shadows turning the thin lines into a map of gullies and riverbeds. I remember back to before Tiro, way back to the night she showed up at our door, raped, her head swollen, the cuts and stitching fresh with pain.

"What are you looking at?" Esther asks.

"Your scars," Iris says simply. "Do they hurt?"

Esther's eyes stay fixed on the firepit. "Depends what you mean by hurt. I don't feel them anymore. Except when

I laugh. Then there's a little pull, and a tingle at the bottom of my lip."

Iris thinks for a long time. "Esther . . ."

"Yes?"

"Esther . . . do you mind being ugly?"

Esther grips her knees. "Sometimes," she says. "Sometimes I see myself in a mirror, and I wish I was dead."

Iris nods gravely.

"But that's only *some*times," she adds. "Other times, I think these scars are part of me. They're part of my life." She hesitates. "Do they bother you?"

"No," Soly shakes his head. "You're Esther."

"Good." Her eyes mist over. She brushes them with her wrist. I put my hand on her shoulder. "It's just the smoke," she says.

There's a pause, then Iris whispers: "You're brave. Soly and me, people talk about us too. Yesterday when we went back to school, Ezekiel Sibanda whispered about our bush brands. He said everyone knew we had them. He said we're animals. The General's animals."

"It hurts, doesn't it?" Esther says. "The talk."

Iris and Soly bite their lips.

Esther's voice goes low. "When people say bad things,

I remember the night I got cut up. I was so ashamed. Now I think, My scars are a badge. They prove I can survive anything."

There's a crackle from the firepit, but none of us move. Esther takes Soly and Iris by the hand. "Here," she says. She runs their fingers gently over the crevice that runs from her forehead, across her eyebrow, cheek, and nose, over her lips and chin, and onto her throat. There's a silence as holy as the moon.

Soly and Iris look at Esther and me. "Would you touch our bush brands?"

Esther and I kiss our fingers and gently touch our kisses to the hurting place. The children's eyes well up, but they don't cry. They cup their hands over ours and press them tight.

"Thank you," Iris whispers. "Thank you."

45

NEXT MORNING, AN ambulance brings Mr. Lesole home from the hospital. Mrs. Tafa's finishing her grand tour when it arrives at his door. She scurries up the road into our yard, dabbing her forehead with her hankie. Esther and I rush to get her a chair and a glass of water. The children hide behind us.

"How's Mr. Lesole?" I ask.

"Who knows?" Mrs. Tafa pants. "His wife bundled him inside with his safari jacket over his head."

"It was like that after the attack," Esther says. "They brought him into the house covered up in a bloody coat."

I can't believe my ears. "You mean no one's seen him since he got hurt? Not once?"

"How?" Esther demands. "At first there were the guards. Then after they left, he kept inside. We figured he wanted to be alone."

Mrs. Tafa plants the tip of her parasol on a paving stone and rests her chins on its handle. "Mr. Lesole was a proud man," she says. "Now his tongue's cut out. His head's deformed. He can't talk. He can't swallow right. No wonder he wants to hide."

"Nobody *wants* to hide," I say. "I'll bet he's just scared of what people will say. Like Mama. Like us. Well Mr. Lesole isn't a secret. He's a friend. Esther, Mrs. Tafa: You of all people should understand." I kneel by Soly and Iris. "The two of you need to see Mr. Lesole. So do I." Their eyes fill with terror. "If you get scared," I say calmly, "just chant the alphabet. It's how I got you home."

We walk alone, the three of us, hand in hand. As we go down the road, the yards go quiet. People pretend to hang laundry, rake the ground by their doors, or darn socks, but the moment we pass they turn and stare. This time, Soly and Iris don't care. Their eyes are glued to the Lesoles' front door. The closer it gets, the more they squeeze my fingers. I squeeze back.

We enter the Lesoles' yard, pass by the hammock, and stand on the threshold. I knock. Silence. The shutters are half-closed. I think someone's watching us from the inside, but I can't tell. I knock again.

Soly tugs my hand. "Maybe we should go."

I'm thinking he's right, when the door opens. Mrs. Lesole stares through the crack. "So you're back," she says.

"Yes."

She glances at Soly and Iris. "We heard these two were in the bush."

"Yes."

An awkward pause. Soly wriggles a toe in the dirt. Iris twists around and looks up at the sky as if she isn't here.

"Mrs. Lesole, we've come to wish your husband a good recovery. The children want to know he's all right."

"Do they." Her breath catches. "Well he's not all right. He'll never be *all right*."

"We're sorry."

"I'll tell him you said so." She grips the door frame. "A few days later, it could have been them that did it."

"Maybe," I say. "But it wasn't."

She wipes her eyes. "He was a beautiful man, my husband. I'll tell him you called." She shuts the door in our face.

"What do we do?" Iris says.

"I guess we go home."

We start to make our way across the yard. As we pass the hammock, Soly strokes Mr. Lesole's pillow.

Then, behind us, a strange sound. We turn around. Mr. Lesole is standing at his front door, in pajamas, slippers, and nightgown. He hides his face behind a park map. We look at each other. He lowers the map slowly. His neck and face are swollen huge. There's bandages over his head and around his mouth and jaw. He motions the children to come to him. They take a few steps and freeze.

Mr. Lesole hesitates. Then he bends over and starts to lumber around the yard like an elephant, his arm-trunk swinging freely. He lifts his hands to his ears. It's Elephant Charge. Soly's favorite. I smile, as he rocks from side to side, kicking the earth behind him. He raises his arm to trumpet. Instead, a mangled cry rips out of his throat.

The children's eyes fill. Mr. Lesole charges. The children know to stay still, but they can't. They turn and run. He catches up, scoops Iris under one arm and Soly under the other. Then he settles onto his knees and hugs them fiercely.

"Mr. Lesole, Mr. Lesole," they say.

He kisses the tops of their heads through his bandages.

"Why aren't I dead?" Soly whispers. "I should be dead."

"Me too," Iris cries.

Mr. Lesole shakes his head, no no no. They hold him tight. They weep into his chest. He weeps too.

46

EVERY DAY WE spend a little time with Mr. Lesole. His love for Iris and Soly has softened Mrs. Lesole. It protects the children from the whispers, too.

The three of us are finally back at school. Iris has the occasional rage, but she's still in my class, and Soly's across the hall, so I get to work and keep an eye on them at the same time. At home, they continue to draw. Mostly the images are terrors from the bush, but every so often there's a surprise. They're with the chickens. Or helping me carry water from the standpipe. Simple things.

This evening they color together quietly. When they're finished, they call me over. They've made a picture of the family. Iris is the biggest, of course. She's smack at the center, standing on my head. I've got Soly by the hand.

Iris points at a bright triangle holding a box to its ear.

"That's Auntie Rose," she says. "And that's Esther. And Mr. Lesole. And Mrs. Lesole."

"It's beautiful," I gasp. "Especially the gold stars around everybody."

"They're for Granny and everybody up in Tiro," Soly volunteers.

"The ancestors, too," Iris corrects. She hesitates, then points to the top of the page. There's a stork flying next to a crow with a clumpy foot. The tips of their wings are touching. "The birds, the birds are . . ." She stops.

"I know," I whisper. "I know."

A family picture isn't the end of our troubles. Mandiki is in their heads and always will be. But at times like this, I know that something else is in there too. I feel myself start to breathe. To dream of a time, sometime, when they'll be well.

We're at the Lesoles' one Saturday afternoon, when Mrs. Tafa runs up twirling her parasol. She calls me aside. "There's a young man got off the truck from Tiro," she says, eyebrows arching off her forehead. "Name of Nelson Malunga. I put him in your front yard." She winks. "You never told me he was so well developed, if you know what I mean. If he wants to stay over, he stays with me and the Mister. You don't want stories getting round."

Nelson's slumped on the wheelbarrow. When he sees me, he gives me a hug. Mrs. Tafa's watching from over the cactus hedge. I bring Nelson to the swings in the empty sandlot. We rock on the wood seats, scuffling the grooves in the dirt under our feet. I can tell there's lots on his mind, but he doesn't know how to say it.

"Your granny says to say hello," he begins. "Your aunties and uncles too. They've sent some things, uh, some dried beef, some preserves. They're in my bag at the house in the shade." He clears his throat. "My sisters-in-law . . . My sisters-in-law, they've gone. They're back with their people. One of them's getting remarried. Maybe the other one, too." He breathes heavy. "Cattle are fine. Your uncles, they help. They've been a big help. They've . . . they're why I could get away."

He gets up and circles the swings in silence, kicking at the odd stone. "It's a nice place you got. Nice place. Nice neighbor lady. She the one who phoned that night?"

"Yes."

A smile flickers on his lips. "Nice lady. Bit strange

though. Told me to comb my hair. Tried to wipe a smudge off my cheek with a dab of spit on her hankie."

"That's Mrs. Tafa—'Auntie Rose,'" I laugh.

"Yeah. Well. She's okay." The smile vanishes. He sits back on the swing.

Silence.

"And . . . ?" I say. I'm afraid to say more.

"And, yeah, well, that's the other thing." He sucks a breath. "That's, well, it's hard. It's hard." He gets up and walks so his back's to me. "He was just a little fellow. He never meant any harm. He was just so, just so . . ."

"Nelson?" I get up. He puts up a hand. I stop.

"He was never really quite right. Not after Papa and my brothers. That time in the bush . . . I don't know how he held up like he did. Back home was another story. He started to fight. He'd fall on the ground and scream. Folks in town, they said he had the bush in him. It wasn't true. I took him to the post. There was no one to call him names there. It was just us and the cows and the herd boys. You knew that the herd boys got saved? All but two of them. It was a miracle. It was—"

I can't hold back anymore. "Nelson. Tell me. Is Pako okay?"

"I hope so . . . I like to think so."

"What do you mean?"

He looks up at the sky. "I thought he was tending the cattle. When they came back to the pen at night without him, I didn't think much of it. I was used to him taking off. Next morning, I headed after him. Same path as always. I got to the waterhole before sundown. His blanket was in the hollow log. I figured he was hiding. I called to him like I always did and waited. Nothing. I went to wash up at the waterhole. That's when I saw it. His bandanna, floating on the surface. He'd filled his pockets with stones, walked into the water, and drowned himself." Nelson pauses. "He liked it there," he says softly. "It was his special place. It was where he felt safe. I hope he's at peace."

We sit very still.

"I can't go back," he says. "I have nowhere to go."

I take his hand. "You have here."

Three Months Later

Ngala's civil war isn't over, but Mr. Selalame says there's hope.

Mandiki's death has been a rock to the rebel beehive. His main army has splintered into three rival factions, led by his brother and two of his cousins. They're so busy killing each other, they don't have time for anyone else.

At the same time, the Ngala government has offered pardons to the child soldiers. Some have left the bush, but not all. Many are orphans, kidnapped when they were little. They have nowhere to go, and no one who wants them. With the rebels, they get food, shelter, and the protection of a gun. Others feel safer in the bush than in Ngala's overcrowded refugee camps, full of war victims seeking revenge. Another problem: There's no pardon for the rebel leaders. If they're captured, they'll be hanged as war criminals. As long as that's true, they won't surrender, and as long as they won't surrender, the Ngala children fear being recaptured and killed if they try to escape.

What to do? Even Mr. Selalame doesn't know. "The horror has to be punished, but the threat of punishment keeps the horror going," he says. "Let's be glad for small mercies. The rebels are back in Ngala. They're too weak and distracted to come here again. At least not for a long while. If they do, next time, we'll be ready."

Closer to home, things have been going well. Nelson's been living with us in a single room beside the shed, built with cracked cinder blocks that Mr. Tafa brought home from his job at United Construction. They're no good for shopping malls, but with a little cement and plaster they're perfect for here. At first, I thought Mrs. Tafa'd have a fit about Nelson staying with us, but Nelson's smart. On Mrs. Tafa's morning walks, he always compliments her on her dresses, and when she's had her hair done, well, he just won't stop!

Nelson does chores and plays with Soly and Iris. He's like a papa and a big brother, both. He also helps with money; he's sold one of his cattle to pay his keep. My uncles tend the rest of his herd in exchange for the use of his land. Sometimes, Nelson gets odd jobs at Mr. Tafa's construction sites, but I know he misses the bush. He may have a chance with the Kenje River Safari Camp. Mr. Lesole's back working again. Since he can't speak, he can't guide, but he's got the best eye up there, so they've kept him as a spotter. He's recommending Nelson for his tracking skills; Nelson would start as a busboy and work his way up, while he learns about the animals.

Thanks to all that Nelson does around the place, I'm finally getting some rest. So much, in fact, I've started to work with Mr. Selalame on finishing my high school. "You'll get that scholarship yet," he beams.

Mrs. Tafa and Esther tease that before that, there'll be wedding bells. They can think what they like. I'm building my dreams one day at a time. Nelson, too. Each night, we sit outside and talk forever. When the air cools, we bundle ourselves together in a light blanket.

I look up at the stars and imagine the ancestors: Mama, Papa, Auntie Lizbet, and the others. Here with Nelson, I can feel them smiling.

Afterword

CHANDA'S WARS TELLS the story of one young woman's heart-break, courage, and hope in the midst of terrible events in a fictional African war. The reasons children are used as soldiers may be complicated, but the effects on them are direct and horrific. Most end up broken by adult wars they cannot hope to understand. A very few, like Chanda and her siblings, find within themselves the resources to resist and to escape with what remains of their tattered lives. Chanda's story reaches to the heart of the terrifying truth about child soldiers in a way that all of us, young and old alike, can understand. It makes it possible for us to imagine the faces of real children caught and trampled by the scourge of war in so many recent and ongoing conflicts in Africa. For those of us working actively to protect children from combat, there is something inspiring in the example

ALLAN STRATTON

of Chanda, who refuses to give in to fear and who risks her life in her quest to save her brother and sister. Ultimately, Chanda's wars are everybody's wars: Every young person stolen and recruited is our brother, our sister, our son, our daughter. We must all join the fight if we are to protect them from the horror of becoming child soldiers.

The Honorable Roméo Dallaire,
Lieutenant-General (retired),
head of U.N. forces during the
Rwandan genocide

Author's Note and Thanks

THE CHARACTERS, COUNTRIES, and story of *Chanda's Wars* are fictional, but the horrors are real. Children and youth are forcibly recruited for combat in strife-torn regions of Africa, as they have been, and continue to be, in conflicts around the world. Despite wars and genocides that demand global action, it must be remembered that Africa is a continent of fifty-four separate countries, most of which, as represented by Chanda's homeland, are at peace. I urge anyone who is tempted to give up hope for Africa's future to consider the past history of Europe.

Work on this novel was made possible by the support and encouragement of friends and acquaintances from Uganda, Eritrea, Sierra Leone, Nigeria, Mozambique, Tanzania, South Africa, Malawi, and Zambia, both living in

Africa and in the African diaspora.

For insight into the psychology of child soldiers, I am particularly grateful to the late Michael Oruni, director of World Vision's Children of War Rehabilitation Centre in Gulu, northern Uganda, and my conversation with former members of the Lord's Resistance Army rehabilitated at the Centre; Dr. Philip Lancaster, United Nations Lieutenant-General Roméo Dallaire's executive assistant during the Rwandan genocide; Tariq Bhanjee of UNICEF; Justin Daniel Peffer of Plan International; Raymond Micah and Amanuel Melles of the African Canadian Social Development Council; filmmakers Oliver Stoltz and Ali Samadi Ahadi, who documented child soldiers along the Ugandan/Sudanese border; Dr. Anne Goodman and Michael Wheeler of the International Institute for Community-Based Peacebuilding; Thomas Turay of the COADY International Institute; Kathy Vandergrift, Rebecca Steinmann, and Ken and Cynthia Jaworko of World Vision; and Barbara Hoffman, director of the Association for the Children of Mozambique. I am also indebted to the wide range of materials available from Human Rights Watch, Save the Children, CARE, Defence for Children International, the Children's Institute, médecins sans frontiers, Amnesty International, War Child, and other NGOs.

The sections about tracking and animal behavior come from my experiences in the bush with Richard Chimwala and Angel M. Gondwe, guides at Wilderness Safaris' Mvuu Camp, Malawi, and with scout Gideon Mpase and guides Ian Salisbury and Alex Cole at Kaingo Camp, Zambia. I also met with Susan Slotar, executive director of the Jane Goodall Institute, South Africa branch.

My observations of village life were deepened enormously by Robert Thomas Gama, who introduced me to rural Malawi, and by Enoch Chidothi, Bakiri Wandiki, and James Asan, who were my hosts during my stay at Ulongwe, and who introduced me to local farmers, villagers, and Ligwang'wa, their late village headman.

I owe my understanding of the power of spirit doctors to visits in Malawi with spirit doctor John Saisa, Father Claude Boucher of Mua Mission, and Felix Chisale of Zomba Plateau, and to earlier visits to spirit doctors in Zimbabwe and Botswana.

Many thanks as well to my Harper editors Lynne Missen (Canada) and Susan Rich and Patricia Ocampo (U.S.); Alexis MacDonald and Christina Magill of the Stephen Lewis Foundation; Harriet McQuire and Althea Tait of Access Africa; journalist Michele Landsberg; and the Canada Council for the Arts, the Ontario Arts Council, and the Toronto Arts Council.

Above all, I'd like to thank all those who invited me into their homes in cities, villages, farms, and cattle posts. I am forever grateful for their generosity of time, guidance, and insight.

Chanda's Wars

An Interview with Allan Stratton

Why do you write?
(*Allan laughs*) I don't have a choice. Writing's like breathing. If I don't write, it's as though I'm suffocating. It's been like that since before I could spell. Mom was a single working parent, so I was on my own a lot growing up. Plus, I had rheumatic fever and three bouts of pneumonia by the time I was five, so I spent chunks of time in bed. To amuse myself, I played with hand puppets and three china elves. I'd make up stories about them, then try to write down the stories by sounding out the letters.

Years ago, I wrote a play called *Papers*. One of the characters is a novelist. He says, "Writing is a sickness, but when it's happening I don't ever want to get better. I'm off in a land where all the unrelated scraps of time and event, all the meaningless odds and ends I waste my life with, have shape. Form. Substance. In my little universe, life has order. Meaning. And I'm free. When I'm with my typewriter, I can take on the world." I still feel that. (*laughs*) Only now I use a computer.

Where did the idea for *Chanda's Wars* come from?

Chanda's Wars grew out of the love and care I developed for Chanda and her family while writing *Chanda's Secrets*. I couldn't stop thinking about them. At the same time, I was reading about child soldiers in the newspapers. One night I woke from a horrible nightmare: There was a fire, Iris and Soly were kidnapped, and I was in a panic, desperate to get them back. Everything flowed from that.

Critics praise your ability to write complex characters, like Chanda, whose lives are very different from your own. How do you get inside your characters' heads?

I've traveled all over the world, lived through all kinds of situations, and made friends everywhere. If life's taught me anything, it's this: Under the skin we're all the same. No matter our age, gender, ethnicity, sexual orientation, or whatever else, we've all felt love, hate, joy, despair—the works. Our common humanity is how we're able to understand and communicate with each other across our differences. It's how we connect to stories and characters no matter when they were

3

written or where they came from. I always ask friends from the communities I write about to read my work to correct any details I've got wrong: Cultural accuracy is important to me. But the human bond—our shared emotional vocabulary—gives me the confidence and comfort to know that if I'm brutally honest about how I'd feel and act as a particular character in a fictional situation, the heartbeat of my stories will be rooted in truth.

That's one of fiction's main benefits, by the way: letting us imagine ourselves in someone else's shoes. Novels increase our emotional literacy; they help us develop empathy. There'd be fewer problems in the world, if people would step back and imagine how they'd be feeling on the other side of an argument. (*Allan smiles*) Think of it: a peace movement based on reading novels.

You started your career as an actor. Do your theater roots help you make imaginative leaps?
For sure. Actors always have to pretend to be someone they aren't. If you're doing Shakespeare, for instance, you may need to imagine yourself as a Danish prince, like Hamlet; an

Egyptian queen, like Cleopatra; or medieval Italian teens in a blood feud, like Romeo and Juliet. Talk about different backgrounds! So, suppose I'm playing Romeo. At the top of each scene, I'll ask myself: What's my situation? What do I want? What am I going to do to get it? As a writer, I ask myself the same questions for each character. It's like I'm doing a solo improv.

What's more important: character or plot?

They're two sides of the same coin. In life, we discover people's characters based on what they do. In fiction, what characters do is the plot. If you start with plot, you have to ask what kind of characters would behave according to your story. If you start with character, you have ask what they're going to fight for, i.e., what's the plot. Interesting people make interesting choices; so the most interesting characters will likely have the most interesting stories. Writers who ignore character end up with bad plots because the stories don't make human sense, they're cardboard. But writers who ignore plot end up with bad characters, because human beings who do nothing are boring.

Can you give a practical example of how plot and character choices worked together in the creation of *Chanda's Wars*?

Absolutely. Let's start with the kidnapping of Soly and Iris. I'm Chanda: headstrong, devoted, and loyal. I feel responsible, panicked, guilty, and overwhelmed that I've broken my promise to my dying mama to keep them safe. I'm obsessed with one goal: to get them back. What will I do to achieve it? Risk my life. That's character.

But as a writer, I know that Chanda's a city girl. She'd never survive alone in the bush. I don't want her dead, so I have to give her a partner who knows how to track, hunt, and keep her alive. Enter Nelson. His character starts as a plot necessity. But it can't end there; I have to make him real. So now I imagine that I'm him. Why do I want to help Chanda? Because my brother was kidnapped too. And I feel guilty I never protected him from our papa. And I don't want to be shamed by the girl I secretly love. Plus, if she gets killed because I do nothing, how will I feel? So now the plot point (helping Chanda) grows from character. And so on, back and forth, until characters and narrative are seamless.

Do you work from an outline?
(*Allan laughs*) I always *make* one, but it changes constantly. To me, an outline is a safety net, not a straitjacket. It's there in case I get stuck, but it never interferes with the free flow of my novel's development.

Here's how that works in practice: Before I write a word, I spend months thinking about my characters and plot, in the way I mentioned earlier in my discussion of Nelson. I make tons of notes. When I have a clear idea of how to tell the story from beginning to end—in other words when I have an outline—I begin.

But once my characters start interacting, they always say and do things I never expect. At that point, I either have to stick to my plan or go where my characters take me. I've learned to trust my characters. Sometimes they lead me up blind alleys, but usually they take me places I'd never have discovered on my own. As the words fly out of my fingers onto the computer screen I find myself laughing, crying, horrified, you name it. At the end of each day, I reshape my outline and regroup.

Maybe the best way to describe my writing journey is to compare it to a road trip from New

EXTRAS

York to L.A. I have an itinerary in the glove compartment, but I don't follow it. Instead, I make constant detours depending on the weather, my mood, and whether or not I come across an interesting side road. Sometimes I find that a town on my route has lots to discover, and I stay a few days; other towns that seemed promising turn out to be washouts, and I drive straight through. And hey, at the end of my trip, if 'Frisco seems like a better destination than L.A., what the heck?

How much do you think about themes?
I never write to make a point or develop a theme. Instead, I let my themes grow naturally from the material. For instance, if Chanda's going to rescue Soly and Iris from a warlord, the theme of war is already in the premise without me thinking about it.

More subtly: As I was developing Nelson's character, I suddenly realized that he hangs around Chanda from the moment she arrives in Tiro because of Granny's secret plans for a prearranged marriage. (Granny had kept these plans a secret from me too! They weren't in my original outline at all!) In any case, this discovery made me realize that Chanda isn't just fighting a war against Mandiki. She's also fighting wars against her family, superstition, and tradition—wars of independence—the universal wars that all teens wage, in one form or another, in their struggle for personal identity. Bingo—while I was focused on character and narrative, the theme of war had taken flight on its own.

One last question, who has been your greatest influence?

My mother. She's the bravest, smartest, most amazing person I know—and probably the reason strong female characters come naturally to me. Mom left my dad when I was a baby, at a time when people didn't divorce. She worked in education; we moved where her jobs took her. There were some challenging times, but no matter what, Mom always made me feel secure. She is unconditional love made human. I am so very, very grateful to have her as my parent, my friend, my guide. She taught me to be open to life, and to think for myself. I owe her everything.

EXTRAS

Sixteen Things I'll Never Forget

1. Encountering a shark while snorkeling off Cayo Largo
2. Wandering alone through the Red Pyramid, in the desert south of Saqqara, Egypt
3. White-water rafting in the Canadian Rockies
4. Taking a balloon ride with my eighty-year-old mom over Cappadocia, Turkey
5. Waking up to find an elephant beside my tent in the bush in Botswana
6. Volunteering at a Baptist soup kitchen while living in Manhattan
7. Undergoing a Santerian purification ritual in rural Cuba
8. Providing palliative care to a friend dying of AIDS
9. Staying overnight in a one-room mud home in the village of Ulongwe, Malawi
10. Sleeping between train cars while traveling by rail through the former Yugoslavia during the Cold War
11. Shaking hands with Pope Paul VI, when I was eighteen, at an audience in Vatican City
12. Meditating in Buddhist temples around Bangkok, Thailand

13. With the imam's permission, climbing the minaret of the Mosque of Qaitbey in Cairo's City of the Dead
14. Skiing opposite the Matterhorn
15. Hiking along the Great Wall of China
16. Eating a mopani worm in Zimbabwe

Drawing by former child soldier Francis, age thirteen. From the book *Where Is My Home?* produced by AVSI, GUSCO, Red Barnet, UNICEF, and World Vision.

EXTRAS

Rewriting the End of *Chanda's Wars*

Editing is one of my favorite parts of the writing process. Why? Because a good rewrite makes a book better. The following scene took place near the end of the novel. After the scene, I'll tell you why I liked it, but why it had to go.

In the villages, there're people who say Mandiki's still alive. By day, they say, he buries himself with the dead things. By night, he jumps over a broom and turns into a ghost crocodile, prowling the posts for stray cattle and children. "Be good," they tell their little ones, "or Mandiki will get you."

I don't believe in village superstition, but I know Mandiki isn't gone. His body's dead. But another part of him lives on. I see it in my family. I feel it in myself.

Last night I had a dream: I'm in the bush. Iris and Soly are crying for me to save them. I run along hippo highways, carve my way through brush. But when I get to where they're crying, they've disappeared, the crying's coming from someplace else. Mandiki's laugh echoes in the night, "You'll never get them back. I'm in their brains. They're mine forever."

I worry it's true. In the weeks since we've been home, Soly hasn't been able to concentrate, and Iris has flown into more rages. Last week, she stuck Paulo Sibanda's head in a pail of shake-shake. I worry what they may do to themselves when they're alone. I've seen them throw stones at each other. And I know they sneak off to the abandoned well at the dump.

Mrs. Tafa thinks I should take them to see Mrs. Gulubane.

"What good can she do? Her magic pouch didn't help Mr. Lesole."

"It most certainly did," Mrs. Tafa huffs, scratching her back with a lemonade straw. "He lost his tongue, but without that pouch he'd have been killed. It saved his life."

I read everything I can on the school's Internet about child soldiers leaving the bush. Soly and Iris aren't alone. All of the children have terrors. In small villages in Ngara, there are purification rituals. The town chants and prays to the ancestors. Then each of the children step on an egg to symbolize a new life, and a goat is sacrificed to kill the evil spirits. They say it helps take away the nightmares. But that's in the villages. They believe more there.

13

*Soly and Iris are from Bonang. It makes a dif-
ference.*

Okay. There were three things in that scene that I
loved: the way parents turned Mandiki into a bogey
man to get children to behave, Chanda's dream,
and the information about purification rituals, which
are based on what happens in northern Uganda.

So why did I cut the page? Well, the Mandiki
rumors were fun, but nowhere near as much fun
as our last image of him being ripped apart and
eaten by wild animals. (Scenes and images need
to build in power, or they drain a book's energy.)
Also, the dream is intense, but Chanda had
already had several, and there were more immediate ways to show Mandiki's continued hold on
the kids. Finally, the purification rituals are interesting, but read like teaching materials; your
characters need to be actively engaged in an
action, otherwise you're not writing a novel,
you're writing a textbook.

I tried to animate the purification information
in a second draft, as follows:

*Later that afternoon, Mrs. Tafa runs over with her
cell phone. Lily and Granny are calling from the*

Tiro clinic to see how we're doing.

"We couldn't be better," I lie. "The kids are at school or I'd get them to talk to you."

"Oh," Granny says, an odd tick in her voice, "well, that's wonderful. We've good news here too. Nelson's herd boys got home safe, all but one. There was some fighting their first day back, but the spirit doctor made them step on an egg, and sacrificed a goat to kill the demons. I know you laugh at country things, but the boys have been fine ever since."

No good. The problem? You guessed it. Same as the Mandiki rumors. Granny on the phone undercuts the power of the last Granny scene in which we see her waving good-bye to her grandkids, maybe forever.

But, hey, you'll notice my cut page wasn't a total loss. See the fourth paragraph where Chanda lists the problems Iris and Soly are having? In the original draft, that's all there was. I took those images and turned them into the first two pages of chapter 43. Compare the two versions. Seeing the stone-throwing in an active, dramatic scene, makes the children's trauma much more horrifying, don't you think?

EXTRAS

Nelson's Recipe for Biltong

So you're going into the bush and you want to bring along some dried meat for a snack, or in case you don't catch anything. Here's what you'll need:

    Beef
    Vinegar
    Rock salt
    Coriander
    Pepper
    Brown sugar (If you have any. Use about a
        handful for every ten pounds.)

What you do:
    Cut the beef along the grain into very thin strips—as thin as the moon of your thumbnail—and about a foot long.

    Dip the strips in vinegar to melt sinew and binding tissue, and to open the pores for seasoning.

    To preserve the meat, coat it with lots of rock salt, put it in a pan someplace cool, like an ice chest, and go do some chores for a few hours.

    Crush the coriander, and mix it with some

pepper and brown sugar. Toss in a little piripiri if you like it hot.

Drain any blood from the meat pan, and scrape excess salt off the meat with a knife.

Roll the strips in your spice mix, or shake them in a paper bag if there's one around. Maybe put them back in the ice chest overnight to absorb the flavor of the spices.

Put the strips on wire hooks and hang on a line in a dry shady place. On the cattle post, we hang ours in a breezy spot under a tree.

Wait a few days till the moisture's all dried out of it. And keep an eye out for bugs. If you're not careful, they'll eat it sure as anything.

Warning from Mr. Selalame: Summers in southern Africa are very dry. In North America, use a fridge to marinate your meat. The U.S.D.A. Food Safety and Inspection Service recommends preheating meat to 160 degrees before dehydrating, and using a food dehydrator that can keep the temperature at 140 degrees throughout the drying process. Their full recommendations to avoid harmful bacteria are at http://www.fsis.usda.gov/FactSheets/Jerky_and_Food_Safety/index.asp.

EXTRAS

An Excerpt from Allan Stratton's Next Book:
Borderline

I'm next door in Andy's driveway, shooting hoops with him and Marty. The holidays are over next week, and we've hardly been together at all. Andy was in summer school for math all July. After that, he and his family took Marty to their cottage on the Canadian side of the Thousand Islands. They just got back yesterday.

I could have gone too, except for Dad. Other times he's let me, but when he heard that Mr. and Mrs. J. wouldn't be there 24/7, he pulled the plug. "You're too young to handle the responsibility," he said.

"What responsibility?" I demanded. "We'll be swimming. Fishing. Dad, please. I'm almost sixteen."

"I've said what I've said."

Yeah, and it's totally not fair. I don't do drugs. I hate booze. And that stuff with Mary Louise Prescott happened over a year ago.

The worst was watching the videos Andy and Marty e-mailed of them hiking, swimming, and cannonballing off the Johnsons' dock. They even got to take the boat out on their own. "So, Sammy, what are *you* doing?" they laughed as they hotdogged through the islands.

But now they're back and everything's fantastic.

At least it *was*. Dad's stepped onto our verandah. The day's been a scorcher, but it seems nobody's told him. Even home, after dinner, it's like he's still at work, supervising the microbe researchers at the lab. His jacket's off, but he's wearing everything else: silk tie, dress shirt, pearl cuff links, and flannels.

I tense as he stands by the railing, watching us play. I was doing great. Now I suck.

"Close, very close," Dad says, as my third shot in a row rockets off the backboard.

I get the basketball before it bounces into the street, pass to Andy, and fix Dad with a stare. "You want something?"

"Can your mother and I borrow you for a while?" Translation: It's time for prayers. Years ago, Mom convinced Dad to give me prayer calls in code, so I wouldn't be embarrassed in front of my friends. But Andy and Marty know the drill.

"You need me this second?"

"Not right away. But, say, in five minutes?" Dad flashes his fake smile, the one where his lips go stiff. "Sorry to interrupt your game."

Go, Dad. Just Go. I shoot out imaginary force fields, picture him flying through the air into tomorrow, but he hangs around like a bad fart.

"You boys have grown this summer!" he says out of nowhere. Dad makes stupid announcements like this almost every time he sees us. It's his idea of Taking An Interest. Well, if he really took an interest, he'd know Andy's been six feet tall since ninth grade; the guys call him Stiltz. And Marty doesn't grow up, just out. Fries, Cokes, chips. If he keeps at it, he'll turn into his parents.

Dad waits for one of us to break the silence. We don't. He bobbles his head like a dashboard ornament, gives us a tight little wave, and finally—*finally*—goes back inside.

We play a bit more, but it's not the same.

Then Dad taps on the living room window. When he was a kid, he fled Iran because of the secret police. So what did he learn about freedom? Not much, apparently. I can't even shoot a private game of hoops with my friends.

"Catch you later," I say.

20